BANG

ALSO BY KERIS STAINTON

KERIS STAINTON

My Heart goes BANG

HOT
KEY
BOOKS

First published in Great Britain in 2018 by
HOT KEY BOOKS
80–81 Wimpole St, London W1G 9RE
www.hotkeybooks.com

A CIP catalogue record for this book is available from the British Library.

ISBN: 9781471406829
also available as an ebook

1

This book is typeset using Atomik ePublisher
Printed and bound in Great Britain by Clays Ltd, Elcograf S.p.A.

Hot Key Books is an imprint of Bonnier Zaffre Ltd,
a Bonnier Publishing company
www.bonnierpublishing.com

For all the girls and women who, like Liane,
struggled to work it out.

SEPTEMBER

Chapter 1

'Are they here already?' Ella asked Lou as they pushed open the front door.

'Dunno,' Lou said. 'Hang on. Can't get the bastard key out.'

Ella glanced back at her friend as she stepped into the hallway. 'Smells better than halls, anyway.'

'Paint,' Lou said. 'Fuck. Me.' Lou turned the key so the deadbolt slid out and in again. 'Can you have a go at this? It's jammed.'

'There's no post on the floor,' Ella said, stepping up to the door and grabbing the key. 'So either the landlord's been in or they're already here.' She waggled the key gently and it slid out. 'Done.'

'Shit, how did you do that?' Lou said, leaving her suitcase in the hall and heading for the kitchen. 'We'll have to get some lube for it. Can't have that every time we come in.'

'Lube,' Ella said, smiling as she followed Lou. The hall was at least one source of the fresh paint smell – it was newly magnolia. When they'd come to look at the place, the walls had been a dingy, stained grey.

Lou threw a grin back over her shoulder. 'You know what I mean. That spray stuff.'

'WD40,' Ella said. 'Please tell me you don't use it as lube.'

Lou laughed. 'Not yet. But the semester is young.'

'It's natural, I think. I read a thing about it once.'

'It worries me that you ever read a thing about WD40, but that is good to know.'

'Kitchen,' Ella said, opening the first door on the right.

'I remember,' Lou said.

The kitchen was bright and white and clean and the rows of empty bottles that had adorned the shelf above the picture rail had been cleared away since the two of them had come to view the house.

'Aw,' Ella said. 'That was one of my favourite things.'

'Just means we have to start our own collection,' Lou said. 'Challenge accepted.'

'What happened to "I'm not going to drink as much" this year?' Ella walked around the kitchen, sliding open drawers and peeking into cupboards. Everything was empty and clean. There was actual liner paper in the drawers. Liner paper!

'"As much",' Lou said. 'Not "nothing". I'm still young. I'm still at uni. I'm still human.' She opened the fridge, which was also clean. And empty. 'Need to do a big shop,' she said. She closed the door and looked at Ella, who seemed to be examining the buttons on the washing machine.

'Do you know which room you want?' Lou asked her as she started up the stairs.

'Don't really mind.' Ella shrugged, following.

'Bollocks you don't.' Lou grinned, stopping on the first landing and pushing open a couple of doors. 'We're here first so we get the two big rooms. Result.'

Ella followed Lou up the next flight of stairs to the main living space. 'Is that fair? I mean, it's completely random that we got here first.'

Lou looked down at Ella. 'Bagsy rules apply, everyone knows that.'

The top floor of the house was the reason they'd chosen it. And the reason there was going to be five of them sharing instead of four, as originally planned. It was all one huge living space with glass doors leading out onto a roof terrace.

'So they're definitely not here,' Ella said, following Lou over to the two huge sofas, arranged in an L-shape in front of the TV. 'Should I text them?'

Lou laughed, flopping down on the sofa nearest the window. 'Why? They'll get here when they get here. You're not their mum.'

'Actually, I haven't even got Paige's number,' Ella said, sitting on the other sofa and immediately turning round to look at the rest of the room.

'Yeah, we'd best make sure we've all got each other's numbers when they do get here,' Lou said. 'Fucking nightmare last year getting locked out and having to track people down.'

'We should put a list on the fridge,' Ella said.

Lou grinned at her. 'Right next to the cleaning rota, yeah.'

'It just makes sense! I know you think I'm a dick.'

'I don't think you're a dick,' Lou said. 'I just think you're old before your time. We're. Here. To. Have. Fun.'

'I'm. Here. To. Get. An. Edu—'

'Yeah, yeah, that too. We passed last year, didn't we? Don't worry so much.'

Ella had passed, but she hadn't done as well as she'd wanted to. At school everyone had kept calling her a big fish in a small pond and telling her how she was going to wow them at uni, but she hadn't wowed anyone. She hadn't wowed anyone at all.

Ella didn't pick the shittest room (the one next to the kitchen), but she did pick a small one. But it was nice. It had a bed and a desk and a window onto the street and that was all she really needed. Unzipping her case, she pulled out the fabric bag that she'd packed her underwear in. She opened the top drawer of the chest of drawers with some trepidation – the drawers in her room at halls had been absolutely disgusting, fag ends in one, an apple core in another – but this was clean, thank god.

She packed away the few clothes she'd brought with her – she still had to get the rest of her stuff from her parents' house in Cheshire – and then sat down on the bed, looking around the room. She didn't want any distractions this year and if that meant living in a room like a cell, that was fine. It was quiet though, just a bit of street noise from outside, which she should like – the noise in halls had driven her up the wall – but it made her feel a bit sad. A bit lonely. A bit lost.

She took out her phone and WhatsApped her brother a photo of the room with the caption 'New home sweet home'. She hadn't expected to hear straight back, but she could see him typing.

'Couldn't find anything smaller?'

She grinned. 'There's a cupboard under the stairs. But there's a boy wizard in it.'

'Typical. U ok?'

'Yeah. Ta. Just feel a bit . . . something.'

'Hate that. Can't ring, sorry. In an interview.'

'STOP TEXTING THEN'

Dylan sent a string of laugh/cry emojis and Ella sent back the same number of eyeroll emojis.

'Call later yeah?' Dylan sent and Ella nodded at the phone before sending a thumbs-up and a heart. She didn't know if he meant he'd call or she would, but it didn't really matter. One of them would. She felt better already.

'Are we allowed to paint the walls?' Lou asked as soon as Ella walked into her room. She'd taken the biggest one on the first floor. 'This room is way too beige.'

'Magnolia,' Ella said. 'Same as the hall.'

'Whatever. I'm thinking bright pink? Or, I don't know, can you do all the walls with blackboard paint? Like the door?'

'If you can paint it – which I doubt – I bet you can't paint it pink or black.'

'Fucksticks. I'll just have to stick a load of posters up then. How's your room?'

'Fine. Small. Plain.'

'Take the big one!' Lou said. 'Seriously. Why do you think one of the others deserves it more than you?'

'It's not about deserving it,' Ella said. 'I just don't need a big room.'

'Well, at least let me do it up.' Lou picked up a handful of lacy underwear and then dropped it on the bed again. 'Put up some fairy lights. Mirror on the ceiling.'

Ella grinned. 'Yeah, that's just what I was thinking.'

'It'd do you good,' Lou said, finally throwing the underwear into a drawer. 'You keep saying you're here for an education.'

'Not about my vagina,' Ella said, crossing the room and looking out of the window. The street outside was quiet. 'They still not here?'

'Don't think so, no. They've got keys though, haven't they? Want to go and get a drink?'

If Ella rested her head on the glass and looked to the right, she could see the beer garden of the nearest bar. But there wasn't anyone sitting out there, because it was drizzling.

'We could go and bring some back . . .' she suggested.

'Morrisons, then? Get some food as well. I'm starved.'

When they got back from the supermarket – Ella carrying two bags of food, Lou carrying two bags of booze – they could tell the others had arrived. Every light in the house seemed to be on and 'Sorry' by Justin Bieber was blasting down the stairs.

'Is that Justin fucking Bieber?' Lou said, her face a picture of horror.

'Issey's here.' Ella grinned.

'We should've got them to put that in the contract – no Justin fucking Bieber.'

'To give him his full name.' Ella ran up the stairs.

'Hiya!' Issey yelled, poking her head out of the door. 'Where've you been?'

'Getting provisions,' Lou said from behind Ella.

Issey ran over and hugged them both at the same time, saying, 'What did you get?' too loud into Ella's ear.

8

'Food,' Ella said at the same time as Lou said, 'Beer. And tequila.'

'Oh shit. I hate tequila,' Issey said. 'Did you get limes and salt?'

'What's it to you if you hate tequila?' Lou asked.

Issey grinned. 'Isn't it great? The house? So much better than last year.'

'Where's Liane?' Ella asked, watching Lou take the bottles out of the bag and line them up on the huge wooden dining table.

'Sleeping,' Issey said. 'She's hungover.'

'Doubt she's sleeping through this,' Lou said. 'Sorry' had ended and 'Baby' had started. 'Do you have to?'

'You knew my feelings about Biebs before you invited me to move in,' Issey said. 'We come as a pair.'

'You wish,' Ella said.

Issey grinned. 'Yeah, I do. Sexy little monkey.'

'Jesus,' Lou said. 'There'd better be a bottle opener downstairs.'

When Lou came back up, Liane was with her, looking rumpled and confused, but still gorgeous, her short afro tied under a red scarf.

'Where were you last night?' Ella asked her, hugging her gently, Liane nuzzling her head into Ella's neck as she always did.

'Leaving do at work. Didn't get home 'til five. We were only meant to be going to bingo.'

'I love your job,' Issey said, throwing herself back onto the long sofa and propping her feet up on the arm. 'Those old ladies really know how to party.'

'They're a bunch of bastards,' Liane said, lifting Issey's legs up so she could sit down and then putting them back over her own. 'I told them not to let me drink too much cos I was moving in today. But they were buying me Long Island Iced Teas all night and then we did shots.'

'Shots,' Lou said, coming back in holding four shot glasses in one hand and a bottle opener in the other, a family bag of Doritos tucked down the front of her shirt.

Ella shook her head, laughing and frowning at the same time. 'That sounds like a very bad idea.'

'Oh, come on!' Lou sat down at the scratched wooden dining table and tipped her head back, her long silver hair falling back over her shoulders. 'It's our first night together! We need to do something to mark it.' She patted the pockets of her dungarees. 'But I need a fag first.' She stood up, stretched her arms over her head and walked out onto the roof terrace, leaving the door open.

'Where's the other one?' Issey said from the sofa. 'What's she called?'

'Paige,' Liane said. 'She said she might be late. And we should wait for her if we're going to do shots. It should be all of us.'

'I've never done shots,' Issey said.

'WHAT?' Liane screeched, before grabbing her head in both hands and muttering, 'Oh my god.'

'Never?' Ella said, sitting down on the armchair next to the TV.

Issey shook her head. 'My dad made me promise. Before I came away. No drugs, no sex, no shots.'

'You've had sex though,' Liane said, her head tipped back against the sofa, eyes closed. 'I've heard you having sex.'

Issey laughed. 'Yeah. S'why it seemed even more important to not do the other two.'

'You smoked weed with me at the end of last term,' Lou called from the terrace.

'That was one time.'

'May as well go for a hat-trick,' Ella said.

Issey snorted. 'Yeah, I guess.' She shuffled back up the sofa, her legs sliding out from under Liane's. 'Sorry, Dad.'

Chapter 2

Paige couldn't get the door to open.

'SHIT,' she said through gritted teeth, kicking the bottom of the door, hard.

'Need a hand there, girl?' someone said from behind her.

'Fuck off,' she said, without turning round.

'Charming.'

Paige leaned forward and rested her head against the door. She'd just wanted to get here, move in, go to sleep and not have to speak to anyone. Was that too much to ask? Instead she'd had to drive her dad to his girlfriend's house because he was still over the limit from last night. Then she'd had to get a cab she couldn't afford to the station, where the train was delayed and the coffee shop was closed for refurbishment when it was only the thought of one of their white chocolate brownies that had got her that far. And then on the Liverpool train she'd had to stand up and listen to a bunch of old fellas arguing about football and politics and calling each other pussies. She'd wanted to lean over and tell them that word was decidedly not an insult because there was nothing stronger than a pussy, but she hadn't been able to make herself do it.

Instead she'd posted a selfie on Instagram and hashtagged it #pussypower. By the time she'd got off the train, it already had ninety-two likes.

She'd had to walk from the station to the house, dragging her suitcase behind her even though one of the wheels was wobbling and it kept hitting her in the back of the legs. She snorted as she passed a 'Gentlemen's Club' and then a ridiculous-looking barber shop, all chrome and blue lights. It was like the eighties here. She loved it even when she hated it.

She took a step back and looked up at the three-storey house she'd be calling home for at least the next year. Lights were on in almost every window so at least she knew her housemates were in. She looked around for a bell and when she didn't see one, knocked first on the door and then on the nearest window. So much for her plan of sneaking in without actually having to talk to anyone.

She was considering giving up and going to sit in a coffee shop for half an hour when the door jerked open and a tiny girl wearing satin football shorts and a loose vest stood there grinning at her. Paige half recognised her from uni, but at uni she couldn't usually see her nipples.

'Are you Paige?' the girl said, her eyebrows shooting up her forehead. 'We were starting to think you weren't coming.'

'Yeah,' Paige said. 'Sorry. I got held up.' She didn't know why she was apologising.

'Come in,' the girl said, leaning forward to grab Paige's bag and giving Paige a clear view down her top. 'We're about to do shots.'

'Great,' Paige said.

13

'You've already met Issey,' Liane said, pointing at the girl who'd answered the door.

'Yeah, but I don't think I said,' Issey said. She was sitting cross-legged on the sofa now, a bottle of beer in one hand, her phone in the other. 'I'm Issey.'

'That's Ella, and Lou's outside having yet another fag,' Liane told her.

'Paige,' Paige said. 'I've seen you around,' she said to Lou.

'Yeah,' Lou said from the terrace door. 'You do look familiar. What are you studying?'

'English and Cultural Studies,' Paige said. 'You?'

'Just English,' Lou said, frowning. Seconds later, she clicked her fingers. 'You go to Bleachers!'

Paige smiled. 'Yeah. Not lately. But I have been, yeah. Your hair's great, by the way.'

Lou pulled her long silver hair up into a ponytail and let it drop. 'Thanks. I get a discount cos I work there part-time.'

'Yeah?' Paige said. She really could do with getting her hair dyed professionally. She'd been doing it herself for a while now and it was OK, but not the same. There was no way she could afford it, but maybe Lou would do it for mates' rates.

'You'd look good violet,' Lou said.

'I was thinking red. Like, bright Little Mermaid red.'

Lou frowned, peering at Paige. 'I think that might be too harsh. Maybe pink? Cerise?'

'Sounds good to me,' Paige said.

'It'll look super-hot,' Issey said, from the sofa. 'But never mind that now . . . SHOTS!'

14

'You're keen, for someone who's never done them before,' Ella said. She was perched on the edge of the coffee table, her elbow on her knee, her chin on her fist.

'You've never done shots?' Paige asked Issey.

'Come and sit,' Lou said, gesturing at the second sofa.

'Nope,' Issey said, popping the 'p'. 'Shot virgin.'

'Or do you want to go and settle into your room first?' Ella asked Paige.

'No, it's OK,' Paige said. 'Ta.'

If anyone had asked her, up to and including, like, five minutes ago, Paige would have said she had zero interest in doing shots with three girls she barely knew and one she . . . actually, four girls she barely knew. But now that she was here and they were friendly and the living room was cosy and her room was empty . . . well, maybe just the one.

Liane dropped down on the sofa next to Issey, who immediately curled up against her, rubbing her head against her neck like a cat, the way Liane usually did. Paige made herself look away.

'So it's shit tequila,' Lou said. 'It's all I could afford. But it'll get the job done.'

She poured the clear liquid into the glasses and they each held one up in front of their faces.

'Hey,' Issey said. 'Aren't we doing the slammer thing? With limes and salt or whatever it is.'

'Oh fuxache,' Lou groaned. 'Do we have to?'

'Shot virgin!' Issey yelled, lifting her hands over her head. 'We have to do it right!'

Lou rolled her eyes, but she got up and ran downstairs to the

15

kitchen, coming back with limes and salt and a roll of paper towels. 'In case you puke.'

'I'm not going to puke,' Issey said, but she looked almost nervous as she arranged the lime and salt on the table in front of her.

'To second year!' Lou said, holding up her glass.

'To our own place!' Liane said.

'To fun!' added Lou and downed her shot.

The others followed, wincing or gasping or laughing. Issey tipped hers back, sucked the lime, licked the salt off the back of her hand and said, 'Fuck me!'

'Good?' Lou asked.

Issey placed the shot glass on the top of her head, her posture perfect. 'Another?'

'Boyfriend?' Lou asked Paige when she was three shots down. She was sitting on the floor between Issey's legs and Issey was attempting to braid her hair. 'Girlfriend?'

Paige shook her head. 'No one.'

'Really?' Issey said. 'But you're gorgeous.'

Paige dipped her head, her hair falling down over her face. It was ridiculous: if someone posted that on one of her Instagram photos, she'd happily reply 'Thanks, babe!' but IRL? Nope.

'She might not be interested, Iz,' Liane said. 'Not everyone's sex crazed like you.'

'I'm not sex crazed,' Issey said. She was lying down now, with her head on Liane's lap. 'I just like boys. Lots and lots of boys.'

'I blame the parents,' Liane said.

Issey laughed. 'Yep.'

16

'They're strict?' Paige asked. She'd only had the one shot – she didn't really like tequila – but she was on her second beer.

'Yup,' Issey said. 'My dad's Greek. And I'm the youngest of five girls. So I was always totally babied and over-protected. So I came to uni and –'

'Went wild,' Lou finished.

Issey laughed. 'Not wild. Not that wild. But wild for me. Wild enough that if my dad knew he'd, you know, die.'

'My dad doesn't care what I do,' Paige said.

'I'm sure that's not true,' Ella said instantly.

'He doesn't even know what uni I'm at.' Paige put the beer bottle down on the coffee table and lined it up with the others, turning them so all the labels were facing her.

'What?' Ella said. 'He must do!'

Paige shook her head. 'He knows I'm at uni, obviously. But I kept waiting for him to ask where and he never did. So I just didn't tell him.'

'And your mum?' Ella asked. She'd moved onto the sofa next to Lou and she hooked her arm through Lou's, cuddling against her.

'Dead,' Paige said.

'Fuck,' Ella said. 'I'm so sorry.'

'I didn't know that,' Liane said, reaching out one perfect leg and poking Paige in the arm with her toes.

Paige shrugged. 'It's never come up.'

'Ella's family is perfect,' Lou said. 'So it upsets her when other people's aren't.'

'Hey!' Ella said. 'That's not fair.' She started to sit up, pulling her arm away.

Lou pulled it back. 'Come on. I'm only joking. But you have to admit your family is like something out of a TV show.'

'So's mine,' Paige said. '*EastEnders*.'

Issey gave one of her honks of laughter that made everyone jump. 'You're funny!' She pointed her beer bottle at Paige. 'I didn't think you were going to be funny!'

'Why not?' Paige asked.

'Because you're so . . .' Issey dipped her head, looked up under her fringe, pouted. She was even pushing her small boobs together with her inner arms.

'Jesus Christ,' Paige said. 'Seriously?'

Liane was crying with laughter. 'Oh my god, Issey! You literally only just met her!'

'I know!' Issey said. 'What's wrong with that? Look at her!'

Liane wiped her eyes with the back of her hands, smearing some mascara onto her cheekbone. She stared seriously across the room at Paige. 'She's just gorgeous,' she said. 'That doesn't mean she's not funny. I thought I told you she was funny.'

'That's what I'm saying!' Issey said. 'I said she's funny!' She clambered up off the sofa, pushing Liane's legs off hers. 'And you didn't say she was funny, you said she was in the shit and we should help her out.'

She half staggered out of the room, bumping into the small table at the end of the sofa and sending all the glasses rattling. 'Just going to the loo,' she told them.

'Sorry about her,' Liane told Paige. 'She's pissed.'

'S'OK,' Paige said. 'I'm glad you asked me anyway.'

It wasn't like she hadn't known. It wasn't as if she'd thought Liane was into her or anything. She'd known Liane had only asked her because Liane was a good person and so one day, after their seminar, when they'd walked to the library together – Liane to meet her friends in the cafe, Paige to stay warm, study, and pretend she'd eaten her lunch already – Paige had ended up telling her too much about her situation. Not everything, of course, but enough.

'Sorry about that. Issey hasn't got much of a brain-to-mouth filter,' Ella said now.

Paige shook her head. 'It's fine. So . . . where are you from?'

'I'm from Lancashire,' Ella said. 'Very small town.'

'And your perfect family?' Paige smiled.

'They're definitely not perfect,' Ella said, smiling back. 'My parents got divorced when I was six. Mum remarried and my stepdad is amazing. I've got a brother a year older and we've got a cat and that's it. Boring.'

'They play Scrabble when they go home,' Lou said, draining a beer and pouring herself more tequila. 'And they've got a family WhatsApp group. They all really like each other! It's fucked up.'

'That sounds great,' Paige said.

'It's not bad,' Ella said, smiling.

'I always wanted a brother,' Paige said.

'You an only child?' Lou said. 'Me too. Sucks. Dylan's, like, Ella's best friend.'

'Yeah?' Paige said, opening another beer.

'We're pretty close, yeah,' Ella said.

'Once,' Lou said, crossing the room to the terrace, pulling a cigarette packet out from the pocket of her dungarees. 'Once when she was drunk, Ella said he was her favourite person in the world. Imagine that.'

'Piss off,' Ella said, laughing.

'Before that, I thought I was her favourite person in the world. But no. It's her actual brother. How wholesome.'

Ella rolled her eyes and Paige smiled at her. It sounded lovely. She couldn't even imagine it.

They moved out onto the roof terrace when the beer ran out. The navy sky was dotted with stars, the air surprisingly warm. Laughter and shouting drifted up to them from the street below. They'd brought pillows and duvets out with them, and were passing the tequila round now, swigging it from the bottle. Paige loved it way more than she'd expected to.

'No relationships for me this year,' Ella said when Liane had finished telling them about the boy she'd seen on the train who'd given her a 'significant look'. 'All work all the time,' Ella added.

'You can't work all the time,' Lou said. 'That's unrealistic.'

'Well . . .' Ella said. She leaned forward to grab some Doritos, but tipped over, ending up with her head in Paige's lap. 'Sorree,' she giggled.

Paige shrugged and helped her back to upright, pushing the crisps closer.

'I'm still going to have fun with you guys,' Ella said. 'But I don't need the distraction of a boy!'

'They are distracting,' Issey said. She was curled up under her duvet like a dog, only the top of her hair visible.

'Well, I'm not giving up boys. Men,' Liane said. 'No fucking way.'

'I'm not giving them up either,' Ella said. 'Just . . . no relationships. I can do . . . casual.'

'You?' Lou said. 'You can do casual?'

'I can!' Ella said.

'Oh, I'm sure,' Lou said, standing up and lighting a cigarette. 'It's just, you know, you never have.'

'I have!' Ella said, shifting so she was kneeling up and looking over at Lou. 'That guy in that bar that time.'

'Oh, yeah,' Lou said. 'I remember him.' She grinned.

'What guy in what bar what time?' Issey said, crawling out of her duvet.

'I can't remember the bar. But the guy was doing a survey? And he came over and started talking to us. Me and Lou. And he asked me to dance. And I danced with him. And then I went home with him!'

'And what happened when you went home with him?' Lou said, blowing a stream of smoke out over the street.

'We fell asleep,' Ella said.

'And in the morning?'

'I left.'

'That does not count,' Lou said.

'It so does!' Ella said, sitting back down and taking the tequila from Paige. 'I went home with someone I'd just met! It counts! Doesn't it?'

'I don't think it does,' Liane said. 'Not if you didn't have sex. Did you do anything? Blowie? Handy? Anything?'

'No,' Ella said, pouting.

'Doesn't count,' Issey said. 'Sorry.'

Ella sighed. 'Well, excuse me if I don't want to just shag random guys I meet in clubs!'

'That's what I'm saying,' Lou said, sitting down next to Ella and wrapping both arms around her. 'You don't do casual.'

'I could,' Ella said. 'I could if I wanted to.'

'What about you?' Liane asked Lou. 'Have you heard from Kyle?'

Lou shook her head. 'Nope. And I don't want to either.'

'You're done?' Liane asked her. 'Really?'

'Definitely,' Lou said. 'This will be a Kyle-free year.'

The five of them sat in silence for a little while, Ella staring up at the stars, Paige scrolling her phone, Issey trying to crawl inside her duvet cover. Liane had her eyes closed and may actually have been asleep. She always fell asleep easily when she got drunk.

'I think this is going to be amazing,' Lou said. 'The five of us. Living here.'

Chapter 3

Issey woke up with a mouth that felt like something was decomposing in it, and a dead arm. She lifted it over her banging head and tried to wiggle her fingers, but it felt really weird. Like it wasn't her arm at all. Like she was wearing a too-tight rubber glove. She grabbed her wrist with her other hand and tried to shake her hand, but it didn't help. She let it drop back down onto the bed.

'Oof. Fuck! Iz!'

Issey yelped, jerking backwards and banging her head on the wall. 'Shitsquirrels. Li?'

Liane rolled over, but Issey could still only see the top of her hair. 'You punched me.'

'I didn't even know you were here. Why are you here?'

'Weird noise. In m'room.'

'Weird smell in mine,' Issey said, shuffling up the bed and leaning back on the pillows. The line through the blinds made stripes on the bed.

'Tequila makes me fart.'

'Nice.' Issey reached for her phone and opened Twitter and Instagram. 'I'm not even hungover.'

'You're prob still drunk.'

'Last night was good, wasn't it?' Issey said, typing Paige's name into the Instagram search box. 'Paige is nice.'

'I told you she was.'

Issey shivered. She shouldn't have left her window open last night. She pulled at the duvet, trying to tug it back up to her chest, but all she succeeded in doing was revealing an undressed Liane.

'Soz,' Liane said without moving. 'Might be naked.'

'You are,' Issey said. 'You are naked. In my bed. Like some sort of perv. What if I was naked too, hmm? That would not be appropriate.'

'It'd be fine,' Liane said. 'S'not like I was going to hump you in your sleep. Anyway, you sleep in shorts and a vest. Always have.'

Issey rolled her eyes. Liane was right. She wasn't that keen on being so predictable. Maybe she'd go out later and buy herself a nightdress or something. Sensible pyjamas like Ella's.

'Anyway. Look at this.' She held her phone up to Liane's face and watched as Liane scrunched her nose up and blinked against the light.

'Is that Paige?' Liane asked.

'Yes!' Issey said, scrolling. 'And look!'

'I know,' Liane said, shuffling up the bed until she was next to Issey. 'I follow her. She's gorgeous.'

The photo showed Paige lying in bed on her front, showing quite a lot of cleavage, her mouth open, staring straight into the camera.

She scrolled past some photos of food and sunsets and clouds and stopped on one of Paige in a bikini, in front of a mirror.

'She looks sexy as fuck there,' Liane said.

'Do you think?' Issey said. She pulled her legs up so she could rest the phone on her knees. 'She's quite big.'

'Yeah, she is,' Liane said. 'But look at her! She's so hot.'

'Do you think?' Issey said again. She took her phone back from Liane. In the next photo, Paige had one hand on her hip, the other pushed into her hair. Again she wasn't smiling, but was looking directly into the camera. 'I don't know.'

'Well,' Liane said, taking the phone again, 'I'm half hard.'

'Oh my GOD, Li!' Issey said, dropping her phone and shoving Liane halfway across the bed. 'Not in my bed!'

Liane laughed. 'God, you're such a prude.'

'I'm not!' Issey said. 'What the fuck? Why would you even say that?'

Liane picked up the phone and scrolled some more. 'Well, OK. You'd never post a photo like this, would you?'

The photo she'd landed on showed Paige sitting in a chair, her legs pulled up to her chest. She was holding a fluffy blanket over herself, but you could see she was naked underneath – the curve of her hip, the side of her boob.

'I might,' Issey said.

'Yeah, right.'

'I might!'

'You're making breakfast?' Paige said, shuffling into the kitchen, wrapped in a huge white fluffy dressing gown, her hair wet and pushed back. No make-up and no glasses. She looked, Lou thought, glancing up briefly from resting her head on her folded arms on the breakfast bar, like an underdeveloped photo of herself. Or like she'd used the wrong Instagram filter.

Ella was standing in front of the cooker, stirring something in a pan.

'Best thing for a hangover,' Ella said over her shoulder.

'I feel like death,' Lou said, without lifting her head. 'Are you rough?'

'I've been better.' Paige sat down and started scrolling through her phone. 'But I've been worse too.'

'We need to all chip in for better tequila in future,' Lou said, reaching for the steaming mug of tea in front of her. 'I can feel my guts rotting.'

Paige laughed.

'There's tea in the pot,' Ella said, bending to pull out the grill. 'Help yourself.'

Paige slid the teapot towards herself. 'I can't believe you made a pot.'

'Ella's a domestic goddess,' Lou said, managing to prop her head on one hand and look over at Paige.

'Apparently,' Paige said. She poured herself a mug of tea and added three sugars. When she looked at Lou, Lou was grinning back at her.

'I like it sweet,' Paige said.

'Apparently.'

'Do you eat meat?' Ella asked, piling bacon onto a plate next to the cooker.

'I eat everything,' Paige said. 'Obviously.'

'Hey,' Liane said, as she and Issey joined the others in the kitchen. 'Don't do that.'

26

'Do what?' Paige asked.

'Put yourself down.'

'Oh fuck, Els, you are a goddess!' Issey said, cuddling Ella from behind.

'Hot!' Ella said, gesturing at the pans in front of her.

'Yeah you are,' Issey said, kissing Ella's cheek and joining the others at the table.

'I wasn't putting myself down,' Paige said. 'I was stating a fact. There's nothing I don't eat.'

'But the "obviously",' Liane said, frowning.

Paige shook her head. 'It's not like I don't know I'm fat.'

'You're not –' Liane started to say.

'I am though,' Paige said. 'There's no point pretending I'm not. But you're perceiving it as negative. I'm just stating a fact.'

'Coming through!' Ella said, hip-checking Issey out of the way and putting a bowl of beans and a plate of fried eggs on the table between them all. 'There's bacon and sausage coming too. And toast.'

'Fucking hell,' Issey said. 'This is mad. You're an angel.'

Ella smiled before turning back to the cooker. 'I thought it would be nice for us to all have breakfast together.'

'You're such a mum,' Lou said.

'Shut it.' Ella brought over the bacon and sausages, piled the toast on a plate, and then joined the others at the table. 'But we do need to sort some house stuff. How we're going to pay bills and who's going to be responsible for different things in the house. That kind of thing.'

'Not now, eh?' Issey said, stabbing a sausage with a fork. 'It'll give me indigestion.'

'Tonight then?' Ella said. 'I want to get it sorted.'

'We're all in tonight, yeah?' Lou said, pouring herself another tea, her eyes still half closed. 'So we can do it tonight.'

Lou spent most of the day in bed, waiting for her head to stop hammering. She spent some time staring at her boring beige walls and boring white ceiling and trying to work out how she could transform her room for not much money. By late afternoon, she'd decided to walk down Church Street and do a bit of shopping. She knocked on Ella's door and pushed it open without waiting for Ella to speak.

'Hey,' Ella said. She was sitting in the middle of her bed with notebooks and uni books spread out around her.

'What are you doing?' Lou asked, horrified.

'What does it look like?' Ella pushed her glasses up her nose and then took them off altogether and dropped them on top of one of the books. 'What's up?'

'But . . . we haven't even started yet. What are you studying?' Lou perched on the end of the bed and then got up again and walked across the room to look out of Ella's window.

'I'm just going over some of last year's stuff,' Ella said. 'Like a refresher.'

'Jesus,' Lou said. 'That decides it.' She turned and leaned back against the window. 'You're coming out with me.'

'I can't,' Ella said. 'I –'

'No, you are. This is mad. I know you're dedicated and everything, but this is too much. You need to live a little.'

'Where are we going?' Ella asked, tidying her books into a pile.

'Primark.'

When they got back – Lou with four bags, Ella with one – 'Can't Stop the Feeling' was blasting from Issey's room and Liane was lying on the sofa in the living room, watching *How to Get Away With Murder*.

'What d'you get?' she asked Lou and Ella, rolling onto her back to look over at them.

'What season's this?' Ella asked, squinting at the TV.

'Two,' Liane said.

'Stuff for my room, mostly,' Lou said. 'And a playsuit. And some boots.'

'And a hat and a onesie,' Ella added.

'Cool,' Liane said, rolling onto her side again.

'Come and help me put the fairy lights up?' Lou asked Ella, who followed her downstairs.

They stopped outside Issey's room, where Issey was standing on her bed and sticking a huge selection of photos to her wall with Blu-Tack.

'Where's Paige?' Lou asked her.

Issey stopped sticking, but stayed on her bed, bouncing gently. 'Work. But she's going to be back for dinner. She said she'll pick up some food from Tesco on the way back and then we can do all the boring shit. My words, not hers. Although I think she said something similar.'

By the time Lou's bags were empty, her room was transformed. A red heart-shaped rug covered the cheap laminate flooring. Six small mirrors were arranged in an artfully haphazard way on the wall behind her bed (which had four new cushions piled on top of the pillows). Flamingo fairy lights dangled from the curtain rail, and disco-ball fairy lights curled around the mirror on the dressing table.

'Are you still going to paint it?' Ella asked.

'Fuck, yeah,' Lou said, lying back on her bed. 'Pink like those flamingoes. Come and have a cuddle. Second year, baby!'

Ella laughed and joined Lou on the bed, snuggling into her friend's side, as Lou squeezed her and kissed her on the temple.

'It's going to be great,' Lou said.

'Yeah,' Ella agreed, half-heartedly.

'It is, you knob. You're brilliant. But you need to relax!'

'I relaxed last night,' Ella said, tipping her head back where some hair had got caught under Lou's shoulder.

'Guess what?' Lou said. 'You can relax more than once a millennium.'

'I'm not that bad,' Ella said.

'Let's go and get a beer,' Lou said.

Ella rolled her eyes. 'Fine.'

Chapter 4

Lou hammered on the bathroom door for the third time since her alarm had gone off that morning. 'For fuck's sake, Liane!'

'Nearly done!' Liane called from inside.

Ella passed Lou on the stairs. She was fully dressed, her hair pulled back in a ponytail, no make-up on.

'She's been in there for, like, forty minutes!' Lou said, turning and leaning back against the door, banging her head on it repeatedly.

'Aw,' Ella said. 'Remember when you mocked my rota.'

'Ella's going to make a rota, Liane!' Lou yelled. 'Then you'll be sorry.'

'I'll make you a tea,' Ella shouted from the stairs.

'Make me one too!' Liane called from the bathroom. The door opened and Lou was enveloped with steam as Liane emerged in full make-up, but with wet hair.

'What have you been doing?!' Lou said. 'You've been in there forever.'

'Had to shave all my bits, didn't I,' Liane said. 'Meant to do it last night, but couldn't be arsed.'

'Oh my god,' Lou said. 'I haven't even got time to wash my hair now.'

'Sorry,' Liane said as she headed up the stairs to her bedroom.

In the bathroom, Lou wiped the steamed-up mirror with her hand and stared at her reflection. She looked tired. And pale. And her hair was a disaster, but if she washed it she wouldn't have time to dry it and it would dry all frizzy and look ridiculous. She'd have to wear a hat. She washed and cleaned her teeth and tweezered the one short sharp hair that always appeared when she was due on. Shit. She was due on. She unzipped her toiletries bag, but there was no sign of any tampons; she'd have to pick some up on the way to uni, giving her even less time. Damn.

'First day back and I look like a proper knobhead,' Lou said, joining Ella and Liane in the kitchen. Ella was sitting at the breakfast bar eating toast. Liane had a bowl of Coco Pops filled almost to the top.

'You look gorgeous as always,' Ella said.

Lou was wearing a T-shirt and tight jeans with boots and a bright-pink beanie. 'I'm worried I'll sweat my head off in this though.'

'Want me to braid it?' Liane asked, leaning over her bowl and shovelling cereal into her mouth.

'Can you do that?'

'Course. French or Dutch?'

'What's the difference?' Ella asked. She stood up, brushed the crumbs off her plate over the bin with her hand, and then held the plate under the running tap.

32

'Dutch is like an inside-out one,' Liane said. 'So it's sort of 3D?'

'That one,' Lou said. 'Please.'

Ella washed the plate and put it in the drainer before turning back to look at Liane and Lou. Liane was standing behind her, running her hands through Lou's hair.

'Your hair is so gorgeous,' Liane said, lifting some and letting it drop. 'It's all silky.'

'Tea?' Issey said, walking in. 'I'm dying.'

'Sit down,' Ella said. 'I'll do it.'

'What's happening?' Issey said, leaning her chin on her hand and gesturing at Liane and Lou.

'Liane's been in the bathroom since the dawn of time,' Lou said. 'So now she's sorting out my hair cos I didn't have time to shower and dry it. Oh, and has anyone got a tampon I can borrow?'

'I have,' Ella said. 'But, you know, I don't need it back.' She picked up her bag and unzipped the outside pocket, dropping two tampons down on the table in front of Lou. 'Is that enough?'

'Yeah, good. Ta. I'm not even on yet. But it's coming.'

'How do you know?' Issey asked, stretching her arms up over her head and rolling her neck. It clicked satisfyingly. 'Mine takes me by surprise every bloody month. Ha.'

'Hag whisker,' Lou said, tapping her lip.

'I know because I want to kill everyone,' Liane said. 'Once I start thinking "why are people SUCH BASTARDS" I know to check the calendar.'

'I'm like that but with crying,' Ella said. 'If I start welling up at adverts. Or, like, seeing old people in the street. I keep meaning to write it down or get an app or something.'

Issey watched Liane braiding Lou's hair, her small hands lifting the strands, nimble fingers crossing them over and tucking them around each other. It was soothing to watch. Liane was frowning with concentration, her tongue poking out of the corner of her mouth.

'I wish my hair was long enough to braid,' Issey said.

'I could braid it,' Liane told her, without looking up from Lou's hair. 'Tiny braids would look so cute. Or one of those crown braids round the front.'

'Yeah,' Issey said, fiddling with her mug. 'That sounds good.'

'Not today though,' Liane said.

'Right,' Ella said, looking from Issey to Liane to Lou. 'I'd better get going. Any sign of Paige?'

'Nope,' Issey said. 'I'll knock before I leave.'

'OK,' Ella said. 'Yeah. See you all later.'

Outside, the air was cold and fresh and the sky was blue and clear. Perfect weather. Ella turned right so she could walk down Bold Street. As she waited to cross the road, her phone buzzed in her pocket.

'Hey!' she said as soon as she accepted the call. 'How are you?'

'Hey,' her brother said. 'I wanted to catch you before uni. You start today, yeah?'

His voice was low and rough. He sounded tired.

'Yeah. I'm just walking up now. You didn't have to ring. Where are you?'

'Uh . . . Hang on . . .' Ella heard a shuffling noise and then her brother was back. 'Brussels.'

'You didn't know?'

'We got here late last night. And I'm still in bed. I couldn't remember . . .'

'God,' Ella said, smiling. 'Your life.'

Her brother snorted. 'I know, right. So are you nervous?'

'Little bit,' Ella admitted. 'I've moved into the specialist department, so it's all going to be a bit new. But, you know, some of the same people, so it shouldn't be too bad. What are you doing today?'

'Don't know,' Dylan said. 'The usual, I should think. Interviews. And then the show tonight.'

'Have you talked to Mum?'

'We texted last night. She's worried about Arthur.'

'I know,' Ella said. 'I need to go over and see them.'

'They've got an appointment, she said.'

'Not for a few weeks though. She said their doctor didn't seem that concerned.'

'That's good. I mean, they probably would get an appointment sooner if they thought it was serious, right?'

'I think so, yeah. Don't you worry about it though. I'll worry about it.'

Dylan laughed. 'I think I've probably got more free time for worrying than you have. You focus on uni.'

'I guess,' Ella said.

For as long as Ella could remember, the two of them had shared out their worries. They were both natural worriers – they got it from their mum – but at some point, when they were both quite little, they'd decided there was no point both of them worrying about the same things and so they'd split them up. Even now Ella would sometimes wake up in the night, think of something troubling and then remember Dylan had taken that one and she'd instantly relax. It was ridiculous really, but it made her feel better. And it made her feel closer to her brother, who she didn't see anywhere near as much as she would like.

'How's the house?' Dylan asked.

'It's good! I think we're all going to get on OK. The one we didn't know – Paige – she seems nice.'

'Hot?'

Ella laughed. 'She is, actually.' Ella crossed the main road, turning to look at the Lucky Penis statue that Lou pointed out every single time they passed it.

'So are you OK, Dyl? Really?'

'I am, yeah,' Dylan said, and Ella could hear him yawn. 'Just tired, you know.'

'I miss you.'

'I miss you too.'

'The boys all OK?'

'Yeah, they're good. Liam's started seeing one of the dancers, so he's always off shagging, but the others are good.'

'And you're using protection and saying no to drugs.'

Her brother laughed. 'Fuck off. You're not my mum.'

'The bus is coming,' Ella said as she reached the stop. 'I'll let you go back to sleep.'

'Hope it goes really well today.'

'Thanks. You too. Break a leg.'

'Love you.'

'You too.'

The bus pulled up and Ella stepped on, dropping her phone back into her bag.

Issey got to the canteen before Liane. She'd had a lecture first and then a seminar and they'd both been fine. More admin and plans for the semester than anything she really needed to think about.

She was waiting in the queue, a sandwich and a bottle of Diet Coke on her tray, when she saw Liane come in. Liane grinned and waved and headed straight over.

'How was your morning?' Liane asked, reaching past Issey to grab a sandwich. Issey felt Liane's boobs brush her arm and she pulled it back and shoved her hand in her pocket.

'Fine,' Issey said. 'Feels like we've never been away.'

'Did you see James?' Liane asked, once they were sitting down.

They'd managed to get one of the booth tables by the window – Issey's favourite, because they looked out over the courtyard and a row of trees. Issey felt like she was in a treehouse.

'Yeah,' Issey said. 'He looked at me and then did this.'

She mimed hiding behind a book. She'd gone out with James a couple of times last term, but then, when drunk, he'd told her that another guy in their seminar group, Conor, fancied her and she actually really fancied Conor, so she'd ended things with James and asked him out. Conor said no.

'And Conor?' Liane asked.

'He wasn't there today, thank fuck,' Issey said. She picked up her Coke and swigged. 'Although it was a bit annoying cos I'd totally prepared myself for seeing him.'

'He probably won't even remember,' Liane said. It had been at the end of term party and everyone had been drunk. Issey didn't think Conor had been that drunk though. She was pretty sure he'd remember.

'Bloody James,' she said. 'I should've known better.'

It had been absolutely mortifying, coming on to Conor, having him say no. She'd even told him that James had told her he liked her. She could still totally see the blank expression on his face, like it had never even crossed his mind.

Mortifying. She was absolutely not going to make a dick of herself over any boys this term.

Ella headed straight for the bookshop as soon as her last lecture was over. She already felt knackered and she still had a seminar and a meeting with her advisor. She'd almost forgotten how hard she had to concentrate in lectures to grasp everything. And how tiring that was. She'd waited at the end to clarify something with the lecturer and she thought she had it now, but she knew she'd still need to go over it a few more times until it properly sank in. Microbiology was really hard. Obviously.

She headed towards the biology department in the back-left corner of the shop. But it wasn't there. The back-left corner was now lit crit. She turned in a slow circle, scanning the shelving for the 'science' signage, but she couldn't see it at all. She was on her second rotation when she noticed a boy staring at her. He was wearing a black T-shirt over black jeans, so it was possible he worked there, but it was also possible that was just his outfit.

'You OK there?' he called out.

'Um,' Ella said, taking a few steps towards him. He was tall. 'I'm looking for microbiology? It used to be here, but now it's . . . not.'

Brilliant, Ella.

'Oh yeah, no,' the boy said. 'Sciences have all moved upstairs.' He pointed at the stairs.

'Oh!' Ella said. 'I didn't realise. Obviously.' She wanted to hit herself in the face.

The boy smiled and dipped his head and a chunk of his floppy dark hair fell down over his face. He pushed it back with his hand. He was wearing rings on almost every finger, Ella noticed. Silver rings, mostly. One of them with something blue. Like his eyes. He had blue eyes. And Ella was still standing there staring at him and not going up the stairs to microbiology. Why?

'I can show you?' he said.

'Oh!' Ella said, shaking her head. 'No. Thanks. I'm sure I'll be able to find it. But thanks.'

She did head for the steps then. She was halfway up the stairs when the boy said, 'Give me a shout if you struggle though. Don't want you to get dizzy.' He started turning in a circle, grinning at her as he did.

'Oh my god,' Ella said and almost ran up the rest of the steps.

Lou thought she'd managed to get to the end of the first day without seeing Kyle. But there he was, waiting at the traffic lights. She'd been planning to walk through the park, since it was a bright, warm day, but no way was she doing that now. Instead she set off down Mount Pleasant, hoping Kyle hadn't noticed her. No such luck.

'Hey, Lou.'

She blew out a sigh and stopped walking, letting Kyle walk around in front of her.

'What?' she said.

He looked better than he had the last time she'd seen him. His hair was shorter, even if it did look a little like he'd cut it himself, and he was clean-shaven. She thought back to the beard burn she used to have after every time they'd been together last year. She didn't miss it. Much.

'Good summer?' he asked.

Lou wanted to tell him to fuck off. She thought she'd made it clear to him at the end of last term that she wasn't interested, but apparently she hadn't been clear enough.

'Yeah, thanks,' she said.

'Where are you headed?'

She was headed home, but she didn't want to tell him that. She didn't want him offering to walk back with her or suggesting they go for a drink. She just wanted him to go wherever he'd been going before he'd spotted her.

'I'm meeting Ella, actually.' She took her phone out of her pocket and glanced at it without really seeing it. 'I'd better go. I'm already late.'

'I'll walk you over,' he said.

'No. Don't.' She sucked in a breath. 'I thought I made it pretty clear last year –'

Kyle shook his head, giving her that crinkly-eyed smile that had won her over in the first place.

'Oh fuck off, Lou. We both know you're going to come back to mine, so why are you –'

'I'm not,' Lou said. 'I told you. I'm not interested. I don't even know why you'd want to when you know that I don't –'

Kyle took a step closer, his face too close. Lou resisted the urge to push him away. She stepped back a little.

'You loved it last year. How many lectures did you miss cos you were sucking my dick?'

Lou shook her head. 'Yeah, exactly. Too many. I told you. I'm not interested. It's over. Please don't talk to me again.'

'Right,' Kyle said. 'We'll see.'

'What's that supposed to mean?' Lou said. 'Actually, never mind. I need to go. Don't follow me.'

'I'm not going to fucking follow you, you stupid cow,' Kyle said, turning back to the traffic lights, as he pulled his own phone out of his pocket. 'Fuck's sake.'

Lou nodded. Right. Her legs were trembling, but she made herself put one foot in front of the other until she was far enough away that she could properly catch her breath again.

She was halfway home when she spotted Paige up ahead. At least, she thought it was Paige. She was wearing the teal leather jacket Paige had had on when she first turned up at the house. She called out her name.

'Hey!' Paige said, as soon as she spotted Lou. 'Were you in that last lecture? The Female Gothic?'

'I was, yeah,' Lou said. 'I didn't see you.'

'Last in, first out,' Paige said. 'I've got work.'

'Now?' Lou asked.

'Yup. No rest for the . . . you know.'

Lou smiled. 'Where do you work?'

'The White Rose?' Paige said. 'Pub. On the corner on the main road.'

'Next to the chippy?' Lou said. 'Is it an old man's pub?'

'It's a bit of a boozer, yeah,' Paige said. 'But we do get students in. It's got a good atmosphere, you should come in.'

Lou must've pulled a face, even though she hadn't intended to, because Paige laughed.

'I mean it. And the drinks are dead cheap. And you can bring the chips in from next door too.'

'You're really selling it now,' Lou said.

'I know, right? But it's good. You should come in. For real.'

They walked on a bit in silence and then Paige said, 'Thanks for knocking this morning.'

'Oh, no probs.'

'My alarm didn't go off. My phone's fucked.'

'Were you late?'

'Yeah. Well, I mean, I skipped the lecture. I'll catch up.'

'What was it? I might have had the same one.'

They waited at the lights by the cathedral while a tour bus went past.

'I don't think so,' Paige said. 'I'm doing English and Cultural Studies, and it was a Cultural Studies lecture this morning. You're just doing Lit, yeah?'

'I am, yeah,' Lou said. 'Hopefully you didn't miss much.'

Paige shrugged. 'I'll catch up.'

42

They crossed the road and walked down Hope Street, past the Everyman.

'You should come and have a drink now,' Paige said. 'You look like you've had a rough day.'

Lou laughed. 'Is it that obvious? Wait. Is it the hat?'

Chapter 5

Paige felt much more at home in the bar than she did at uni. At uni she constantly felt like she was bracing herself against something, but she didn't even know what. She was waiting for someone to catch her out, to tell her she shouldn't be there, she never should have been there, it was all an administrative error. Or maybe for her dad to turn up and drag her home. She still had nightmares about that sometimes, even though she knew he didn't care enough to even look for her, never mind take her back home. It was a relief. But also not.

But as soon as she walked into the pub, she felt like she could breathe, as clichéd as she knew that was. She'd felt like that from the first time she'd stepped inside it last year, when she'd seen the scrap of paper with 'Help wanted' written on it stuck to the inside of the window with Sellotape. She hadn't thought about working in a pub, and had been leaving her feeble CV at coffee shops and fast-food places, but the pub had turned out to be perfect.

Jonny behind the bar was always pleased to see her, but not too much. He said hi, asked her about her day, but then expected her to just get on with working, which she was happy to do. And he always tried to squeeze extra shifts in for her when she was desperate.

Paige loved the regulars – Alan and Donnie, who'd had a pint, just the one pint, every night after work and had been doing so for years. They showed Paige photos of their grandchildren, their new cars, their frequently redecorated kitchens. And they always offered to buy her a drink, but were never sleazy about it (and she never accepted). Jean, who lived alone with her dog, had a missing front tooth and drawn-on eyebrows, and, Paige guessed, was horribly lonely. Paige suspected she may be the only person Jean ever spoke to. It made her heart hurt.

Billy, who was loud and Scottish and asked Paige out every single time he saw her, but was always funny and charming about it. And Paige wondered what it would be like. She thought he'd probably be pretty good – enthusiastic, not too serious, and he had nice hands – but she wasn't going to risk it, not with someone who came in the pub. It was her safe space and there was no room for sex in the safe space.

Right now it was pretty quiet, the lull between lunch and the end of the work day. Apart from Lou, who was sitting on a stool at the bar, alternating between talking to Paige and fiddling with her phone. Lou was the one Paige had been the most nervous about getting to know – she just seemed so cool. And while she was cool – effortlessly so, apparently – she was also warm and funny.

Paige was wiping the counter down, lifting the soaking wet bar towels and polishing the beer taps, when she saw Issey and Liane standing in the doorway, Issey's eyes wide, Liane looking bored and slightly disgusted.

'I WhatsApped them,' Lou told Paige. 'That's OK, right?'

'That's fine, yeah,' Paige said.

Issey spotted the two of them and her face lit up. Paige was grinning back at her before she even realised. There was something about Issey's enthusiasm and naivety that completely charmed Paige, ridiculously. If someone had described Issey to her, she'd have stuck her finger in her mouth and pretended to gag herself, but in person Issey was just kind of sweet.

'Hey!' Issey said, clambering up on the bar stool next to Lou, directly in front of Paige. 'So this is where you work!'

'Yup,' Paige said, dropping the cloth under the counter and wiping her hands on a tea-towel. 'This is where the magic happens.'

'How was your first day?' Liane asked Lou, who held up one finger and carried on texting, a little frown line between her eyebrows.

'You look good behind the bar,' Issey said, leaning back a little and narrowing her eyes at Paige. 'It suits you.'

'Buxom wench,' Paige said. 'Yeah, I've heard.'

Issey actually blushed, her eyes flickering down to Paige's boobs and then back to her face again. Paige laughed. This happened sometimes when someone found her Instagram – they started superimposing the semi-naked pictures over her real, fully dressed self.

'What are you drinking?' Paige asked. 'First one's on me.'

Issey and Liane both got beers. Liane hadn't sat down; she was still standing, next to Issey, half leaning against her.

'Is Ella coming?' Paige asked Lou, after she'd taken someone else's order. She pulled open a bag of crisps and put it on the bar in front of Issey and Liane.

46

'I love you,' Issey said, immediately shoving crisps into her mouth. 'M'starving.'

'She's on her way,' Lou said, putting her phone down on the bar then picking it up again to make sure it hadn't been in a puddle.

'I like this place,' Issey said. 'It's cosy.'

'That's why I like it,' Paige said. 'Let me see if the snug's free.'

She walked to the end of the bar and round a corner and then came back and gestured at Issey, who hopped off the stool, steadying herself on Liane's arm, and walked to the end of the bar.

'Open the door,' Paige told her. 'And then the next door on the left.'

Issey followed Paige's instructions, Liane behind her, and they found themselves in a tiny separate room with its own access to the bar. Where Paige was standing, grinning at them.

'Oh my god,' Issey said, turning in a circle. 'This is perfect! Can we keep it permanently reserved? Like the sofa in *Friends*?

Paige laughed. 'I don't think so. But it's actually almost always empty, except when we're really busy. No TV in here.'

Issey sat on the sofa under the window, dipping her head under the net curtain to look outside.

'Can we get rid of this?' she asked Paige.

'Bloody hell, Iz,' Liane said. 'You can't redecorate.'

'We can, actually,' Paige said. 'I don't even know why that's there – the window's half frosted anyway.'

Issey kicked her shoes off under the table and stood up on the chair, looking out of the top half of the window. 'This is much better. Ooh! There's Ella!' She knocked on the window, while Liane opened the door to the snug and went out to find Ella and guide her in.

'Can we have our own bell?' Issey said, sitting back down. 'On the bar here. So we can call you when we need you.'

'Don't push your luck,' Paige said, but she was still smiling. She'd thought it would be nice to have the girls here while she worked, but she hadn't actually realised it would feel this nice. She shook her head at herself – she was turning into a sap.

Chapter 6

They barely saw each other for the rest of the first week back, and by the weekend they were all more than ready to wind down and get completely hammered. Together. Everyone gradually drifted out onto the terrace as they made it home from uni, bringing drinks, snacks, blankets, cushions and, in Ella's case, one of her textbooks that she knew, in her heart, she wasn't actually going to look at.

By eleven, it was cool and dark, and they were all various stages of drunk.

'Shit!' Ella said as she knocked over her drink. She sat up, looking around for something to mop it up with.

She was just reaching for one of the blankets when Paige said, 'Here!' and pulled a magazine out from where it had been stuck under one of the table legs.

'Hey!' Lou said, grabbing her own drink. 'I was leaning on that.' She tipped her head back and blew her smoke up into the dark sky.

Ella dabbed at the pool of beer with the magazine. 'This is useless. I'm going to go and get some kitchen roll.'

She stood up and staggered a little, banging into the table with her hip.

'Hey!' Lou said again, picking up her own bottle. 'Respect the booze!'

'Listen to this,' Issey said from the floor, her face right next to Ella's spilled beer. 'There's an article called "The Fuck It List".'

'God, what magazine is it?' Liane asked.

Issey squinted at it. 'Can't tell. It's all wet.'

'I'll read it,' Paige said, reaching out and taking it from Issey. 'And then I need to take my contacts out. My eyes are burning.'

Ella came back through and mopped up the beer before flopping down on the floor again.

'Jesus, listen to this,' Paige said. '"There are some men every woman should sleep with, even if she knows she shouldn't. Often the sexual encounters you know you shouldn't have had are the ones that linger in your memory. The hottest. The weirdest. The ones you wouldn't tell your mother about."' Paige looked up at the others. 'Do people generally tell their mothers about their sexual encounters?'

'Ella probably would,' Lou said. 'If she ever had any.'

Ella hit her with a cushion.

Paige looked back at the magazine. 'Yadda yadda . . . sex with people you shouldn't have sex with is hot, you get the drift. And then there's a list. Of people you should have sex with before you get married. Because, you know, everyone has to get married.' She rolled her eyes.

Issey crawled out of her duvet, tenting it over her head. 'Here for the list.'

'OK,' Paige said. 'But I'm warning you, this looks like total bullshit. Number one: sleep with a man with a tattoo.'

'We've all shagged someone with a tattoo, surely?' Lou said.

'I haven't,' Ella said.

'Of course you haven't,' Lou said, kissing the top of Ella's head.

'I have,' Issey said. 'Actually, I don't think I've had sex with anyone who didn't have a tattoo.'

'Same,' Liane said without opening her eyes.

'Gavin had a tattoo?' Issey said.

'Shit one,' Liane said. 'Yin yang thing on his arm.'

'God,' Issey said.

'"Sleep with a waiter",' Paige read. '"Sleep with a Greek waiter".'

'It is weird that she feels the need to specify,' Issey said. 'If you do the Greek waiter first does it count for both?'

'"Sleep with someone off a reality show",' Paige continued. '"Sleep with a man who once went to jail".'

'I think I prefer the crim to, like, someone off *TOWIE*,' Lou said.

'"Sleep with a cab driver".'

'I don't understand what's wrong with these people,' Issey said. 'What magazine was this in?' She reached for the page, squinted at it, turned it over, and then, finding no info, handed it back.

'Nothing's wrong with them,' Lou said. 'They're just blokes to shag.'

'But it does sort of read like a list of people your parents are meant to disapprove of,' Paige said.

'Oh well, I've never worried about them when choosing someone to shag,' Lou said. 'Ella?'

51

'Piss off,' Ella said, mildly.

'But I mean my parents wouldn't disapprove of any of them,' Issey said. 'My dad's a cab driver and he's got a tattoo.'

'Ooh!' Lou said, leaning forward to look at Issey. 'Can I shag him? Tick two off.'

'Fuck. Off.'

'So what do you want on the list?' Lou asked Issey. 'Like, an MP? A public schoolboy?'

'Ugh god, no,' Issey said. 'What about someone who doesn't speak English?'

'Fantasy of yours?' Paige asked her.

'Maybe,' Issey said, straightening up and grinning. 'Don't you think it would be hot, though? Like, it would all be physical.'

'There's more on this list,' Paige said, wafting the paper in the air. '"With another girl, with a friend's brother, with someone in a band".'

'That's more like it,' Lou said.

'Which one?' Issey asked.

'Any of them.'

'You haven't had sex with a girl,' Liane said, turning to look at Lou. 'Have you?'

Lou shrugged. 'Not yet. I'm just saying I'm not ruling it out. I've done the other two though.'

'I've done the brother,' Issey said.

'And I've done the band,' Paige added.

'Oh my god,' Ella said, reaching for the tequila again. 'I haven't lived.'

'Well, here's your guide,' Lou said, taking the article off Paige. 'Laminate this. Tick them off with a Sharpie. No relationships, all casual sex. Plenty of time to "focus on your studies",' she said, doing air quotes. '"Have sex with your teacher or boss",' Lou read. 'See? Perfect for uni.'

'God,' Ella said. 'Don't get this tequila again, it's rough as.'

'It was eight quid,' Lou said.

'Is that the end of the list?' Issey asked.

Lou held the article up under the fairy lights. 'Someone twice your age. Done that. Someone in uniform. Ooh. Would like to do that.'

'Firefighter,' Liane said.

'Soldier,' Issey said.

'Pilot,' Paige said.

'There's a hot security guard at Primark . . .' Issey said. 'Bit more realistic than pilot.'

'Do we need to be realistic?' Ella said. 'I thought we were just . . . you know.'

'I don't know,' Lou said. 'Don't you think it could be fun? See how many we can tick off before the end of year? Winner gets . . . I don't know, what does the winner get?'

'Chlamydia?' Paige said and the others laughed.

'Every time we tick one off we put a tenner in a jar. Winner takes all.'

'So you're telling me it's going to cost me a tenner a shag,' Liane said. 'I need a better job.'

'What do you think?' Lou said. 'Up for it?'

'I am,' Issey said. 'And now I'm going to bed.' She stood up, her duvet curled around her like a turtle's shell. 'Night, sluts.'

'Ugh, I hate that word,' Ella said. 'You can include me if you want, but you should keep expectations low.'

'They are the lowest,' Lou said, kissing Ella's temple.

'Yeah, why not?' Liane said.

'Paige?' Lou asked.

Paige tucked her phone inside her bra and said, 'What the hell.'

The others followed Issey's lead, standing up and heading back inside the house. Ella picked the article up from the floor and started to fold it before saying, 'Hey, wait. Missed one.'

'What?' Lou said, stopping in the doorway.

'Sleep with your best friend,' Ella read. She snaked her arms around Lou's waist from behind, dipping her head to rest her forehead between Lou's shoulders. 'Want to do it now?' She tried to sound sexy, but started laughing halfway through.

Lou laughed. 'Oh my god. See, it's already getting you frisky. This is an excellent plan.'

Chapter 7

On Sunday, Lou made a curry and they all sat around the huge table in the living room together. Issey and Liane had both had hangovers all day and had spent most of it on the sofa watching *How to Get Away With Murder* and napping. Paige had been at work. Ella had made a start on her course reading. And Lou had slept in until just after lunchtime and then joined Issey and Liane in Shondaland.

'So I've been thinking about that list,' Lou said, dipping naan into her curry. 'I think we should do it. For reals.'

'Seriously?' Ella said.

'Yeah, I think it could be a laugh. We don't all have to shag everyone on it. Just, you know, if you fancy a shag, have a look at the list for ideas.'

Issey laughed. 'I like that idea. Like a menu. A menu of men. A MEN-u. Fuck it, that doesn't work.'

'Don't you think it's kind of . . . sleazy?' Ella said.

Lou rolled her eyes. 'Yeah. But in a good way. Just . . . we all want to have sex, yeah?'

Ella shrugged, but the others agreed.

'This way we get to have sex, but without the bullshit.'

'Leaving us free to focus on our studies,' Paige said, looking at Ella over the top of her glasses.

'Exactly,' Lou said. 'It's genius, really.'

'I guess,' Ella said.

'I can't believe it was the "focus on your studies" bit that convinced you,' Lou said.

'I didn't say I was convinced.' Ella stabbed a piece of carrot and popped it in her mouth. 'Just that I'll give it a go.'

'I'm up for it,' Liane said. 'Definitely. Last year was a dis-as-ter, boys-wise. This year I need a plan.'

'Excellent,' Lou said. 'Are we happy with the full list?'

'What was it again?' Paige said. 'Where's the magazine?'

'I think I stuck it back under the table.' Issey pushed her chair back and headed out onto the terrace, coming back in holding the magazine at arm's length between her fingertips. 'It's wet. And gross.'

'Don't put it on the tabl—' Ella said, as Issey flopped it down on the end of the table where no one was sitting.

'Read it out, Iz,' Liane said.

'Right,' Issey said, leaning over the table so she could read it without touching it. 'Tattoo, a waiter, Greek waiter, someone off a reality show, a man who once went to jail, cab driver, another girl, a friend's brother, someone in a band, your teacher or boss, someone twice your age, someone in uniform, your best friend and we were going to add someone, weren't we?'

'Someone who doesn't speak English?' Lou said. 'For Issey.'

'Yes!' Issey grinned. 'Get in.'

'Can we make it gender neutral?' Paige asked.

'Are you gay?' Issey asked, before she could stop herself.

Paige shrugged. 'Queer. Bi, I think. Or maybe pan.'

'What's pan?' Liane said.

'Gender is irrelevant,' Paige said. 'I'm more interested in people than genitals.'

'God, I love a good genital,' Lou said, closing her eyes and smiling.

Paige laughed. 'So you're all straight, then?'

'I am,' Ella said. She'd got her notebook out and was writing in it on the table next to her plate.

'Of course you are,' Lou said. 'And are you seriously writing the Fuck It List down in your bullet journal? Have you got the washi tape for that?'

'Fuck off,' Ella said. 'And you're straight too!'

'I have been so far, it's true,' Lou said. 'But I'm open to new experiences.'

'That's what uni's for, isn't it?' Liane said. 'Trying this stuff out.'

Issey chewed the corner of her mouth. 'I've only been with boys,' she said. She wanted to say that she thought about being with girls, but she couldn't make the words come out of her mouth.

'Cool,' Paige said. 'So if we just make it gender neutral, yeah?'

'So when do we start?' Liane asked.

'Tomorrow?' Lou suggested. 'I would've said first day of term, but we've missed that. Sooner the better. Strike while the iron's hot and all that.'

'And it ends?' Paige asked.

'End of second year,' Lou said.

'Agreed,' Issey said.

Liane held up her beer bottle. 'Works for me.'

Paige leaned forward and clinked her own bottle against Liane's, inspiring Lou, Issey and Ella to do the same.

'To the Fuck It List!' Lou said. 'May the odds be ever in your favour.'

'Or your pants,' Issey added.

OCTOBER

Chapter 8

Ella sighed as she lifted the pizza box out of the recycling and put it on the counter. Someone in the house was absolutely crap at recycling, but Ella really didn't want to be *that* housemate. She started to pull apart an empty Cheerios box, before realising the plastic bag was still inside. She flattened it, along with a teabag box, pulled out some yoghurt cartons and put them in the bin (they hadn't even been rinsed) and then opened the pizza box. There was still pizza in it. She closed her eyes, took a breath, and put the kettle on instead.

'Ooh, are you brewing up?' Issey said, joining Ella in the kitchen. She opened the fridge and just stood there, staring.

'I'll make a pot,' Ella said.

'Whose cheese is this?' Issey asked.

'Mine,' Liane said from the doorway. 'Touch it and I'll kill you.'

'Okeydoke,' Issey said. 'Is there any bread?'

She didn't wait for an answer, just opened the bread bin and started to rummage. Ella focussed on putting teabags in the pot and milk in the mugs.

'How was your day?' Issey asked her, giving her a quick

squeeze as she passed her, before sitting down at the breakfast bar with a slice of bread and jar of peanut butter. No plate.

'Good,' Ella said. 'Long. Had two lectures and a seminar and a tutorial. My brain is burning. You?'

'I caught my jumper on a shelf in the library and pulled a row of books down,' Issey said through a mouthful of peanut butter sandwich. 'Which was fucking mortifying. But then this boy – Mickael – came over and helped me pick them up. I think he does speak English, so he might not strictly count for the list, but he has a really strong accent and I couldn't really understand anything he said so I'm counting him anyway. He asked me to meet him for a drink tomorrow. I think. It wasn't entirely clear.'

'Excellent,' Liane said. 'I blew Tom from my seminar in the loo. Does that count or does it have to be full sex?'

'Jesus,' said Issey.

'Who's Tom?' Lou asked, joining them. 'On the list, I mean. Greek waiter? Twice your age? In uniform?'

'He's in a band,' Liane said. 'They sound godawful, but still.'

'I think it counts,' Lou said. 'Should we vote on it?'

'Oh my god,' Liane said, putting her head down on her arms on the table.

'Oh, shut up,' Ella said, sliding a mug of tea towards her. 'It counts.'

'Yay me!' Liane said, sitting back up again and punching the air.

Lou put her hand out. 'Tenner.'

The Fuck It List was stuck to the fridge with alphabet magnets that had come in someone's cereal box, and they'd washed out an Illy coffee can with a screw-top lid for the cash.

'Oh, shitballs,' Liane said. 'I forgot about that. I can't believe I've got to pay a tenner for a blow job.'

She folded the note up and dropped it in the tin.

'Did you at least get off too?' Lou asked her.

'Nope. Had to go to a seminar.'

'A sexy seminar?' Issey joked, waggling her eyebrows.

'If you find performance management in the workplace sexy. Which I very much do not.'

'Oh, I don't know . . .' Issey said. 'It could be. Bend me over the desk and manage my performance . . .'

'Christ,' Lou said. 'So Liane's got the first tick then? No one else has anything to share?'

'Paige might have,' Ella said.

'Where is she?' Issey asked. 'I've hardly seen her all week.'

'Work, I think,' Lou said, adding sugar to the tea Ella had passed her. 'She's always at work.'

'We should go and see her,' Issey said.

'Can't tonight,' Liane said. 'Massive essay. But yeah, we should.'

'When does Paige do her uni work?' Ella asked, moving the toaster so she could wipe the counter.

'No idea. Never see her doing any,' Liane said.

'Maybe she can do some at the pub?' Lou suggested. 'I get some done at work sometimes. When it's quiet.'

'Yeah,' Ella said. 'Maybe.' She rinsed the cloth under the tap and put it on the draining board, before turning to look at the other three. 'Can I add someone to the list or is it too late?'

'Ooh,' Lou said. 'Go on . . .'

63

'I was just thinking maybe someone from a bookshop,' Ella said.

'Got someone in mind?' Lou grinned. 'Do you have sexy librarian fantasies? Actually, that does sound like you . . .'

'Not a librarian,' Ella said, straightening the toaster so she didn't have to look at Lou. 'A bookseller. Because we're going to be spending a lot of time –'

'And money,' Liane interrupted.

'And money – in bookshops, so I figured this would make it interesting.'

'I like the way you think,' Issey said. 'Maximise our flirt hours.'

'I think we should put "bookseller or librarian" though,' Lou said. 'Keep our options open.'

'Or someone we met in a library . . .' Issey suggested.

'Fine,' Ella said. 'Not yours, Iz. That could basically be anyone.'

'And he's already covering "doesn't speak English" anyway, no?' Liane said.

'S'pose.' Issey stuck out her bottom lip and then curled it like Elvis.

'You can do it, El,' Lou said, gesturing at the list on the fridge. So Ella did.

Liane went straight from uni to work for an evening shift at the supermarket – six 'til ten. She was on with Colette, who was her favourite. She was old enough to be Liane's mum, but always up for a chat and a laugh.

'Someone who's been to jail?' Colette said, leaning her

elbows on the counter and craning her neck out over the store. 'Think that's probably your best bet here, tbh.'

'Did you really just say "tbh"?' Liane asked her. She was crouching down under the counter, looking for the box of paper receipt rolls she knew was under there, but couldn't seem to find. She looked up at Colette.

'I did, yeah,' Colette said. 'And don't even start. I've had our Owen telling me I'm too old to say "fam", too old to listen to fuckin' Lady Gaga, too old to wear thigh-high boots.'

Liane stood up and smiled at Colette. 'You're not too old for any of that. Don't listen to Owen.'

'I never do, love. Hey, he's got a tattoo – he any good to you?'

Liane crouched back down and knelt in front of the cabinet so she could reach in further. 'I don't think so, Col. Thanks, though.'

'Hey, he's not a bad catch,' Colette said. 'I mean, he's not a *good* catch. And you might actually catch something . . .' As she laughed at her own joke about her own son, Liane reached behind a roll of blue paper and screamed as her hand touched something furry.

Liane pulled her hand out of the cupboard and looked at it. She didn't even know what she was looking for. Maybe a flashing light that said 'you just accidentally touched a dead rat'. She shuddered, took a deep breath, and finally pulled the roll of paper out of the cupboard.

'What about him?' Colette said, pointing at a guy standing in front of the chiller cabinet looking puzzled.

'Is it because he's black?' Liane asked, biting the inside of her mouth to stop herself smiling.

'Oh my god!' Colette shrieked, as Liane had known she would. 'No! You know I'm not like that. He's cute. He comes in here a lot. Although . . .' She stared over at him, frowning. 'He did buy condoms once.'

'Stop talking now,' Liane said.

The boy came over, carrying two tubs of Ben & Jerry's: one Caramel Chew Chew and one Phish Food.

'Can I ask your advice?' he said, once he was in front of them.

'Not me, love,' Colette said. 'I've got to nip to the ladies. You'll be all right on your own, Liane, yeah?'

'Fine, yeah, thanks,' Liane said through gritted teeth. She was going to kill her.

Colette lightly slapped Liane's bum on her way past and then disappeared through the door to the staff room.

'Which one of these is nicer?' the boy asked.

'Caramel Chew Chew or Phish Food?' Liane said, redundantly. It wasn't as if he was asking her about his hands. They were both nice, although one had a wide silver ring on the middle finger. She probably liked that one better.

'I like them both, actually,' Liane said. 'But Phish Food is my favourite. Caramel Chew Chew can be a bit too . . . caramelly.'

The boy smiled and his face transformed. He was cute before, but smiling made him quite ridiculously gorgeous. Liane mentally ran through the Fuck It List – she couldn't see any tattoos, didn't think he'd been on reality TV, hoped he hadn't been in prison, maybe he was a waiter? – but then she realised she was being ridiculous. She could go out with him, list or no list.

66

'Right,' he said. 'Too caramelly could be a problem, I guess.'

'Phish Food has more variety,' Liane said, glancing towards the door and saying a little prayer that no more customers would come in. 'You've got caramel in there too. But you've also got marshmallow. And the little fish.'

'Everyone likes the little fish,' he said, turning the tub of Phish Food around in his hand.

'I think so,' Liane said. 'Only a monster wouldn't.'

The boy laughed. 'You're right. I'll get the Phish Food.'

He put the tub in front of Liane and took the Caramel Chew Chew back to the freezer, putting it back exactly where he'd got it from. Liane shouldn't have been impressed – it was basic good manners, obviously – but she'd spent enough time tidying people's shit in the store that it was a definite point in his favour.

'So,' he said, arriving back at the till.

'Thanks for that,' Liane said, nodding at the freezer.

'Oh right,' he said. 'No problem.'

He was staring at her. And she stared back. Should she just go for it and ask him out? Or maybe she should wait and see if he was going to ask her.

'Sorry,' he said. 'Can I . . .'

Liane swallowed hard. 'Yeah. I was just going to –'

'I don't want it to melt,' he said, with an apologetic little shrug.

'Oh, fuck,' Liane said, and then clamped one hand over her mouth. 'Sorry. You didn't hear that. Shit. Sorry!'

He was laughing again. And he had dimples.

'God,' Liane said. 'I'm sorry. That's four pounds. And do you need a bag?'

'Is card OK?' he asked. 'And yes to a bag, please.'

'It'll be four pound five then, is that OK?' Liane said. Like an idiot. She wanted to crawl into the cupboard under the counter, dead rats and all.

He nodded and Liane realised he was still holding out his card. She couldn't see the card machine so she took his card off him, which they weren't supposed to do. God, what if he was from Head Office and this was a test. She'd failed miserably. She found the card machine and pushed his card in, glancing at his name before handing the whole thing to him.

He put his number in while she found a bag and then there was nothing left to do.

'Thanks for your help,' he said, taking the bag.

'No problem,' Liane said. 'Let me know how it goes.'

He grinned. 'I will.'

And then he left.

'So?' Colette said, slamming back through the door practically before he was out of sight.

Liane shushed her.

'Did he ask you out? Did you ask him out? Are you going to eat the ice cream together with two spoons like *Lady and the Tramp*?'

'None of the above,' Liane said. 'I made a tit out of myself.'

'I'm sure you didn't,' Colette said, hip-checking her. 'And even if you did, I bet he didn't care. You're gorgeous.'

'Hmm,' Liane said. She didn't feel gorgeous. Not in her supermarket uniform, a scarf tied round her hair. She had make-up on, at least.

'Did you get his name?' Colette asked, heading back to her own till.

'Yep,' Liane said. 'Alfie.'

'Well, there you go,' Colette said. 'That's a start.'

It was, Liane thought. It was a start.

Chapter 9

Lou had been reading *Moll Flanders* for so long that her eyes were starting to burn. She closed the book, stretched her arms over her head and squeezed her eyes shut. She wanted to rub them, but she was wearing make-up. She pressed her fingertips to the outer corners anyway. Someone had told her that was a shiatsu move for tiredness. Or something like that, anyway. She packed up her books and stretched again before shouldering her bag. The light had changed outside – there'd been bright sunshine when she came into the library; now it looked like rain was threatening. And she didn't have an umbrella or even a hood on her coat. Great. If she got a move on, maybe she could get home before it started tipping down.

It was already spitting when she pushed out through the main doors. She stopped and rummaged through her bag to see if she still had the hat she'd worn last week, but no, she must've left it at home.

'Fuck,' she muttered, seeing Kyle standing in the archway opposite, staring straight at her.

Had he been waiting for her? But how could he have known

she was in there? She turned left without looking at him again and started walking.

'That's not very polite,' Kyle said, appearing alongside her.

'Piss off, Kyle,' Lou said without looking over at him.

Lou pulled her bag up on her shoulder and held on to the strap to hide the fact that her hand was shaking a little. She wasn't scared – it was still light, there were plenty of people around, she didn't think he'd actually hurt her. But he was just intense. And she wanted him to leave her alone.

'I don't get why you're being like this,' Kyle said.

As they turned onto Brownlow Hill, Lou glanced at him out of the corner of her eye. He wasn't looking at her, just staring straight ahead. She stopped at the traffic lights and got her phone out, opening WhatsApp and typing 'anyone near the library?' into the house group chat.

'Come for a drink,' Kyle said.

'Sorry,' Lou said. 'I've got work.'

'Listen, do you want to tell me what this is about?' Kyle said, exasperated. 'Cos I'm really fucking confused.'

Lou shook her head. 'I told you. I told you last term.'

'That we didn't go out? That I didn't want you to see your friends?'

'That you were possessive, yeah.'

'Because I like you. I think that's normal.'

Lou looked up from her phone. Kyle actually looked genuinely confused and something softened inside her chest. They had had some good times. And he'd been amazing in bed. Maybe he genuinely didn't get it.

'I just . . . It wasn't right between us. I'm sorry.'

'Right,' Kyle said, nodding. 'Right.'

Lou's phone buzzed and she glanced down to see a reply from Ella: 'Am at the bookshop.' Just over the road. Perfect.

'OK, so I'm going,' Lou said, starting to walk in the opposite direction.

'I guess I'll see you around,' Kyle said.

Lou kept walking.

From her spot in the seating area between History and Travel, Ella saw Lou come in the main door of the bookshop and immediately looked over at the boy to see if he was watching her. Lou was really pretty and totally striking with her silver hair: of course he would be looking at her. But he wasn't. In fact, Ella thought he might have been looking in her direction until she looked over at him. Now he was fiddling with a pile of paper on the desk, his cheeks flushed.

'Hey,' Lou said, dropping into the seat opposite Ella. 'What are you doing here?'

Ella held up the book she was reading, so Lou could see the cover.

'*Essential Skills for Life Sciences*,' Lou read. 'Gripping.'

'It actually is,' Ella said. Or it would be, if she hadn't been half keeping an eye and ear on the boy the entire time.

'Are you going to be much longer or are you going home?'

Ella flipped through the rest of the chapter. 'Five more pages and then I'm done.'

'You know this isn't the library, right?' Lou said.

Ella bit her lip. 'I know. It's out at the library. I'll buy it as soon as I can.'

Lou shrugged. 'Hey, I don't care. It's just a bit daring of you.' She grinned. 'I'm going to go and see if they've got that play I need.' She started to stand up and then flopped back down again, taking her phone out of her pocket. 'Actually, I'd better check which one I do need.' She waved a hand at Ella. 'Carry on. I'll be very quiet.'

Ella had read two more pages by the time Lou got up. But instead of heading to the Literature section, Lou went straight over to the desk. To him.

Ella watched as Lou leaned against the desk and the boy smiled at her, running one hand through his hair. Shit.

She turned back to her book. Once she'd read the same two sentences three times, she gave up and looked up again. Lou was laughing. The boy was smiling. Ella wanted to throw up. She should have known not to let Lou come and meet her. Though that was ridiculous – it was the campus bookshop, so even if Lou hadn't come to meet Ella, she would have come and met him eventually. She might even have met him already. But then if she had, she would have mentioned him, surely. Although Ella hadn't.

'Fuck,' she muttered to herself.

And she had added 'someone in a bookshop' to the Fuck It List. So not only had she brought Lou here and practically introduced her to the only boy she'd been interested in for ages, she'd given her an incentive to ask him out. She was a complete idiot.

She watched as the boy came out from behind the desk and he and Lou headed upstairs. Even though Literature was downstairs. They were probably going to go and shag between the bookshelves. Ella wanted to slam her head between two halves of the textbook. Instead, she photographed the last few pages she needed with her phone and texted Dylan while she waited for Lou to come back from the sex section. She'd texted him a couple of times already today and he hadn't replied, which wasn't like him. But he was probably busy with work. He worked too hard.

'He was cute,' Lou said as the two of them walked home.

'Who?' Ella said, stupidly.

Lou laughed. 'Come on. I saw you peering at us.' She pulled a pained-looking face, eyes squinted, lips drawn into a line.

'Oh god, tell me I didn't look like that!' Ella said.

'You didn't *not* look like that,' Lou said. 'I should've known when you added to the list. I should've known you had someone in mind.'

Ella wanted to say she hadn't, that it was a coincidence, but it was pointless. Lou knew her better than that.

'So go get him, tiger!' Lou said. 'What are you waiting for?'

Ella shook her head. 'I can't just ask him out.'

'Why not? You thought I was asking him out, right?'

'Well . . . yeah. How did you know that?'

Lou did the pained face again and Ella groaned.

'He was looking at you too, you know,' Lou said. 'When I first walked in. You were staring down at that Life Skills book –'

'Life Sciences.'

'Whatever. You were staring at the book and he was staring at you. Like this.' She pretended to rest her chin on her hand and did full heart-eyes at Ella.

'He wasn't.'

'He bloody was. Would I lie to you?'

'Probably.'

'Well, I'm not now. You should just ask him out. Then shag him and put a tenner in the pot.'

'I'll get right on it,' Ella said.

Both of their phones buzzed at the same time and they laughed as they stopped and checked their texts.

Ella's was from Dylan. She turned it so Lou couldn't see the screen, hoping Lou would assume the light was shining on it. The text said 'Sorry. TV today. Will call later. Love u.'

'Who is it?' Lou asked.

'Just my brother,' Ella said, sticking her phone back in her pocket. 'Yours?'

'Hmm?' Lou said, still staring at her phone.

'Who's the text from?' Ella asked.

'Oh,' Lou said, dropping her phone in her bag. 'No one. Automated charity thing.'

Issey stood in front of the mirror in her bedroom. She'd brought it from home last year, took it back in the summer, and her dad had dropped it off again last weekend. She'd found it in a charity shop and even though it was all bubbly and brown round the edges, she loved it. It was shaped sort of like a curvy shield and it made her feel like a superhero when she looked at herself in it. She put her hands on her hips and pushed her chest out, grinning at herself. She could see her nipples through the vest top she'd worn in bed. She turned to one side and then the other and then reached for her phone. She leaned forward so the reflection was looking down her top and quickly took a photo. It was crap.

She pushed her vest off one shoulder and tried again, pouting. That was even worse. She deleted it immediately. She pulled her vest over her head and looked at herself topless in the mirror. She had good tits. Small, but nice. She'd always liked them, once she'd got over them not getting any bigger. She held the phone up next to her and took a photo, looking at her own face in the mirror, as if the phone was taking the photo on its own, nothing to do with Issey, nothing to see here.

She looked at the photo. It was good. She looked serious and sexy. She almost wished she had someone to send it to. She thought for a sec about sending it to Liane with 'See! Not a prude!' but that was weird. Liane probably didn't even remember the conversation they'd had about Paige's Instagram. But Issey had looked at it so much that it came up at the top when she hit search. Plus, she'd never sent a tit pic to anyone; she couldn't send her first to her best friend. She picked up her vest and held it over her boobs, turning to the side slightly so she could see her waist and hip and side-boob, like Paige had done in her photo. It looked good. She dipped her head forward and looked up under her fringe like Paige, but that just made her laugh. What a knobhead. She tipped her head back, her bob hanging down between her shoulder blades. Maybe she should grow her hair again . . . No. It got straggly when it got longer; she needed to keep it short-ish.

Straightening up again, she stared at herself in the mirror. Then she held the phone up and took another photo. That was the one. The phone was hiding half her face, but showing the tiny star tattoo on her shoulder. And her skin looked good. She posted it to Instagram with 'love my new mirror' and a row of laugh-cry emojis.

Lou shut her bedroom door, put her TV on loud, and sat back against the headboard of her bed, pulling her knees up to her chest. It hadn't been an automated charity text. She didn't know how she'd managed to even speak to Ella after she'd asked. And she was so glad Ella hadn't looked at her phone. If she'd been with no-boundaries Issey, there's no way she'd have got away with it. But she had. Ella hadn't seen it and Lou hadn't told her and if she deleted it, maybe she could pretend it hadn't even happened.

She opened the text again.

It was from Kyle. And it was a photo. Of her. Asleep, on her back, completely naked, along with 'I've got loads like this. See you tonight?'

'Fuck,' Lou said, her eyes burning with tears. 'Fuck.'

She couldn't believe he'd taken photos of her asleep. Or that he'd kept them after she'd ended things. But what she really couldn't believe was that he was sending them to her now to try to blackmail her into going out with him. She scrubbed at her eyes with the heels of her hands. What a piece of shit.

Chapter 10

'This is just the best,' Issey said a few nights later, rolling her beer bottle between her hands and grinning at the other girls. 'Like our own personal pub!'

'Jonny asked when you were next in,' Paige said from the other side of the bar.

'Aw.' Lou grinned. 'He missed us!'

'The brewery have been wanting to get rid of the snug for years. Knock it all out, give the place a gastropub feel. Now he's got you in there, he feels like he was right to say no.'

'God,' Ella said, 'that's terrible. This pub's got so much character!'

'That's exactly what he says,' Paige said. 'Do we have "publican" on the list?'

'Fuck off,' Ella said, her cheeks flushing.

Paige grinned. 'Anyone made any progress?'

'Issey had a shit date,' Liane said. 'Tell 'em.'

'With the guy who doesn't speak much English?' Ella asked.

'Nah,' Issey said, fiddling with a beer mat. 'Different one. And it wasn't exactly shit. It was just . . . meh.'

'Sometimes they're even worse,' Paige said. 'Like, you get all dressed up and it's only OK.'

'Yeah,' Liane said. 'I wouldn't say worse, though. I mean, I'd rather it was only OK than completely fucking awful.'

'At least if it's awful you get a good story out of it,' Lou said.

'That's what I was thinking!' Issey said, leaning forward in her seat. 'Like . . . give me something to work with here. Even if it's that you've got a crush on your sister or you like to pee in car boots or something.'

'Seriously?' Lou said, staring at Issey with one eyebrow raised.

'I don't know!' Issey said, shrugging.

'What's the worst date you've ever been on?' Liane asked them all, as she started to peel the label off her beer.

'I kissed this boy and he had a spider in his mouth,' Issey said, reaching for a crisp from the torn-open packet in the middle of the table.

'What?' Ella said.

Issey blinked at her.

'The thing I love about you, Iz,' Lou said, 'is how you can say that as if it's a perfectly normal thing for a person to say. And not totally batshit cray.'

Issey shrugged. 'It was a thing he did.'

'Wait,' Ella said, frowning. 'He had the spider in his mouth on purpose?'

'I don't know that he could have had a spider in his mouth by accident . . .' Liane said.

'It was a thing,' Issey said. 'He still does it, as far as I know. They call him Spidermouth.'

'Jesus fucking Christ,' Lou said. 'What is wrong with people?'

79

'Shame they didn't call him that back then,' Paige said from the bar. 'You'd've known not to kiss him.'

'I probably still would've,' Issey said. 'I was desperate. And he was hot.'

'Hot enough to make up for the spider?!' Ella said, appalled.

'No one's that hot,' Lou said.

'Dylan Jewell is,' Issey said, cramming more crisps into her mouth. 'He could kiss me with a tarantula in his mouth. Or a whole nest of spider babies. Poisonous spider babies.'

'You're so fucking weird,' Lou said.

'Which one's Dylan Jewell?' Paige asked. 'I get all your boy-toys mixed up.'

'From Bang!' Issey said, picking up her phone and swiping it open.

'What, the band?' Paige asked.

'I'm still stuck on the spider in the mouth, to be honest,' Ella said. 'Like . . . was it a pet?'

'Look, though,' Issey said, holding her phone out to show Paige a photo on Tumblr of Dylan Jewell wearing a sheer black shirt, his tattoos showing through it, his head hanging down, long hair covering half of his face.

'He's got tattoos,' Issey said. 'I could tick him off the list.'

'And he's in a band,' Lou said. 'Two birds, one stone.'

'Imagine,' Issey said. 'Except he'd ruin me for other men. But it'd be worth it.'

Ella stood up. 'Anyone want a drink?'

'Beer for me, please,' Lou said.

'I want a cig,' Issey said, standing up too. 'I've been looking at this photo too long, I've flustered myself.'

'Come on,' Lou said, shuffling her bum along the bench seat. 'I can spare you a fag.'

'You OK?' Liane asked Ella, who was still standing up, not looking like she had any intention of moving. 'You don't need to go round. Just wait for Paige to come back.'

They'd all got used to Paige disappearing to deal with other customers and then reappearing at their bit of the bar to join in the conversation as if she'd never been away.

'Actually, I need the loo,' Ella said.

'I'll get the drinks in then,' Liane said, getting her own phone out. 'No worries.'

They stayed in the pub until the end of Paige's shift and walked home together. It was only two streets away, but the other four girls were pleasantly drunk and giddy and Paige found herself wanting to link arms with them, maybe sing something. It was very much not like her.

'I'm glad I moved in here,' she said, as they stopped at the front door and Lou wrestled with the sticky lock.

'We are toooooo!' Issey said, wrapping both arms around Paige's waist and half nestling herself in her cleavage.

'Jesus,' Paige said, bracing herself against the wall to keep her balance.

'Fuck me,' Lou said, glancing over her shoulder. 'I think you're the one trying to tick off "sleep with a girl", Iz.'

'Piss off,' Issey said, straightening up, her cheeks flushed. 'I'm just being affectionate. That's allowed, isn't it?'

'Course it is,' Ella said, draping one arm around Issey's shoulders and hugging her. 'Ignore the sex fiends. They're all obsessed.'

81

'Are you seeing anyone?' Issey asked Paige as they all fell into the house.

'Not really. There's a girl I see sometimes. Sharda. But I haven't seen her for a while.'

'Girlfriend?' Lou asked. 'Or just like a casual thing?'

'Definitely casual,' Paige said.

Issey was just falling asleep when Liane crawled into her bed.

'Whatsup?' she mumbled into her pillow, shuffling over towards the wall.

'I'm going home this weekend,' Liane said. 'Tomorrow.'

'Oh yeah,' Issey said blearily. 'Forgot.'

She felt the mattress dip behind her and then Liane said, 'I don't want to. That's bad, isn't it?'

Issey rolled over to look at Liane. 'No? I mean, it's not your fault.'

Liane sighed, one arm over her face. 'I get jealous sometimes, you know? Of, like, Ella's family. How they all love each other so much. And you and all your sisters.'

'We fight like bastards.'

'Yeah. But you love each other.'

'Your mum loves you,' Issey said. 'I bet.'

'She does,' Liane said, dropping her arm and rolling over so she was facing Issey. 'In her own way. It's just that her way makes me feel like shit.'

'I'm sorry,' Issey said, her face serious.

Liane shook her head. 'No, I'm sorry. Sorry to be such a fucking downer. It's only two days.' She rolled onto her back again and stared up at the ceiling. 'What do you think of dick pics?'

Issey snorted, rolling onto her back too. 'Not much. Why?'

'This guy from my seminar sent me one. I haven't even spoken to him.'

'Put a Snapchat filter on it and send it back,' Issey said. 'Is it nice? Can I see?'

'It's all right, I guess,' Liane said, passing her phone over.

Issey shuffled up against the pillows and looked down at the photo. Toned abs. And a hard dick in white Y-fronts.

'Retro,' Issey said.

'I just . . . Am I meant to like this?' Liane said. 'Like, is this something I should be cool with? Cos I feel like it's gross. And you know me, I don't mind dicks in general.'

'I think it'd be different if you knew him,' Issey said. 'Or liked him. Or asked for it!'

'Yeah. Like, I'd never send him one back, you know?'

'I don't think fanny pics are a thing, are they?' Issey frowned. 'Maybe they are and it's just that no one's ever wanted one of mine. I did take a tit pic though. And, you know, I'm a prude. Sometimes.'

Liane laughed. 'You took one? Who for?'

Issey's face heated. 'Not for anyone. I mean, just for me. I posted that one in the mirror on IG and took some for myself.'

'Was that because I called you a prude?' Liane leaned back and Issey could tell she was looking at her, but she couldn't bring herself to look back. 'You know I was joking, right?'

'Yeah,' Issey said. 'Not cos of that, really. More cos . . . Paige's photos are nice. And I wanted to see what I'd look like . . . like that.'

'Lemme see!' Liane said, shuffling up the bed.

Issey pulled the duvet over her head. 'No!'

'Aw, come on!' Liane said, yanking it away again. 'I showed you mine!'

'That's not the same!' Issey said.

'Come on, Iz,' Liane said. 'I wanna see! The one you put on Insta was so nice.'

'Nooooo,' Issey said. 'Go back to your own bed.'

'Let. Me. See,' Liane said, punctuating each word with a poke to Issey's side.

Issey curled against her friend's fingers. She was really fucking ticklish and Liane knew all her spots.

'OK, OK,' Issey said, pulling her phone out. 'But you can't laugh.'

'Why would I laugh?' Liane said. 'Show me.'

Issey unlocked her phone and clicked on the photos, then closed her eyes and just held her phone over her head for Liane to take, before pulling the duvet back over her face.

'Oh wow,' she heard Liane say.

She pulled the duvet closer until all she could hear and feel was the cotton fabric and her own breath. What had she been thinking? Showing Liane? What had she been thinking taking them in the first place?

'Iz,' Liane said.

Issey could feel her trying to pull the duvet away.

'Let go!'

Issey relaxed her fingers a little, just enough to let Liane pull the duvet free.

'You look so fucking gorgeous,' Liane said.

'Shut up,' Issey said.

'You do,' Liane said. 'Like a model.'

'A tiny tit model,' Issey said.

'Shut up. You've got lovely tits.'

'Oh my god,' Issey said, rolling over and burying her face in the pillow.

Chapter 11

Liane decided to walk home – *home* home, as she'd started thinking of it – from the station. Usually she'd get a taxi or her mum would pick her up, but it was actually a lovely autumnal day, sunny and brisk, and walking would take fifteen minutes longer than driving so it was absolutely preferable.

She'd hadn't really expected anything to have changed since she'd only left the previous month, but it had. New trees had been planted in front of the station. Small ones, saplings. She walked round the huge roundabout and along the main road, trying to work out how many times she'd done this walk in her life. To school, to the library, to McDonald's to meet friends, to the station to get out of there. She couldn't begin to imagine. And she couldn't believe she was back so soon – she hadn't planned to come back until Christmas, put off by the prospect of the three-hour train journey, and she hadn't even been sure about Christmas. But her mum was having 'a thing' and insisted she be there.

She turned right at the dry cleaners, which had closed just before she'd left, but was actually boarded up now. Her mum wouldn't like that, particularly not tonight with people coming round. Liane was sure she would have contacted the estate agents to try to get the boards removed. She rolled her eyes, even though there was no one to see her.

She stopped at the gate and looked up at the house. At the tiny balcony off her bedroom, where she'd spent so long sitting and looking down at the street and thinking about leaving. For as long as she could remember. Since before she even had an idea of where she might like to go, or be able to go.

Her mum's car wasn't on the drive, so Liane's shoulders weren't quite as tense as they could have been, but she still had to take a big breath before opening the front door. The hall smelled the same: furniture wax and money. She dropped her keys in the glass bowl on the round 'telephone table' and took her bag up to her room, dropping it on the bed before crossing to the window with the balcony. She pulled, but it didn't open. She paused a second, thinking she'd just forgotten exactly how to open it, but no. It was locked. It had never been locked, not for as long as she could remember. She rested her head on the cool glass instead and looked at Zack's house opposite. His balcony with its curled wrought iron, unlike the plain white wood of hers. And the tree in the garden had already grown slightly taller than it. If he was still there, he'd have to hold the branches out of the way to look across at her. But it didn't matter. Because he wasn't there.

She unpacked her bag and lay on her bed staring at the ceiling. She felt heavier already and she'd only been home five minutes. She took out her phone and texted the girls' group chat.

'Home. I'm so cold and all alone.'

'Babe,' Issey replied instantly. 'Is it "Take That lyrics" bad?'

'Always,' Liane said.

'You mean Sure,' Issey replied.

'At least you're not Back for Good,' Ella posted and Liane laughed out loud. That was a very good point.

Issey: 'Ella's right. Have a little Patience.'

Ella: 'How's your mum?'

Liane: 'Not home yet. Just me here.'

Issey: 'So you can Do What You Like?'

Liane: 'I think it's actually Do What U Like. But yes.'

Lou: 'Aren't you embarrassed to know that?'

Liane: 'Nope. What are you all doing?'

Issey: 'Watching *Scandal*.'

Liane: 'NOT WITHOUT ME'

Lou: 'We wouldn't dare. Paige is making a veggie curry.'

Issey: 'It smells fucking amazing.'

Liane: 'I can't believe I'm missing it.'

Issey: 'I bet we can get her to make another.'

Paige: 'As long as you're all suitably impressed with this one. I'm slaving over a hot stove here!'

Issey: 'And we love you for it!'

Ella: 'Will you be OK?'

Liane: 'Yeah. I'll be fine. It's only a couple of days, like you said. I Can Make It, I know I can.'

Issey: 'Fuck. Deep cut.'

Lou: 'We're here for you. Never Forget.'

Liane: 'Lou! Did you google Take That songs?'

Lou: 'Might've.'

Liane: 'I appreciate it.'

After letting the girls go, she scrolled Twitter for a while, before heading downstairs to make herself a drink. The kitchen was pristine as always. She made a coffee and turned the TV on in the adjoining room. They used to call it the family room until her dad left. Then her mum started calling it the snug and Liane thought of it as the TV room.

She flicked pointlessly through the channels, stopping to watch a couple of videos on the music channel and a bit of a *Grand Designs* repeat, before getting up again. The house was too quiet. It had always been too quiet. She wondered about texting her mum to tell her she was home, but decided against it. She made herself a sandwich, ate it on her bed, showered, and tried to sleep, but she couldn't stop thinking about Zack.

She'd spent so long thinking she was in love with him. She'd told herself she was. She'd thought about telling him so many times. She'd acted it out in her head: what she'd say, how he'd respond, what they'd do about telling his girlfriend. His girlfriend who Liane also really liked. But they'd only ever been friends. And she wasn't sure now if she'd ever been in love with him. But she really missed having him as a friend.

'What time did you get back?' Liane asked her mum at breakfast. She was sitting at the dining table with a newspaper in one hand and an apple in the other, a piece of cheese on the side plate in front of her, next to a cup of black coffee.

Her mum glanced up briefly before looking back at the paper. 'About eleven, I think. I told you I was at Mo's gallery opening.'

She hadn't. Liane loved Mo; she would have remembered. She might have wanted to go, even. Maybe.

Liane ate her own toast and drank her tea while her mum finished her apple and cheese and coffee and paper and only then looked over at Liane.

'Any news?'

'About what?'

Her mum sighed as if Liane was being deliberately dense. 'University? Your courses? Your friends? Your job?'

'It's all good,' Liane said. 'Not much to report. We've really only just got started.'

'The house is comfortable?'

'It's great,' Liane said, smiling at the thought of the girls. 'The other girls are great. I think we're going to have fun.'

'Not too much fun,' her mum said, as Liane should have known she would.

'Perish the thought,' Liane said.

Her mum raised one eyebrow. 'So. This evening. I think we have about forty people coming.'

'Here?'

'Of course. It may be more. Jackson had a couple of investors he was talking to. But it certainly shouldn't be more than fifty. The caterers will be here by six.'

'Right,' Liane said. 'So . . . what's it for?'

'I told you,' her mum said briskly. 'The new gallery.'

'You and Jackson?'

'What about Jackson and I?'

'You're opening a gallery? Together?'

'Hoping to, yes. Assuming we can get enough investment.'

'And I'm here because . . .' She tipped her head on one side. 'Because you're my daughter.'

Because I'm Charles Coonce's daughter, more like, Liane thought, but didn't say. She'd got used to these so-called parties when her dad was still at home, but it was new for her mum to be throwing one. And it would probably be all the same people, having all the same conversations. Wanting to tell her how beautiful and charming and poised her mum was. How they'd been sorry to hear about her dad, as if he was dead. Her mum had worked alongside her dad at their gallery – Liane had always thought of it as their gallery, but from the moment divorce had first been mentioned, it had become his gallery – and was now apparently desperate to establish a gallery of her own. Liane didn't care. She didn't care that her mum had been pushed out of the Coonce Gallery. Didn't care that she might start a new gallery with her friend (or boyfriend, she didn't care about that either), Jackson. Didn't care that her dad had sent money for university, but hadn't actually called. She didn't care about any of it.

For years now, she'd only cared about Zack. But he was gone. And he wasn't coming back.

'Can you take the coats and get people drinks?' Liane's mum said that evening as they waited for the guests to arrive. She was standing at the kitchen counter, rearranging the canapés.

'Seriously?' Liane said.

'You know what you need to do, Liane. I don't have time for this.'

Liane stalked out of the room, almost slamming the door behind her, but catching it with her foot at the last minute.

It had a glass panel and if it smashed, the evening would be ruined and her mother would never recover.

She ran upstairs, patted water on her face, stared at herself in the mirror and then sat on the loo and texted Issey. 'I am staff tonight. It's just like being at work, but I don't get paid. Not even in dented tins.'

'But you can drink, right?' Issey replied immediately.

Liane grinned at the phone. 'Right.'

'And your mum buys good stuff, yes?'

'Yes.'

'Get hammered then.'

'I'll do my best,' Liane replied.

She stood up and reapplied her scarlet lipstick. Her mum had suggested something more subtle, but there was no way she was tackling this evening without armour lips. She actually felt better already, just from talking to Issey, knowing that she had another life away from her mother, away from this house. That's what Zack had been for a while – an escape. But now she actually had escaped. She needed to remember that.

She batted her eyes at herself in the mirror, pulled the neckline of her little black dress a little lower and headed downstairs.

NOVEMBER

Chapter 12

'That boy from the bookshop was in my Soul Cycle class last night,' Lou told Ella, as they queued for jacket potatoes in the cafe in the Design Building.

Ella stopped shuffling forward so suddenly that Lou bumped her back with her tray.

'Seriously?'

'Yup.'

'Did you talk to him?'

'Yeah. I said "My mate fancies you".'

'You did not.'

'Course I fucking didn't. He said hi; I nodded at him.'

They'd reached the front of the queue and they both requested their potatoes before shuffling onward to the till. They sat in a window seat with a view of the sculpture garden outside. Rain tapped against the floor-to-ceiling windows and wet leaves swirled over the flagstones. But inside it was warm and bright and almost cosy. Almost.

'He said hi to you?' Ella said. 'He recognised you? From the bookshop?'

'I assume so,' Lou said. 'Either that or he was just being friendly.'

'Well, that's that then,' Ella said, digging her fork into her potato. Melted butter ran down and pooled on the plate.

'What's that then?' Lou said, scraping out the middle of her potato with her fork.

'He fancies you.' Ella ate a forkful of too-hot beans and then fanned her hand in front of her mouth.

Lou laughed. 'Because he said hi? Come on, Ella.'

Ella shook her head. 'He fancies you. I can tell.'

'What if he fancies you? What if he's getting up the courage to talk to me, so he can say, "You know that girl who keeps coming in my shop and reading the books for free and staring at me creepily? Can you give me her number?"'

'I don't stare at him creepily,' Ella said. Even though she'd been worrying about exactly that.

'Just ask him out,' Lou said. 'If you want to go out with him. Or just, you know, say 'I think you're really hot . . . have you heard of something called a Fuck It List?"'

'Oh my god,' Ella said. 'No.'

'So you're just going to wait? Wait and see if he's interested?'

'That's the plan, yes,' Ella said. 'Now shut up and eat your potato.'

Out of the corner of her eye, Issey watched the boy watching her. All around the shop. She'd come into the shop – one of her favourites on Bold Street – to buy a card for her parents, but she was distracted by pretty much everything else. She picked up some novelty egg cups and laughed when she saw the little knight came with a little trident fork. She sprayed some sort of tropical (it had palm trees and pineapples

96

on the packaging) perfume on her wrist and sniffed it. It smelled like her nan's bathroom spray. She turned on a set of pineapple-shaped fairy lights and thought she might actually buy them for her room. Until she saw the price. All the time, he was watching her.

She'd been failing miserably at the list lately. Uni was busy – she seemed to be constantly trying to catch up. She'd known that second year was going to be more pressurised than first, but she still hadn't expected the constant deadlines. She hadn't gone out – or got off – with anyone for weeks. It was getting ridiculous. But now this boy was watching her. And he was cute. She didn't know if he'd fit on the list, but she could always draw a tattoo on him, if nothing else.

'Hey,' he said when she went up to the cash desk.

Issey had an anniversary card to send to her parents. She had originally planned to go home for their anniversary, but she couldn't really afford it. So. A card.

'Hi,' Issey said.

Up close, he had really nice eyes. Blue. Very blue. And blond hair. Looked like natural blond hair – he was very fair-skinned, so maybe it was. It was nice anyway. It looked soft.

He put the card in a small paper bag and leaned forward over the desk. 'You're very pretty,' he said quietly.

'Oh!' Issey said. His cheeks had flushed pink and blotchy. 'Thank you. You're . . . you have lovely eyes. I was just thinking that.'

The blush spread down his throat. Issey kind of wanted to reach out and see if it had made his skin hot to the touch.

'That's two forty-nine.'

'What?'

'For the card.'

'Oh yeah. Sorry.'

Issey handed over the fiver she'd already taken out of her purse.

He opened the till and handed her the change and receipt.

'I'd ask you out if I thought you'd say yes,' he said.

Issey smiled. He was so cute. 'Yeah? I'd say yes if you asked me out.'

He glanced towards the back of the shop and then grinned at Issey. 'Would you like to go out with me?'

'No,' Issey said. His face fell. His mouth actually dropped open. 'God, sorry,' Issey said. 'I'm joking – yes. Yes, I'd like to go out with you.'

'Damn, that was cold,' he said, but he was grinning.

'Listen to this,' Lou said after college, dropping onto the sofa next to Liane, who was watching yet another episode of *Scandal*. 'And then we need to talk about your Shonda Rhimes obsession.'

'We don't,' Liane said. 'Shonda is a goddess. End of.' She paused the TV and sat up, leaning against the arm of the sofa.

'There's a boy Ella likes –'

'Oh yeah?' Liane said, just as Ella said 'Lou!'

'Shush,' Lou told Ella. 'We need a second opinion.'

Ella pulled a cushion up to her stomach and rolled her eyes at Lou. 'Fine.'

'OK, so Ella likes this boy,' Lou repeated. 'But she thinks he fancies me.'

'Why does she think that?'

'Because I saw him at Soul Cycle and he said hi. To me.'

'And then asked you to peel off his lycra?' Liane said, grinning over at Ella. 'Offered you a sniff of his sweaty towel?'

'Nope,' Lou said. 'He just said hi.'

'Ella, do you think everyone who says hi to you fancies you? Because I'm sure I've said it a few times, and while I love you a lot –'

'Shut up,' Ella said. 'I don't think that. It's just . . . it's Lou.'

'Aw,' Lou said. 'That's bullshit though.'

'Has he ever said hi to you, Els?' Liane asked.

Ella peered at her from over the top of the cushion. 'Yeah.'

'So then you're even. You can fight over him.'

'I'm not interested though,' Lou said. 'He's not my type.'

'Cos he's the type to go to Soul Cycle?' Liane said, nodding.

Lou snorted. 'No. He was sort of . . . bumbling and geeky.'

'Ohhhhh,' Ella wailed, flopping over and resting her head on the cushion.

'What?' Liane said.

'Bumbling and geeky is Ella's kryptonite. She loves a great gormless dork.'

Liane laughed. 'Yeah. I can see the appeal. There was a guy at school – he was on the football team, but he was absolutely shit. Like his legs were too long and he was always falling over. Like they were new and he hadn't got used to them. I don't know what it was about him, but I used to get the full-on horn watching him running around like a baby deer.'

'You'd better stop talking about him, Li, Ella might start humping your leg.'

'And on that note, I'm going to go and phone my mum,' Ella said, throwing a cushion at Lou as she left.

'Tell her hello from us,' Lou called after her.

Ella had been talking to her mum for about twenty minutes before either of them mentioned Arthur, her stepdad. Ella felt awful because it was the first thing she wanted to know. Or rather, she knew it should have been the first thing she asked. It was the most important thing. But if she asked about Arthur, the whole conversation would be about Arthur, she wouldn't really get to talk properly to her mum, and also all the oxygen would be sucked out of the room. She couldn't do it.

So first she let her mum tell her about the Macmillan Cancer collection she'd done at Argos last weekend, and how the cat had got her paw caught in her new collar and hopped all round the house to find her, mewling pitifully. How the neighbours had moved out and the landlord had found a 'weed factory' in the loft, and how she'd got a manicure that was meant to change colour with her mood, but only seemed to change when she did the dishes. Only then did Ella ask, 'How's Arthur?'

'You know,' her mum said, even though Ella didn't. 'Pretty much the same.'

'Have you had a hospital appointment?'

'We got one, yes. But it's a while off. Dylan's sorting one out for us in London. Next week, I think.'

'That's good.' Dylan sorting it meant Dylan's PA sorting it and Dylan paying for it.

'It is, yeah. And we're just trying to . . . stay positive, really. He played golf last week, did I tell you?'

'Yeah, you did,' Ella said, rolling onto her stomach and pressing her forehead against her pillow. 'That's really good.'

'It was. It cheered him up. He hates being shut up in the house all day.'

'I could come home at the weekend?' Ella said. 'We could go for a drive. To Lytham, maybe?'

'That sounds nice. But not this weekend. He needs to take it easy, I think. Rest up ready for London.'

'Oh yeah,' Ella said. 'OK.'

'I'll let you know how we get on. You know. In London.'

'God,' Ella said. 'Yeah. Of course.'

'Do you think he's OK?' her mum said.

'Arthur?' Ella asked, confused.

'No. Dylan. I know he's busy, but I've spoken to him a few times lately and he's sounded a bit . . . I don't know, just not quite himself.'

'I think he's just busy,' Ella said. 'And worried about Arthur. But I can talk to him if you like?'

'No. No, don't worry. I'm sure he's fine. Just busy, like you said.' Down the phone, Ella recognised the sound of the back door opening and knew her mum was letting Dipsy the cat out. It made her feel homesick. She should try to get home this weekend. Maybe.

'How's everything with you?' her mum asked.

And they spent the next ten minutes talking about Ella's course and her housemates and whether she was eating enough fruit or if her mum should buy her a NutriBullet with her Nectar card points. It was lovely.

Chapter 13

'So your mum's got a gallery?' Colette asked Liane as she restocked the cigarettes.

'Not yet. But that's the plan.'

'So she was – what? – trying to get investors?'

Liane nodded and then realised Colette couldn't see her. 'Yeah. And also I think just to get the word out? Get a bit of buzz going.'

'Oh, aye. Like that new bar on Seal Street. They had men in short shorts handing out shots.' Colette turned and leaned back on the counter, grinning at Liane.

'Just like that, yeah,' Liane said. 'Only with no joy or fun. Or short shorts.'

'Booze, though?'

'Oh yeah.'

Liane flashed back to an image of herself in the garden of the house she grew up in, some guy's hands up her skirt, her head tipped back and banging on the trellis. She'd kept worrying that some of the flower heads would get knocked off, which was a really weird thing to have worried about. She hadn't asked his age, but from the looks of him he was easily mid-forties, so she got to tick someone twice your age off the Fuck It List at least.

If her mum had seen them – if the man mentioned it – Liane's life would effectively be over. But last weekend, she'd drunk enough that she didn't care. She didn't feel great about it. But this was why she hadn't wanted to go home.

'So what's she like?' Colette said. 'Your mum?'

A customer came then and tried to use the automatic checkout, even though Colette and Liane were standing right there. They stopped talking and just watched and waited for the inevitable 'unexpected item' alert. Once the customer had left, Colette said, 'So? Your mum?'

'She's . . . not like your mum.'

Colette rolled her eyes. 'God. Who is?'

Colette's mum came into the shop every week. She brought Colette a dish of food – she called it leftovers, but Colette strongly suspected she made it especially – and talked them through pretty much every step of her week since she'd last been in: which neighbours she'd chatted to, what she'd watched on TV, everything she'd eaten, whether or not she'd been able to 'go' that day. (The first time she came in, Liane had innocently asked 'Go where?' and Colette and her mum had almost peed themselves laughing.)

'She doesn't act like a mum,' Liane said now. 'I mean, obviously I don't have anyone to compare her with. But she doesn't act like mums on TV. Or my friends' mums. She kind of treats me like an irritating employee.'

'Fuck,' Colette said simply. 'I'm sorry. Has she always been like that?'

'She's never really been affectionate . . .' Was that true? Liane tried to think back to the last time her mum hugged or kissed her beyond a perfunctory air kiss whenever they met, and she couldn't remember. 'There's photos of me sitting on her knee and stuff when I was little, but that's all really. For Mum, it's all about appearance. And achievement. She's got worse since Dad left though. Definitely.'

'Isn't that your boyfriend?' Colette said, nodding at a guy standing in front of the beer fridge.

'Not my boyfriend,' Liane said. It was Alfie though, she was pretty sure.

'Nice little arse,' Colette muttered, just as the guy turned round.

His eyes actually lit up when he saw Liane. They definitely did. She saw it. No question. He was happy to see her.

'Hey,' she said, holding onto the edge of the counter. 'How did the Phish Food go down?'

'Yep,' he said, nodding. 'Very popular choice. I've been back for more, but you weren't here.'

He'd noticed, Liane thought. He'd noticed she wasn't there.

'Oh yeah,' she said. 'I went home for the weekend.'

Alfie was standing next to the trolley with the reductions on it and he turned a pack of yum yums around to look at the price before putting them in his basket.

'Yeah?' he said, looking around absentmindedly before focussing on her again. 'Where's home?'

'Richmond,' she said. 'Surrey. How about you?'

'Here, actually. Well, Crosby. But I live in town now.'

'Cool,' Liane said. 'Me too. Bold Street.'

He stepped up to the counter then. 'Yeah? I work there. In Bean? The coffee shop?'

'Oh, yeah!' Liane said. 'I've been in there! I've never seen you.' I would've noticed, she wanted to add, but couldn't.

'Well, next time you come in, coffee's on the house,' he said. 'I mean, as long as I'm there.' He grinned and Liane stared at his dimples. They were huge.

'You are so in there,' Colette said as soon as Alfie had gone.

'He's just being polite,' Liane said, but she was still staring at the door.

'What did he get?' Colette said.

'Um . . . beer. Yum yums.' Liane hadn't been paying attention, she'd just scanned the stuff and bagged it up.

'Tomatoes, burgers, bread rolls,' Colette said. She'd lifted the flap on the till and was reading the receipt. 'Paracetamol, cheese . . . No condoms, that's good.'

'I would've noticed if he'd bought condoms.'

'I don't know. You looked pretty out of it.'

'Did I?' Liane shrieked.

'Calm down, love. Not like he'd've noticed. But, yeah, you looked pretty smitten.'

'Shit,' Liane said.

'That's a good thing,' Colette bumped her with her shoulder. 'You want him to know you're up for it, right? For whatever he's offering?'

'He's really cute.'

'He is, yeah. You need to go to that coffee place tomorrow.'

'Tomorrow? Do you think?'

'Yep. Get it while it's hot. And before someone else sweeps in.'

Liane nodded. She could go and get a coffee in the morning. That would be fine.

Chapter 14

'That girl is living the life I want,' Lou said, as a girl went past on a bike. She was wearing a fake fur coat and a beret and had a bowling bag over her shoulder.

'What's wrong with your life?' Ella asked Lou.

Lou shrugged. 'No, you're right. It's fine. It's just . . . I always think about different lives I could have. Don't you?'

'Not really,' Ella lied. 'I think you have to live the life you have.'

Lou reached out and pinched her cheek. 'And that is why I love you.'

'Why?'

'You're so . . . straightforward.' Lou tore open a sachet and emptied the sugar into her latte.

'Oh my god,' Ella said, veering away from Lou's hand. 'That means boring.'

'No! You're not boring. I love you. You're sensible. Steady. Smart.'

'Ugh,' Ella said. 'I'm nineteen. I shouldn't be any of those things.'

'Like, if it wasn't for me, you'd be at home drinking latte

from a sachet instead of out here in the world throwing caution and £2.59 to the wind.'

Ella stuck her tongue out at her, before lifting her latte and taking a sip. Ella did think that paying for a drink they could make at home was a waste. But she'd started telling herself the drink was free and she was paying for the experience of sitting in a cafe with her friend and people-watching. It helped. The cute guy behind the counter didn't hurt either – she'd seen Lou eyeing him earlier.

'Is there a barista on the list?' Ella asked, jerking her head back towards the counter.

Lou grinned. 'Can't remember. But he's cute, isn't he? Dimples.'

'Ask him out.'

Lou shook her head, her long earrings jangling. 'Nah.'

'Why not?'

'He looks too nice.'

'Oh god,' Ella said. 'I don't understand you. I thought you got that out of your system with Kyle.'

Lou slurped some coffee, shaking her head. 'Stop trying to change the subject. We were talking about you.' She tapped Ella's coffee cup with a teaspoon. 'You're happy, aren't you? You don't want to be different. You don't want to be wild. You can do shorthand, for fuck's sake!'

Ella looked down at the table where her notebook and pen from that morning's lecture were laid out. 'It's useful!'

'I know it is. That's what I'm saying. I come out of lectures and I can't read my notes. Or I lose them. Or I forget my laptop. You come out of lectures with perfectly ordered notes that are actually helpful.'

'Wow,' Ella said. 'Hot.'

Lou grinned at her. 'Do you want me to Rizzo you, is that what you're saying? You're Sandra Dee and you want the leather kecks and the cig and the "Tell me about it . . . stud".'

'No,' Ella said. 'God, no.' She picked up her pen and doodled a 3D box in the corner of the page. 'Maybe . . . a bit.'

'Your hair?'

'What's wrong with my hair?!'

'Nothing's wrong with it. It's lovely. It's just a bit . . .'

'Boring.'

'I think you'd look great with brighter hair, is all I'm saying. Maybe pink? You mentioned that before. And the Christmas party's coming up. Bookshop Boy might be there . . .'

'Oh god.' Ella twisted her mouth to the side as she tried to picture herself with pink hair. 'What about lavender? Like yours?'

Lou had decided the silver was too high-maintenance and had gone lavender the week before.

'You want us to go around together with matching hair?'

'Oh yeah,' Ella said. 'Maybe not.'

'Pink then,' Ella said. 'But not, like, baby pink. Brighter.'

'Like this?' Lou said, holding up her beanie that had been resting on top of her bag on the table. 'Raspberry?'

'Yeah,' Ella said. 'Raspberry. Would that look good, do you think?'

'I think it'll look gorgeous,' Lou said. 'Come and get it done tonight – I'm working 'til nine.'

Liane walked in and did a double take at Ella and Lou

before walking over to join them.

'We were just admiring the barista,' Lou told her, nodding in the direction of the counter.

'That's why I'm here, actually,' Liane said. She gestured at Lou's coffee. 'Can I? I'm gasping.'

'I'll get you one,' Ella said, shoving her chair back. 'Unless you . . . ?'

Liane shook her head. 'That's not him. And don't worry, I can go.'

'You're fine,' Ella said, heading over to the counter.

'How is she always so nice?' Liane asked Lou.

'No idea,' Lou said. 'She makes me sick.' She slid her coffee back and took a quick sip before pushing it back to Liane. 'So. How's things with you?'

'Confusing,' Liane said, scrunching her face up. 'Do you ever think . . .' She shook her head. 'This is going to make me sound insane.'

Lou shrugged. 'Go for it.'

'I have, like, all this stuff in my head. And I don't know how much of it is real and how much I'm making up, you know? Like . . . I spent ages, years, thinking I liked this guy. And now I'm not sure I ever really did. So now I like this other guy –'

'The barista?' Lou asked.

Liane nodded. 'His name's Alfie. But how do I know if I really do? Or if I'm making it up again?'

Lou frowned. 'I think you just have to try anyway? And see where it goes. And try to be honest with yourself about what you want.'

'Historically,' Liane said, finishing Lou's coffee, 'I have not been good at that.'

'Fuck,' Lou agreed. 'Me neither.'

The salon Lou worked in looked like a cross between a junk shop and a tattoo parlour. The walls were covered in framed paintings and neon signs. A huge, squashy, patterned sofa took up most of the back wall and was piled with cushions. The sinks and units were reclaimed from a 1950s beauty salon. Only the client chairs were modern and even then they were bright pink leather.

Lou pasted the dye over Ella's hair, while telling her about a client they'd had the previous night who'd wanted rainbow hair and had brought a My Little Pony with her to show them the colours.

'I think Katie Price killed off the whole looking-like-My-Little-Pony thing,' Lou said. 'That and the bronies.'

'What?' Ella said. Her phone was buzzing in her pocket.

'Jordan. You know? She did a book launch dressed as a My Little Pony. With the hair and an actual horse body.'

Ella pulled her phone out of her pocket. 'She had a horse body?'

'The back of one. You know, like a cyclops. No, not a cyclops. Centurion. No. What the fuck's it called?'

Ella shook her head, feeling her hair tug in Lou's hands, and then answered the phone, holding it an inch or so away from her ear so as not to get dye on it.

'Sid?' Lou shouted to the back of the shop. 'What's the thing called that's half man, half horse?'

'Is this a cock question?' Ella heard Sid say and then her brother said, 'Heyyyyyyy!'

Ella laughed. 'Are you drunk?'

'Sooooo dunk.'

'I'm getting my hair dyed bright pink,' Ella said. 'Right now. In Lou's salon.'

'Hot Lou?' Dylan said. 'And high.'

'Did he just say 'Hot Lou'?' Lou said, her eyes meeting Ella's in the mirror. 'Who's that?'

'Are you saying hi or that you're high?' Ella said, frowning into the phone.

'Centaur!' Sid yelled. 'I googled.'

'Centaur, that's it,' Lou said. 'Els. Who is it?'

'It's my brother,' Ella said. 'Can I just . . .' She started to get out of the seat. 'For just a minute?'

'Seriously, just a minute though. Or you'll come out patchy. Apache. Is that another horse?'

'Palomino,' Sid said, before disappearing into the back room again. 'And don't google bronies, for fuck's sake.'

Ella walked to the front of the salon and opened the door, stepping outside onto the street. 'Dylan? Did you say you're high?'

'Just a bit, yeah. Was it Hot Lou?'

'Yes, that Lou. How are you? Who are you with?'

'The boys! Noah. And Calum.'

'Don't let them leave you on your own though, Dylan. Promise me.'

'They're not going to leave me on my own,' Dylan mumbled. And then he shouted, 'THEY LOVE ME.'

'Jesus Christ,' Ella said. 'I love you too. And I know what you're like when you're high. And you need to not be on your own. Can I talk to one of them? Put Calum on the phone.'

'Fuck off, Els. You sound like Mum. They'll all take good care of me, don't worry.' He snorted.

'God,' Ella said. 'I'll ring you later then. Make sure you're still alive.'

'I might not answer though. I might've pulled. Calum met these girls and –'

'Oh my god, shut up,' Ella said. 'As if I want to hear about that. I'm going back in now, before I fuck my hair up. Promise me you'll be sensible.'

'Sensible is no fun!' Dylan almost shouted.

Ella turned to open the door and it was only then she really realised she'd been standing out in the street with pink dye plastered to half of her head. And of course it was also exactly then that she saw the boy from the bookshop walking towards her.

'Oh shit,' she muttered. 'Fucking shit.' The door wouldn't open. Of course it wouldn't open.

'Are you OK?' Dylan said. 'Is your head burning? That happens to Noah sometimes when –'

'No, Dyl. It's fine. Just . . . call me later, yeah. Even if you pull.'

'Hey,' the boy said, as he walked past.

'Love you,' Dylan said.

Ella wanted to bash her head against the door, but she didn't want to get dye on the glass.

'Love you too,' she said into the phone.

She pulled at the door again, resisting the urge to boot through the glass. And then Lou was walking towards her and opening the door.

'You could've just tried pushing,' Lou said.

'Fuck,' Ella said.

Chapter 15

'You seem excited,' Liane said. She'd come back from Bean, having failed to even see Alfie, had a shower, called home, and decided to spend the evening doing absolutely nothing. She leaned against Issey's doorway wearing a T-shirt and nothing else.

'He's cute,' Issey said, shrugging.

'Who is he? Can you tick him off the list?'

'Not sure yet. He works in that shop – you know, the one with all the lit-up signs in the window? I'm hoping he's got a tattoo at the very least.'

'Where are you going?'

'I don't know. We just said we'd get some food.'

'So you're not going to be late? Cos we've got that essay and you said –'

'Yeah, I know. We're not going to do it tonight though, are we? Tomorrow morning?'

'Yeah, I was just thinking . . . if you were hungover . . .'

'I'll be fine,' Issey said. 'You?'

Liane shook her head, as if to clear it. 'Yeah, sorry, m'fine. Just talked to my mum and she was a bit . . . you know.'

'Ugh,' Issey said. 'Parents.'

She posed, pouting, with one hand on her hip, the other pushed into her hair. 'How do I look?'

She was wearing a short black dress with a black leather jacket and motorbike boots.

'Gorgeous,' Liane said.

Issey blew her a kiss.

'What?' Paige snapped, looking up from her laptop.

'Two pints of lager and a packet of crisps please,' the man said. He was young. Probably not much older than Paige. Shaved head, angry eyebrows. Just the kind of bloke she would've shagged without hesitation in the past. But now? She couldn't be bothered. When had that happened?

'Seriously?' Paige said.

He frowned. 'Yeah. Why?'

'It's the name of a TV show,' Paige said, closing her laptop and reaching for a pint glass. 'I used to watch it when I was a kid.'

'Never heard of it,' the man said. 'Was it good?'

'Can't remember,' Paige said. 'Which crisps?'

She got him the drinks and the crisps and he said, 'Have one yourself,' which she thought probably meant that he would also be up for a quick trip to the loos, if she was so inclined. But she needed to finish her essay and every time she was interrupted she had to go back to the beginning. Postmodernism fucked with her head.

She opened her laptop to find the screen covered in flickering multi-coloured lines. 'Fuck,' she muttered, tapping the space bar. 'No. No no no no no.'

'Paige?' Jonny said from somewhere over her shoulder.

'Hang on,' she said, trying to remember when she'd last hit save. 'Look at this. Do you think it's fucked?'

'Have you got the charger?' Jonny said. 'Take it in my office and put it on charge. Sometimes that helps.'

''K,' Paige said. 'Thanks.'

In Jonny's small and sweat-scented office, Paige plugged the laptop in and watched the screen turn black and heard the fan stop whirring.

'No,' she said, her eyes filling. She scrubbed at them with the heels of her hands. 'For fuck's sake.' But it was a 3,000-word essay. And she'd done maybe 2,500. And she had no idea if she'd saved it and even if she had, if her laptop – her ancient, on-its-last-legs laptop – was fucked, then she was too. She closed it, leaned over and banged her head on the desk a few times. She opened the laptop and held her breath while it flickered back to life.

'Thank fuck for that,' she said.

'Do you really love it?' Lou asked again as she and Ella walked back up Bold Street towards home.

'I do,' Ella said, glancing at her reflection in a shop window. Her hair was a brighter pink than even she'd expected. 'I promise. I love it.'

Ella had stayed 'til the end of Lou's shift, reading over some notes on her laptop and making a plan for the essay she had to write by the end of the following week. The salon hadn't been busy, but there had been a fairly steady stream of customers, though not enough to distract her. What had distracted her though was worrying about Dylan. Dylan somewhere off in Europe, pissed and high.

Dylan was utterly hopeless with drugs. Always had been. He got dopey and clingy, loved everyone and thought everyone loved him. Which was pretty similar to his personality when he wasn't high, but both drink and drugs heightened it and lowered his common sense. Ella was fairly confident the other boys would look after him, but she still had an image of him wandering lost and alone in some strange city, being taken advantage of. It was ridiculous. He was her older brother, ffs.

'You OK?' Lou asked, as they turned off at Wetherspoons. 'You seem distracted.'

'Just worrying about my brother,' Ella said. 'He's pissed.'

'Pissed off or drunk? Oh and hey, I totally forgot. Did he say "Hot Lou"? Did he mean me?'

Ella rolled her eyes. 'God. Yes. He saw a photo of you on my phone once and got all creepy about it.'

'Is *he* hot?' Lou asked. 'Show me a photo. Actually, I can't believe I've never seen a photo of him! Does he look like you? I could totally go for a boy version of you.' She bumped Ella's shoulder.

'He does look a bit like me, yeah,' Ella said. 'I haven't got any photos of him on my phone though.'

'Piss off, you must have!' Lou said. 'I bet you all took a family one at Christmas, didn't you? In front of the tree, all in your Christmas jumpers, reindeer antlers on.' She tried to grab Ella's phone out of her hand, but Ella yanked it back and dropped it in her bag.

'I haven't, honest! I'll find one next time I go home, promise.'

'Your brother thinks I'm ho-t-t,' Lou sing-songed.

118

'Only because he hasn't met you and doesn't know how annoying you are.'

'You love me,' Lou said, hugging her.

'I do love you.'

'And your hair. You love your hair.'

'Yes,' Ella said. 'I do love my hair.'

'How did it go?' Liane asked without turning over.

'Sorry,' Issey said, climbing into bed behind her. 'I didn't mean to wake you up.'

'I was awake. Mostly.'

She'd watched two episodes of *Grey's Anatomy*, searched AO3 for some fanfic and stumbled guiltily across the Addison/Callie tag. That had been highly enlightening and distracting. But she'd decided she'd have to think about it some other time. She had enough to be dealing with right now.

'So?' she asked Issey. 'Do you have something to tick off the list?'

Issey rested her forehead between Liane's shoulder blades. Liane was still wearing the T-shirt she'd been wearing earlier that evening.

'Nope. No tick for him.'

'What happened?' Liane asked, starting to turn over.

Issey put her hand on her back to stop her. 'Don't laugh.'

'What? Why would I laugh?'

'He's sixteen.' Issey buried her face in Liane's pillow, embarrassment overwhelming her once again. When Daniel had told her – in the restaurant, as they were having coffee – she'd wanted to just get up and run straight home.

'Oh my god!' Liane said, laughing.

'You said you wouldn't laugh!' Issey howled, face still in the pillow.

'I didn't. You just told me not to. Oh my god, Iz!'

'I knowwwwwww. Shut up. God, I want to die.'

'You didn't do it, did you?' Liane said. Issey could tell she'd rolled over now – her voice was right next to Issey's ear.

'Fuck off. God. No. But imagine if I had. Jesus.'

'Did you kiss?'

'No.' Issey couldn't breathe. She turned her head to one side. Liane was right there. Head on the pillow next to Issey's, face just inches away. 'We didn't do anything.'

'Well. That's OK then,' Liane said.

'Yeah. It's just, god. I was so embarrassed. What was he thinking?'

'Did he know how old you are?'

Issey tried to shake her head even though she was lying down and it didn't work. 'He said he'd guessed I was older, but he didn't know. I told him. When he told me. I think he was pleased. Probably going to go and brag to his mates.'

'The playground'll be buzzin' at school tomorrow,' Liane said and grinned.

'Fuck. Off,' Issey said, but she could feel laughter bubbling up inside. 'Oh my god.'

'I hope he doesn't tell his mum,' Liane said, face serious.

'You're not funny.'

'I am though,' Liane said. 'I'm hilarious.'

'You keep telling me that,' Issey said.

'Cos it's true. I'm hilarious. And smart. And hot,' Liane said.

Issey's eyes flickered down to Liane's lips and she closed her eyes rather than look back at her.

'Want to stay here?' Liane asked, her voice low.

'No,' Issey said. 'I'd better not.' Not when she was scared to open her eyes and see Liane right there in front of her, her face on the pillow, soft and sleepy.

'You can do,' Liane said. 'I don't mind. Even though you snore.'

'I don't snore,' Issey said. 'And you fart in your sleep, so you've no room to talk.'

'That's it,' Liane said. 'Offer rescinded. Get back to your own room.'

Issey rolled over, opening her eyes only once her back was turned to Liane. 'I'm going, I'm going.'

'Essay in the morning,' Liane said.

'Wouldn't miss it.'

'Sweet dreams about your toyboy,' Liane said, as Issey opened the door.

Issey grabbed a cushion from the floor and threw it at the bed.

Chapter 16

'I love your hair.'

Ella had been concentrating hard and jerked forward with shock, banging her forehead on the shelf.

'Shitballs,' she muttered. The book she was reading hit a lower shelf and started to slip out of her hand. She floundered, managed to grab the cover and then wailed 'Noooooo' as the cover ripped off in her hand and the rest of the book tumbled to the floor.

'I'm so sorry!' the boy said.

Ella didn't even need to turn round to know it was THE boy.

'I'm buying it,' Ella said. 'I mean, I was already going to, but I'm definitely going to now.'

'Is your head OK?'

Ella became aware of a slow throbbing between her eyebrows. She reached up and touched it tentatively with her fingertips. 'I think so.'

'Can I see?' the boy said. 'I'm a first aider.'

Ella closed her eyes as she turned round. She was mortified.

'It doesn't look too bad,' she heard him say. 'Let me just . . .'

She sucked in a breath as she felt his fingers on her cheek

and then he turned her head into the light. She could tell because it was bright through her eyelids. 'It's probably going to bruise though. It's already looking a bit blue.'

'Great,' Ella said. 'That's all I need. A bruise on my forehead, of all places.'

'Could be worse,' the boy said. 'Can you open your eyes? Cos if the light's hurting them it could be a sign that –'

'No, no,' Ella said, opening her eyes.

His face was very close. His eyes were dark brown in the middle and lighter brown around the edges. His hair looked like the crest of a wave.

'I feel like I need one of those pen lights,' he said. 'I could say "pupils fixed and dilated". Like on *Grey's Anatomy*.'

'I think that would mean I was dead. Pupils fixed and dilated, I mean.'

'Shit, really?' He bit his lip and his cheeks flushed pink. 'Are you a med student?'

'Microbiology. But I've read that somewhere. I think it's "pupils responsive", maybe. If you're not, you know, dead.'

'I'll remember that,' he said. He took a step back and stared at her. 'You don't feel dizzy or anything, do you? Can I get you a glass of water? Or a cup of tea?'

'No, I'm good, thanks. I'll just pay for this and then I need to go.'

'You don't need to pay for that,' the boy said. 'It was my fault you dropped it. I startled you.'

'No, I shouldn't have been reading it here anyway.'

'Oh, everyone does that. Half these books have got bookmarks in. Seriously, if you were really planning to buy

123

it then fine – I'll do you employee discount – but if you just needed to read that bit, leave it. It's not a problem.'

'Are you sure?' Ella said. It was a £24 book.

'Positive,' the boy said.

'I do need to get this one though.' Ella picked up the book she'd left on one of the chairs, on top of her bag.

'Cool,' the boy said. 'I'll leave you to it then.'

'No, it's fine,' Ella said. 'I'm done. I can just . . . pay. Now.'

He scanned the book through and it came up as twenty per cent cheaper than the marked price.

'Is that . . . did you do your discount?' Ella said.

'Yeah. I said I would.' He put the book in a bag. 'Not going to charge you the five p for that either.' He grinned.

'But the discount was for the other book.'

'Don't worry about it,' he said. 'Perk of the job. If you maim a customer, you get to give them a discount. It's written in the shop's constitution.'

Ella's mouth twisted into a smile. 'The shop has a constitution?'

'Oh, yes. It's there on the wall.' He gestured across the room and Ella actually turned to look, before realising and looking back at him. He was grinning.

'Made you look.' He handed her the book.

'Oh my god,' Ella said, passing him her debit card.

'I'm Nick,' he said, as he pushed the card into the machine. He didn't look up.

'Ella.'

'Could I have your number?'

Ella turned the card machine towards her and tapped in

her PIN. The screen flashed up that she should take her card and she took it and dropped it back into her bag.

'Thanks again,' she said, smiling at him. 'And I'm really sorry again. About the book.'

'I'm sorry about your head,' he said. His cheeks were definitely pink.

'It's fine,' Ella said, unconsciously reaching up to touch it again, forgetting the bag with the book was hanging on her wrist. It swung and hit her in the jaw.

'Oh my god,' Ella said. 'I'd better go before I do actually brain myself. Thanks! Again!'

She turned and headed for the door, praying she didn't trip over her own feet or walk into a table or humiliate herself in any other ridiculous way.

'Your hair really does look good,' she heard him call as she was almost out of the door.

Chapter 17

Lou filled the kettle and switched it on, then remembered there was beer in the fridge. Beer would be better. She opened the beer, grabbed a bag of crisps from the house cupboard and headed upstairs. She'd been planning to take the tea to her room and maybe do some work, but she didn't want to sit in there drinking alone, so she kept going up to the living room.

Paige was sitting at the dining table in front of her laptop, her glasses pushed up into her hair, her face pale.

'You OK?' Lou asked her, flopping down onto the sofa.

'Laptop's dying,' Paige said. 'Just need to finish this essay. Please don't put the TV on.'

Lou had just picked up the remote, but she put it back down again. That was fine. She could go on her phone. It might actually be OK checking Kyle's messages with Paige here. She didn't want to tell anyone about them, didn't want to talk about them at all, but she hated being alone with them too.

Lou had turned off sounds and notifications when the ping of a new message had started to make her feel sick. She'd blocked Kyle's number after the second text, but it didn't stop him.

After he'd sent five more photos using five different phones, she gave up blocking and started avoiding her messages.

She was going to have to talk to him. It was the only way to get him to stop. Either that or she'd have to go to the police. But she didn't want to do that unless she absolutely had to.

She was surprised none of the other girls had noticed how little she looked at her phone any more. Especially Ella. Lou had been such a social media addict, but she hadn't posted on Instagram for a couple of weeks now, hadn't been on Twitter at all. She only kept up with Facebook because her mum would notice and worry if she didn't.

She tapped the messages icon and scrolled through Kyle's latest series of messages. More photos of Lou sleeping. One of her awake that she remembered him taking – she was sitting up in bed, her hair in a knot on the top of her head, no top on, one hand covering one boob, but the other boob bare. She was looking straight into the camera and laughing. She remembered him taking that one: they'd just had really good sex. Kyle had been slow and caring and attentive, which he wasn't always. He'd made her laugh and they'd been planning to go out after and get some food and maybe go on and meet her friends in whatever bar they'd ended up at. But in the end, they hadn't. Kyle had decided he didn't want to 'waste' time with Lou's friends when he could be spending time just with her. And so she'd made herself some toast while he watched an old episode of *Top Gear* and fell asleep.

Lou pictured the hot guy in the coffee shop, the one Liane was keen on. She bet he didn't watch *Top Gear* (not least cos it was often racist). And he was a barista. He'd probably make her coffee and a panini in the morning. She wasn't sure about the sex though. He seemed too nice. She definitely had to stop thinking that nice blokes wouldn't be good at sex. That was part of what got her in trouble with Kyle in the first place.

And maybe it would be good to just sleep with someone and tick them off the Fuck It List. She was probably the only one in the house who hadn't yet. Apart from Ella. Obviously. She should go and check the list, but it was all the way downstairs and she couldn't be bothered getting up now. She screenshotted Kyle's messages and put her phone down on the coffee table, groaning as she stretched her arms over her head.

'Fuck,' Paige said, as an error message popped up on her laptop screen. Out of the corner of her eye, she saw Lou sit up on the sofa, but she couldn't look away from the screen.

'FUCK!' she yelled, tapping CTRL-S compulsively.

'What's happened?' Lou said.

'FUCK!' Paige yelled again, standing up and pushing her chair back. 'No. No no no.'

'What's up?' Liane asked, coming to stand next to her. Paige hadn't even known she was home.

'Laptop crashing,' Paige said, her breathing coming fast. 'It did a thing earlier, but I thought I'd managed to – Fatal exception. Right. So that's it. Dead.'

'Shit,' Liane said. Lou came over from the sofa and the two of them stood either side of Paige, all three of them staring at themselves reflected in the black screen.

'Oh, fuck,' Paige said, sitting back down. 'I'm fucked.'

'You can take it to that guy by the canteen,' Liane said. 'Don't panic.'

'I can't afford it,' Paige said. 'I've literally got, like, twenty quid to last me 'til payday.'

'I can lend it to you,' Liane said. 'I mean, depending how much it is. I think he charges thirty-five quid to look at it and do a diagnostic thing.'

'I'll go halves,' Lou said. 'Don't worry.'

'I don't even know when I'd be able to pay you back though,' Paige said. 'Literally all that money is gone already. I mean, not gone. But I know where it's going.'

'The next one then,' Liane said. 'Don't worry about it. You need a laptop.'

'Yeah,' Paige said. 'Thanks. You're great. I just hope they can fix it.'

Liane shrugged. 'If not, you can use mine. I mean, when I'm not using it. And I bet the other girls'll say the same.'

'Seriously?' Paige said, pushing her chair back away from the table again. 'You'd do that?'

'Course,' Liane said. 'Obviously I need it, but you usually stay up later than me, so you can have it after I go to bed. I'll set you up a login thingy. Need a cup of tea first. Want one?'

'I do,' Lou said.

'That's really lovely of you,' Paige said. To her embarrassment, she was starting to tear up. 'Thanks.'

'S'just tea,' Liane said, bumping Paige's with her shoulder.

Paige laughed again. 'I meant the laptop. But the tea too. Thank you.'

In the kitchen, Liane tried to remember what she'd done with her old laptop. The one she'd had before she'd come to uni.

When they'd found out she'd got in, her dad had bought her a MacBook and she suspected she'd stuck her old Toshiba in a drawer and just left it there. If she'd known Paige's was knackered, she could've brought it up for her last time she'd gone home. Maybe she'd ask her mum to send it up, if she could bear to.

She opened the fridge for the milk and, as she closed it, the Fuck It List fell off and skidded across the tile floor. Putting the milk on the counter, Liane picked it up and stuck it back on.

She'd only ticked two off so far, but 'someone with a tattoo' had three ticks, 'waiter' had one, 'someone in a band' had one, and 'someone in uniform' had one. She didn't know who'd ticked them off or if they'd put the tenner in the pot each time. They should probably have a house dinner and talk about it. She'd suggest it next time everyone was home at the same time.

She wondered if Alfie had a tattoo. She thought probably not, but maybe he was really surprising under his clothes. She needed to find out. She needed to stop bottling it and actually ask him out. Although maybe she was putting off talking to him because of what had happened with Zack. Because she'd spent so long thinking she'd liked him and now realised she didn't know if she ever really had. How did anyone know their own minds well enough to actually take action? Liane had no clue.

Chapter 18

'Do you ever see things in the ceiling?' Liane asked. 'Like shadows and cracks and stuff?'

'Sometimes,' Issey said.

They were both in Issey's bed again. Issey had been about to go to sleep – or at least to read some Bang! fanfic, have a wank, and go to sleep – when Liane had come in and just clambered under the duvet like it was her room too. Not that Issey minded. At all.

'In my room, if a car goes down the street with the lights on, I get little light shapes on the ceiling,' Liane said. 'I like it.'

'Once I saw a light darting around on my wall,' Issey said. 'And I couldn't figure out where it was coming from. It was a reflection from my phone. I was watching it like a kitten. Dickhead.'

Liane laughed. 'Turn the fairy lights off.'

Issey rolled over and reached down the side of the bed to click off the switch on the extension cord. Her room was completely dark – she had lined curtains, so once the lights were off that was it.

'So dark,' Liane said. 'I can't even see my hand.'

131

'My room was like this when I was little,' Issey said. 'I used to wake up in the night and I couldn't tell if my eyes were open or not. And then I'd start to worry I was trapped or dead.'

Liane laughed. 'I used to tell myself I'd been kidnapped and I was on, like, a tanker or something. And that once it was light I'd see that I wasn't in my room at all, but in the middle of the ocean.'

'I used to pretend I'd teleported. I would wake up in New York or Paris or somewhere. I used to lie there and plan the things I'd do for the day. First I'd get breakfast and then I'd go to the Empire State Building . . . And then it'd be morning and I'd have to just get up and go to school.'

'Rubbish,' Liane said. 'I always wanted to just go to the airport and get on the first plane, no matter where it was going. Have an adventure.'

'Me too,' Issey said. 'Or stick a pin in a map.'

'Yeah,' Liane said. She'd moved without Issey realising – her voice was closer.

'Iz?'

'Yeah?' Issey put her hand on her own chest. She could feel her heart racing.

'Can I ask you something?'

Issey nodded, before realising Liane couldn't see her. 'Course,' she managed to squeak out.

'Have you ever kissed a girl?'

Issey's heart was thumping so loudly that she was sure Liane would be able to hear it.

'No,' she whispered. 'Have you?'

'No. But . . .' Liane shifted on the bed. 'I've been thinking about it. Lately. I don't know if it's just cos of living with Paige . . . I was thinking that . . . You know when you're with a guy? Are you, like, always thinking about him? Like his body or whatever? Cos when I'm with a guy, I . . . I can't believe I'm telling you this. It's good and everything. I like it. And I get turned on. But then when I want to actually . . . you know? Get off? I think about girls. When I'm on my own too. I mean . . . is that normal?'

Issey's mouth was so dry she wasn't sure she'd be able to speak. She licked her lips, but she still heard her mouth make a clicking sound. 'I think that's normal, yeah. I mean, I think anything's normal really. It doesn't necessarily mean you're not straight? But maybe you're not. And that's OK too. Yeah?'

'Yeah. I know that. I just . . . I don't know if it's, like, fantasy or if it's something I really want to try.'

'Right,' Issey said. 'Yeah. I get that.'

'I haven't told you about Zack, have I?' It wasn't really a question; Liane knew she hadn't.

'Not really,' Issey said. 'Only that he was your friend and he died.'

Liane sighed. 'We were really close for a while. And then he was out with some friends and they got into a fight with this group of guys. It wasn't about anything big, I think they said they'd pushed into the taxi queue or something? It was just shouting, I think. And then one of them pushed Zack and he fell and hit his head on the kerb and that was it. Died instantly.'

'Oh my god,' Issey said, reaching out and wrapping her fingers around Liane's wrist before she even had time to think about it and stop herself. 'That's awful. I'm so sorry.'

'Yeah. It was . . . rough. But also . . . I wasn't just friends with him. I was friends with his girlfriend too. Emily. And I thought I was in love with him. But . . . I don't know. I've started to think maybe it was more . . .'

'Her?'

'Yeah,' Liane said. She couldn't quite believe she was talking about it. She probably shouldn't have been.

'Are you still in touch with her?'

'No,' Liane said. 'And I wouldn't . . . I mean, it's not something I'd ever . . . I just wonder. You know?'

'Yeah,' Issey said, quietly. 'I know.'

DECEMBER

Chapter 19

'Have you seen the guy with the tattoos?' Lou said, her mouth against Ella's ear. 'Might not have been such a bad shout after all.'

It was the last night they'd all be at home before Christmas and they were in the club five minutes from their house. Lou had wanted to go somewhere else – she thought it was horribly cheesy with its LED lighting, exposed brick and chrome bar – but it was near, played decent music, and the drinks weren't stupidly expensive, so she'd been overruled. Exams were over, uni was winding down for Christmas, and they'd all (apart from Paige, who was working, as usual) decided it was a good time to go out and get hammered.

Ella shook her head and then tried to follow where Lou was pointing. Eventually she saw him. He was small and wiry, but hot, wearing a sleeveless black vest and with tattoos all down both arms and across his chest.

'Will you be OK?' Lou yelled.

Ella glanced over her shoulder at Liane and Issey and then nodded at Lou. 'Go get him, tiger.'

'What?' Lou yelled.

Ella shook her head. She hated trying to have conversations in clubs.

'Where's she going?' Issey yelled into Ella's other ear.

'Tick off someone with tattoos.'

'Ohhhhh. He is HOT,' Liane said. 'Wish I'd seen him first.'

'Let's dance!' Issey shouted, grabbing Ella around the wrist. Ella let herself be tugged out onto the dance floor and told herself to relax. And then she downed some of her beer to help.

Issey danced like a toddler after too much candyfloss and before long Ella found herself letting go and letting the music take over. Liane was an amazing dancer and seemed to be somehow effortlessly sexy; she moved like a cat, Ella thought. A sexy cat.

'Is Paige coming?' Issey yelled after a few songs and another beer.

'I don't think so,' Ella shouted back. It felt wrong to have their last night out without Paige. But Paige had insisted she had to work; she needed the money. Which was fair enough. But still.

'Get it, Lou,' Issey said, pointing.

Ella looked past her to see Lou and the boy with the tattoos. He had her pressed back against the railing of the raised platform, his hands on her waist, his mouth on her neck.

Ella wondered what Lou had said when she'd gone over. And then she wondered what she would have said if she'd decided she wanted to get off with him. Probably something ridiculous and embarrassing. Or the way things had been going recently, she probably would have tripped up the step and headbutted him or something. She realised she was still staring at her best friend getting off with some random bloke, so let her eyes drift away.

They landed on the boy from the bookshop – Nick – who was standing right next to them, holding on to the railing and looking directly at Ella.

'Fucksticks,' she said.

'WHAT?' Liane bellowed in her ear.

Ella wanted to turn and leg it off the dance floor. Possibly out of the club. The city. The country. Instead she forced herself to look back at him again. He was still looking at her. She smiled. He smiled back and raised his hand.

'Who's that?' Issey yelled. She'd actually turned all the way round to look at where Ella had been looking.

'Iz!' Ella hissed. 'For fuck's sake.'

'He's cute!' she shouted.

Ella shook her head. She should go over. Should she go over? Like Lou had done. Just walk over and say, what? 'Fancy seeing you here'? 'I'd really like to lick your face'? She was still staring at him, oh my god.

'Go over,' Liane said, giving her a little shove in the small of her back. Once they were home and sober, Ella was going to have to talk to her friends about appropriate behaviour, god.

She took a couple of steps, but then realised Nick had disappeared from the platform. She looked around a little wildly and then spotted him on the dance floor. He was weaving between the dancers, but still looking over at Ella.

'Fucksticks,' she said again. She turned to her friends for some moral support, only to find they'd both disappeared, the absolute bastards.

* * *

Paige was trying to decide between a packet of cherry tomatoes for 99p, some marked-down bananas, or a packet of noodles. The noodles would last longer. But the tomatoes and bananas were healthier and she didn't want scurvy. Maybe the marked-down bananas and some cheaper SuperNoodles would be a good compromise? She wasn't sure. She'd decided to definitely get the bananas and was heading for the aisle with the noodles when she saw Sharda. She was standing in front of the chiller cabinet, a supermarket basket over one arm, a black beanie with ears pulled down low.

'Hey,' Paige said, without moving.

They hadn't seen each other for months and Paige couldn't actually remember how they'd left things. So she was relieved to see that Sharda was already smiling as she turned round.

'Heyyy!'

One of the things Paige had really liked about Sharda was how she'd always been pleased to see her. It had never seemed false or fake. It made something tug in Paige's chest now. She couldn't remember why she'd stopped calling. Because she was pretty sure she was the one who had stopped calling. It seemed like something she would do. She took a few steps until she was standing right in front of her.

'How's things?' Sharda asked.

Paige noticed her glance down at her basket and was briefly embarrassed about her sad, browning bananas. Which was ridiculous.

'Not bad,' Paige said. 'You?'

Sharda sighed, looking down at her own basket. 'Buying a

meal for one. Should we go and get dinner somewhere instead? I haven't seen you for ages.'

Paige bit the inside of her cheek. 'That would be really good. But I've literally got, like, a pound. I can totally offer you a banana. But that's it.'

'I can pay,' Sharda said instantly.

Paige was already shaking her head, when Sharda reached out and grabbed her arm at the elbow. 'Come on. I've got some money. I can't let you go home and eat a banana. I'd feel terrible. You can pay me back when you've got some funds. OK?'

Paige wanted to say no. She couldn't believe she was even considering it. But Sharda was great. She'd definitely been great. Most of the time. And Paige really hadn't been looking forward to a SuperNoodles and banana dinner.

'OK,' she said.

'You're hot,' the boy said, his lips on Lou's ear.

'Come and dance?' Lou tugged at his arm.

He shook his head. 'I don't dance.'

'Not even at Christmas?' Lou pointed at the mistletoe hanging above the bar, the huge tree where there were usually two sofas and a low table.

'S'not Christmas yet,' he said, his eyes sparkling.

'Come on,' Lou said again.

He shook his head and pressed her up against the pillar. 'We can just dance here.'

Lou laughed. She wanted to dance. She did. But he didn't. And he was hot. And she liked how his fingers felt on the back of her neck. So she tipped her head back and brushed her lips across his jaw. He groaned and dipped his hips, rubbing against her.

'Want to get out of here?' he said.

'Bloody hell!' She ducked out from under his arms. 'You're keen!'

'You're so hot!' he said again.

'Dance first and then maybe we can go,' she said.

He shook his head, rolling his eyes. 'OK.'

'OK?'

'OK.' He let her tug him down the steps to the dance floor. She twirled under his arm, laughing. He was actually a pretty good dancer, and Lou slipped her fingers into his belt loops to pull him closer. His hands pressed into the small of her back and he swung her around, laughing.

Which was when she spotted Kyle.

She stopped dead. 'Shit.'

'What?' the guy said. 'Did I hurt you?'

'No. Sorry. Just . . .' She didn't know whether to tell him or not, but she liked him so far. And she didn't want to make things weird. 'Just my ex. He's kind of a dick.'

'The guy in the Kappa shirt?'

Lou squinted. She hadn't noticed that, but he was indeed wearing a Kappa shirt: black with a high neck. It made him look a bit French. She would've been into it this time last year. And she knew Kyle knew that too. Was he here cos he knew she'd be here? Or was it a coincidence? He wasn't looking at her; she didn't even know if he'd seen her. She wanted to leave, but at the same time, why should she let Kyle spoil her fun? She turned around so her back was to him and carried on dancing with tattoo guy.

* * *

Ella kept staring at Nick and he kept coming closer. He had a small smile on his face, but Ella wasn't sure what her own face was doing. He was wearing tight black jeans with the knees ripped out and battered brown boots. His hair was even higher than it had been in the shop and she wanted to stroke it. She was staring at him. Still staring at him. And he was still coming towards her.

'Hey!' he shouted when he was just a few feet away.

Ella tried to make herself smile, but she couldn't seem to manage it. 'Hi,' she said, but not loud enough for him to hear. She hoped he could read lips. Or got the gist anyway.

He was still coming closer. He was standing right in front of her. She could hook her fingers through the belt loops of his jeans. She could just press right up against him. She could loop her arms around his neck and press her face into the curve of his shoulder. She could see one of his collarbones where the neck of his T-shirt was stretched out and she thought about putting her mouth on it, running her tongue along the length of it.

'Are you stalking me?' Nick said, his mouth right against her ear.

She shook her head. Still couldn't speak. And then she turned a little. 'I could ask you the same!'

Nick grinned. 'Maybe we're stalking each other? Can I get you a drink?'

They were still standing in the middle of the dance floor, bodies moving around them. Ella felt like she was in the eye of a hurricane. Or in a film where the main characters see each other and the world stops while they just stare. No, the opposite of that – Nick and Ella had stopped and no one else had even noticed.

She wanted to look for Issey and Liane, but she didn't want to burst the bubble.

'Yes,' she answered. Finally.

And then his hand was on her arm, just about her elbow, his fingers curving around, pressing heat into her bare skin. He steered her through the crowd. Someone was flailing their arms around, laughing, head thrown back. Two boys were pressed up against each other, dancing but barely moving, their hands pressing and pressing. Two girls were pretending to grind on each other, one of them bent at the waist, the other pretending to slap her arse, while they both laughed hysterically.

Ella glanced up at Nick – he was so much taller than her – and he was looking down and smiling. He raised one eyebrow and Ella wasn't sure whether she wanted to run out of the club and never look back or jump up into his arms like a monkey and tell him to take her home.

They walked up the three steps to the raised area and then he guided her to the bar, his hand large in the small of her back.

'What can I get you?' he said. Ella leaned against the bar for support, curling her hands around the metal bar running along the edge.

'Beer!' she yelled back, mostly because it was easier than wine. Wine usually involved further questions, some sort of conversation.

Nick nodded and then stretched across the bar to yell at the guy behind it. And then he was laughing, they were both laughing, having a conversation, even though Ella had no idea how they could possibly hear or understand each other.

The other guy passed Nick two beers and Nick handed one to Ella before reaching out and tapping the neck of his own bottle against hers.

'Do you want to go outside?' he said.

At least, that's what Ella thought he'd said. But where?

She nodded. And then they were moving again, towards the main doors, and then out into the lobby. Ella hadn't even thought about the lobby. It was still pretty loud, but nowhere near as loud as the club itself, and red velvet seats curved around the walls.

Nick wasn't touching her any more, but he glanced over to her to indicate where he was heading – which was the sofa in the darkest corner. There were a few other people around – a couple of girls talking to the security guys on the door, a clearly too-drunk guy sitting on the other side of the room, alternating between hanging his head down between his knees and leaning back against the wall to groan.

'Here OK?' Nick said, gesturing at the sofa, and Ella nodded.

They both sat down. They both drank some beer. They looked at each other.

'Do you have someone?' Nick said.

Ella frowned. Had he come over because he thought she was alone? Had he come over to take care of her because he thought she couldn't look after herself? Oh my god, was this a charity thing? Some sort of intervention? Was he going to ask her if she'd ever thought about taking Jesus into her heart?

'I came with friends,' she said, her voice sounded strained and feeble. 'I was dancing with them just before you came over. I don't know where they went.'

Nick's eyebrows pulled together in a small frown and he shook his head. 'No. Not tonight. I mean . . . You have a boyfriend? Or . . . girlfriend? Someone . . .'

Ella shook her head. She was frowning too. She tried to stop, to straighten out her own forehead, but she wasn't sure how successful she'd been.

'I . . .' Nick shook his head again, laughed a bit. 'I wanted to find a way to ask you that didn't involve me saying "I earwigged when you were on the phone the other day" but I've got nothing.'

'Oh!' Ella said, her face heating when she pictured herself standing in the street, pink hair plastered to her head, talking to Dylan. She'd been talking to Dylan.

'No! No, that was my brother. I was talking to my brother. I don't have . . . I'm not seeing anyone.'

She was half expecting Nick to do what so many boys had done in the past – pretend they were only asking casually, not that they were really that interested – but instead Nick's face broke open into a huge smile. His mouth was massive. Ella hadn't noticed before. She stared at his bottom lip and thought about grabbing it between her finger and thumb. Or maybe sucking on it. Was that weird? That sounded pretty weird.

'Oh hey, is your brother OK? I know it's none of my business, but I just remembered you saying something about drugs? And you sounded worried.'

Ella shook her head. 'He's fine. He was with friends and I just . . . worry about him. When he's drunk or stoned he gets very . . . affectionate. And I worry someone will take advantage of him.'

'You sound like an excellent big sister.'

Ella laughed. 'He's older. He's just . . . I've always been the sensible one.'

She wanted to kick herself immediately. Why had she said that? She didn't want Nick thinking of her as sensible, for fuck's sake. She wanted him to be thinking about pushing her back on the sofa and getting his hands in her pants.

She looked at him and caught him looking at her mouth. His eyes immediately flickered back up to hers, but something had changed. Something was crackling between them. She could feel it. It felt so strong that she was amazed she couldn't actually see it. In her mind, there were white jagged lines joining their bodies and actually vibrating with electricity. She could tell Nick felt it too, and even that was odd because normally she wasn't good at picking up those kinds of cues.

'Do you want to get out of here?' Nick asked.

Chapter 20

'So what have you been up to?' Sharda asked Paige, once they'd been seated.

They'd only walked a little further down Bold Street to the Moroccan place. They'd been here before, Paige realised as they'd walked in, the first night she'd met Sharda, through someone else on her course. They'd all gone out for a drink and ended up here, ordering too much food. Paige hadn't been able to enjoy it because she'd worried about the bill the entire time.

'Not much,' Paige said now. 'Working. And uni. You know.'

'How's your dad?'

Paige had forgotten she'd told Sharda about her dad. She couldn't remember exactly what she'd told her, but it was probably more than she'd wanted to – they used to get stoned together and Paige talked when she was stoned.

'The same,' Paige said.

'I'm sorry.' Sharda reached over and touched the back of Paige's hand with her index finger. Her nails were long but squared off at the tip. She was wearing bright purple polish. Paige flashed back to that first night again – the boy from her seminar rubbing his knee against hers under the table while

Sharda sat opposite and every time Paige looked at her she was looking right back. The guy had dropped out of the course last year. Paige couldn't even remember his name now.

'How about you?' Paige asked Sharda. 'How are things?'

'Good,' Sharda said. 'Went out to San Francisco to see Lola a couple of months ago.'

Lola and Sharda had just split up when Paige and Sharda first met. Or 'sort of' split, as Sharda had put it. Lola was working away for a year and while they wanted to be together, they didn't think it was practical while on opposite sides of the world.

'She loves it out there. She was talking about staying.'

'Wow.' Paige reached for the menu and ran her fingers around the edges. Her stomach was rumbling.

'I know. I think I'd try to move out there too, if she did.'

'Yeah? That's big.'

The waiter appeared and they both ordered, Sharda encouraging Paige to get more than she really wanted. Or more than she wanted Sharda to have to pay for, anyway.

'So it's really serious with you two then?' Paige said, once the waiter had gone.

'Oh, yeah. I mean, it has been all along, really. I love her.'

Paige nodded. She'd met Lola once and she was fucking awesome. She wasn't surprised to hear Sharda planned to uproot her entire life for her.

'But while she's away . . .' Sharda said and hooked her ankle around Paige's under the table. 'I mean, we agreed it would be unrealistic for us never to see anyone else.'

Paige grinned at her. 'Good to know.'

Nick pushed open the door of the restaurant, and the smell of spices made Ella's mouth literally water. How had she not known she was hungry? She couldn't remember having been this hungry for ages.

They were shown to a booth table and Nick let go of her hand so they could both sit down.

'Beer?' Nick said and Ella realised she'd only had one sip of the last beer he'd bought her. She didn't even know what she'd done with it. Had she just left it on the floor in the lobby?

'Please,' she said.

'Text your friends,' Nick said. 'I'm going to pop to the loo.'

Nick got up and Ella watched him walk to the bathrooms at the back of the restaurant. She liked the way he moved. Like all his limbs were a bit more loosely attached than other people's. Was it called 'loping'? she wondered. She thought maybe he loped.

She texted Issey and Liane to tell them she'd left and then texted Lou: 'With a boy. I like him. Tell me not to fuck it up.'

Lou replied immediately: 'Don't fuck it up! You're gorgeous. He's lucky to be with you. Get some. It's been too long :)'

Ella was smiling at Lou's reply when Issey's popped up: 'Woo! We saw you go. HE'S HOTTTTTT', and then another came through: 'B careful. Text again later so we know you not murdered.'

'Helpful,' Ella muttered, smiling.

'All OK?' Nick said, sitting down opposite her. The waiter arrived with the beers and put them down on the table, asking if they were ready to order.

'Sorry,' Nick said, smiling brightly. 'Haven't even looked yet. Maybe some prawn crackers and sauces.'

The waiter nodded and left and Nick said, 'Have you texted?'

'Yeah,' Ella said. 'My friend Issey wants me to text again later to tell her I'm still alive.'

'Sensible,' Nick said, smiling. 'I thought you were the sensible one.'

Ella smiled. 'I am. Usually. And Issey definitely isn't. But . . . I don't want to be sensible all the time.' She looked down at her hands on the table and then up at Nick.

'I was always the sensible one too,' Nick said. 'At school. Like . . . I've got a younger brother and he just did what he wanted, didn't even think about it. But I worried about what my parents would think. Or that someone they knew would see me and it would get back to them . . . I went out with a girl once. From school. I didn't really like her much, but she liked me and my friends couldn't understand why I didn't want to see her. So we went out. Like, just to this square where everyone used to sit around drinking and smoking and getting off with each other.'

His eyebrows flickered up as he looked at Ella and she smiled back at him.

'So we were all there, right? And I knew she was waiting for me to kiss her. And the others were too – they'd been going on about it all day, you know, like "Nick's on a promise" and telling me "You're going to get your –"' He stopped, his cheeks flushing pink. 'You know the kind of shit people say.'

Ella nodded.

'And the longer I left it, the harder it was to actually make a move. Cos everyone was looking, waiting, getting impatient.

Actually . . .' He sat back in his seat, still looking embarrassed. 'I'm wishing I'd never started telling this story.'

Ella smiled. 'No! You have to tell me now. I won't judge. Actually, that's a lie. I probably will judge. But I'll try to be OK about it.'

Nick picked up his beer by the neck. Ella watched him turn it in his fingers and then forced herself to look up at his face.

'Cut a long story short,' he said. 'I pretended I had the shits.'

Ella let out a yelp of laughter. 'Oh my god.'

'I know.'

'But . . . why didn't you just kiss her?' Ella asked, picking up her own beer.

'I . . . I mean, that would've made more sense, right? I just . . . I didn't like her. I didn't like her as a person. I didn't find her attractive. I only agreed to go out with her cos my friends said I should. If I'd kissed her it would only have been to stop me looking bad in front of my friends and that just didn't seem like a good enough reason to kiss someone. It's a true story, I promise,' he said, his face gentle now. 'You can ask my mum.'

Ella laughed again. 'You told your mum?!'

'One of her friends told her. The mum of one of the other kids. She tried to make out she was concerned, like "I hope your Nick's feeling better", but she just wanted to mock me. And then my mum and dad thought it was hilarious and they mocked me too.'

'It sounds like a very upsetting experience,' Ella said, trying not to laugh.

'It was,' Nick said, his face serious. 'It really was.' And then he grinned.

They stared at each other and Ella felt the electricity thing happen again. It was as if it was running up her arms from her fingertips, lighting her skin up. She wanted to ask Nick if he could feel it too, but what if he said no? What if it was just her?

'I kind of want to say let's get out of here,' Nick said, still staring. 'But I'm starving.'

Ella nodded. 'Me too.' She stared at their hands on the table and then said, 'You can feel it too, right? The thing?'

'Fuck yeah,' Nick said. 'I've been feeling it since you came in the bookshop.'

'Oh my god,' Ella said.

'That wasn't a line,' Nick said. 'Did you think that sounded like a line?'

Ella shook her head. 'I thought it sounded amazing.'

Liane was dancing with a boy Issey thought might be Tom from her seminar. He was shorter than she'd expected him to be. And his hair was stupid. But Liane had hooked her hand around his wrist and was grinding up against him. He looked at Issey and smiled as if he expected her to join them.

'Are you drunk?' Issey asked her.

Liane shrugged. 'Tom had some stuff.'

'What stuff?' Issey looked at Tom, but he had his eyes closed and his face turned up to the lights as he danced.

'Come and get some water,' Issey said, tugging at Liane's other hand.

Liane frowned and then said, 'Yeah. I'm thirsty, actually.'

She pressed her mouth up to Tom's ear and Issey watched

153

him smile, but then Liane let Issey lead her across the dance floor to the bar.

'It's sweet that you worry about me,' Liane said once they got there, dropping her head down on Issey's shoulder.

'You know I love you, right?' she said, against Issey's neck. She'd flopped almost entirely against her now, they were pressed together from chest to knee. Issey started to wriggle away, but Liane just made herself even heavier.

Issey could feel sweat prickling the small of her back. She wanted to push Liane away and tell her not to be so dramatic, but she also wanted to keep her close, keep her safe.

'Let's go home,' Issey said. 'This is shit.'

'I want another drink!' Liane said, her lips sliding over the hollow under Issey's ear. 'And I said I'd go home with Tom.' She squinted out onto the dance floor where he was already dancing with someone else. 'Actually, fuck him.'

'We've got stuff at home.' Issey straightened up and Liane staggered back. 'We can take our duvets out on the terrace and drink all of Lou's tequila.'

'That,' Liane said, holding up one finger, 'sounds like a plan.'

Paige was in the kitchen making herself a coffee when she heard a door slam overhead, followed by heavy footsteps on the stairs.

'What the fuck?' she said, as a strange guy appeared in the doorway.

'Your mate's a fucking psycho,' he spat.

'You scared the shit out of me,' Paige said. 'Who even are you?'

'Your mate. The one with the purple hair. She's a fucking psycho.'

'You're the one acting like a psycho,' Paige said. 'Why are you even here, talking to me?'

'She told me to get out.'

'So get out,' Paige said, taking a couple of steps closer to him.

'Don't tell me what to do, you fat bitch,' the boy said.

'Are you joking?' Paige walked right up to him. She was only very slightly shorter than him, just a couple of inches. She was wearing her tartan pyjamas and flip-flops and he was fully dressed. Although now she was up close, she could see that he wasn't wearing anything under his stupid hipster cardigan and it was buttoned up wrong.

'If Lou told you to go, you need to go,' Paige said. 'Before I call the police. Or just open the front door and scream – the security over the road's usually pretty quick. And very protective.'

'You're all fucking mental,' the boy said, staring down at her. 'She brought me back here. If she didn't want to fuck –'

'Clearly she didn't,' Paige said. 'Or she'd have fucked you. So off you go.' She pushed past him and opened the front door. 'And don't come back, eh?'

'Fucking lezzers,' he said as he left. Paige resisted the urge to kick him up the arse. But only because she was wearing flip-flops.

Once he'd gone and Paige had locked the door and put the bolt on, she kicked off her flip-flops and ran up the stairs to Lou's room. She knocked and Lou said, 'Who is it?'

'It's Paige. He's gone. You OK?'

Lou pulled the door open. She looked pale and smaller than usual.

'Did he hurt you?' Paige asked.

Lou shook her head. 'Can you come in for a bit? Do you mind?'

She took a couple of steps back until the bed hit the back of her legs. She sat down and scrabbled up towards the headboard. Paige sat cross-legged at the foot of the bed.

'Who was he?'

'I just met him tonight. It was stupid. I wasn't going to bring him back, I was just going to dance. But then my ex was there. And he's . . . I mean, he's a dick. He's been kind of . . . I don't know, bothering me a bit. Sending messages and stuff. I keep telling him it's over, but he doesn't believe it's over. So I thought if he saw me leave . . .'

'Right,' Paige said.

'I mean, that's not the only reason. That guy was cute. In the club. And hot. And I haven't had sex for fucking months.'

'Hey,' Paige said. 'No judgement.'

'It was stupid.'

'It wasn't. It was the same thing people do literally every weekend. And certainly every Christmas party.'

'You saw him, right? When he left?'

'Yeah, he came down to the kitchen and yelled at me.'

'Fuck, I'm sorry.' Lou tipped her head back and rubbed her hands through her hair, before turning slightly to look at Paige. 'You didn't want to come to the party?'

Paige shook her head. 'Nah. Not a big Christmas fan, to be honest.'

Lou snorted. 'No. Me neither. Although it's not as bad as New Year's Eve. That's the fucking worst.'

Paige held up one hand and Lou high-fived her, smiling.

'Have you been here the whole time?' Lou asked her.

'Nah. Had dinner with a sort of ex. And then she came over for a bit. She's gone now. I was just getting a coffee when I met your friend.'

'Coffee? Now?'

'Got an essay to finish,' Paige said. 'But I can leave it if you want me to stay.'

Lou shook her head. 'Thanks, but I'm OK. Nothing even really happened. I don't know why I . . . I mean, it was fine. He was a bit of a shit kisser, slobbering all over my face, and then he started taking his clothes off and I just . . . I couldn't do it. I didn't want to do it. So I told him and I apologised. And he –'

'Didn't take it well,' Paige finished. 'He was a right prick.'

'Yeah,' Lou said. She rested her chin on her knees. 'And I'm still horny.'

Paige laughed. 'I mean . . . I could help you out there, but it might make things awkward in the house.'

Lou laughed, and looked better than she had since she'd opened the door to Paige.

'You could help, actually. Have you got any AA batteries?'

Chapter 21

Ella held on to the belt loops of Nick's jeans as he struggled to open his door.

'Our door sticks too,' Ella said, her cheek resting on the bit between his shoulder blades.

'It doesn't usually,' Nick said. 'I think . . . my hands are shaking.'

Ella turned her face and pressed her forehead against his back. How could he just say that? How could he tell her that and not even be embarrassed?

'I probably shouldn't have said that,' he said.

'No,' Ella said. 'No, it was good. I'm glad you're nervous too.'

Nick laughed. 'Shitting myself. Not literally. This time. Again.'

Ella snorted, hiding her face against him again. 'Do you want me to try?'

'Shit, no,' Nick said. His hands dropped down by his sides. 'I feel like if I can't even get a key in a door, you're not going to want to have sex with me.'

Ella laughed again. 'Turn around.'

'You think I can do it with my hands behind my back?'

'Shut up. Turn round.'

Nick turned around and looked down at her. His eyes were wide. They looked grey in the semi-darkness of the street.

Ella tipped her head back, but he was so much taller than her.

'Hang on,' she said. 'Swap places.'

'I can open the door, El! Let me try again.'

'Swap places,' she said again, raising one eyebrow.

Nick stepped down and Ella stepped up. She curled her hands into the front of his coat. It was soft. Warm. And then she tugged him towards her a little. And he finally got it. He was staring at her mouth. She stared back at his. Her heart was rabbiting in her chest and she could hear herself breathing quickly.

'I don't know why I feel like this,' she said, raising one hand to brush her thumb over his cheekbone. 'I hardly even know you.'

'You know enough,' he said, his voice low. 'And don't get ahead of yourself. We might be really bad at kissing. Each other.'

Ella laughed. 'I don't think so.'

'Come on then,' he said. 'Let's see what you've got.'

Ella grinned. 'You're annoying.'

'I've been told.'

She moved her hand over his cheek, stroking her thumb over his bottom lip. He shuffled closer on the step until his face was so close she couldn't even bring it into focus. She closed her eyes. And touched her lips to his. Gently at first and then more firmly. She heard herself gasp. Wanted to pull him hard against her, have him press her back into the door. He turned his head, fitting their mouths together more neatly. She could feel his tongue running along the seam of her lips and she opened her mouth, still gasping. Her hand was on the

159

back of his neck, even though she didn't remember moving it there, and she could feel his hands on her waist, squeezing, his fingers pressing.

'I need –' Nick said, against her mouth. 'I mean. We need to –'

'Yeah,' Ella breathed. 'But –'

Nick pulled away and for a second Ella followed him involuntarily, before leaning back again, tapping the back of her head gently against the door. Fuck.

'I know,' Nick said. 'I'll do the door. I'm confident this time.'

Ella didn't move. She wasn't sure she could. She felt boneless, like if she lost the support of the door, she'd just slide down the steps into a puddle in the gutter.

Nick reached past her, bracing himself against the door with one hand, the key in the other. He put it in the lock. And it turned.

'Yesssss,' he hissed under his breath.

Ella leaned forward and kissed his jaw and he turned his head and pressed his lips to hers again, quickly.

'You taste soy saucy,' he said.

'Oh my god,' Ella said, blushing.

'I should've saved that 'til I'd got you inside, right?' he said as he pushed the door open. 'Should I call you a cab?'

'Shut up,' Ella said. And followed him inside.

Issey had one arm around Liane's waist as she guided her out of the club. Some girls hanging out with the bouncers jeered at them, but they literally only had to cross the road to be home, so Issey couldn't bring herself to care. Liane kept giggling and staggering and Issey had to keep tight hold of her. She felt warm and heavy and smelled of beer and coconut shampoo.

'I'm so tired,' Liane said.

'Well, you can go to bed in about five minutes,' Issey said.

'Nah,' Liane said. 'Tequila!'

Someone in the street shouted 'TEQUILA!' back at them and Issey laughed as she shut the door.

'Shush,' she said to Liane. 'The others might be asleep.'

'They're probably still out,' Liane said. 'Just us two sad-arses home already.'

The two of them bumbled up the stairs, giggling as Liane's foot slipped and she grabbed Issey's dress, pulling it down off her shoulder.

'God,' Issey said. 'You're wrecked.'

'Tom brings the good shit,' Liane said. 'Shame his dick's so sad.'

'Sad?' Issey said, turning Liane towards her room.

Liane made some hand gesture Issey couldn't interpret and then said, 'No! The terrace! You promised.'

'Fucksake,' Issey said.

She steered Liane outside and then went back in for cushions and blankets, fully expecting Liane to be asleep when she made it back out again. But instead she was sitting on the picnic table, trying to take a selfie.

'S'too dark,' Liane said.

'That's cos it's the middle of the night,' Issey said. She took Liane's phone back inside and then curled up next to her on a beanbag.

'I'll miss you,' Liane said. 'Over Christmas.'

Issey laughed. 'You'll be having too much fun.'

'With my mum? You've got to be joking. I wish I could come home with you instead,' Liane said. 'I bet your family's fun.'

'They're an absolute shambles,' Issey said. She slid further down the beanbag and tipped her head back, looking up at the stars.

'I'm glad we moved in here,' Liane said.

'Me too,' Issey said.

'I have good ideas.'

'It was my idea!' Issey yelped, turning, indignant, to look at Liane.

She was right there. Not even inches away. Her eyes wide and bright. Issey's breath caught in her chest. 'You should go to bed. You'll be fucked tomorrow.'

'Nah,' Liane said. She licked her lips and Issey heard herself gasp.

Liane's fingers skittered up Issey's bare arm under the blanket and then her hand was tangling in the back of Issey's hair. Issey shivered.

'Are you cold?' Liane said.

Issey couldn't speak. She shook her head.

And Liane kissed her.

Chapter 22

'I don't even know your surname,' Nick said, and then ran his tongue over the shell of Ella's ear.

She shivered. 'I thought you would have looked on the card. I was thinking that you would have looked on the card and then used it to find me and ask me out.'

Nick shifted on the bed and kissed down the side of her neck.

'I did ask you out.'

Ella pulled her head back so she could look at him. 'You did not!'

He grinned. 'I did! In the shop!'

'I think I would've remembered.' She let her head drop back on the pillow again.

He kissed across her chest to her other collarbone. 'I asked for your number.'

'When?'

He moved back again to dip his tongue into the hollow of her throat and she bucked up against him involuntarily.

'Shit,' she murmured. 'Sorry.'

'Don't apologise,' he said and she could hear the smile in his voice. 'Do it again.'

'God,' she said.

She pushed one hand into the back of his hair. It was so soft. Ridiculously soft. Softer than hers. She'd have to ask him what conditioner he used. She tightened her fingers and he groaned.

'I like that,' he said, kissing back up the other side of her neck.

'Nick.'

'What?' He lifted up and looked down at her. He had really pretty eyes.

'I'm not good at this,' Ella said.

'You're doing pretty well so far,' he said. 'I'm all flustered.'

She laughed. 'You're so weird.'

He kissed her quickly on the mouth. 'And you're so fucking gorgeous I can't believe I'm here with you. I've had a raging crush on you since you first came in the shop and did your turn. I've been thinking about this for so long that I'm half worried this is actually a dream and I'll have to wake up and seduce you all over again.'

Ella laughed. 'You seduced me?'

'Well . . . I'm not done yet. But I'm working on it.' He kissed her quickly again. 'How am I doing so far?'

Something that felt like butterflies ran through Ella's body and she gripped Nick's arms to ground herself. 'Pretty good.'

'Good,' he said, his face turning serious. And then he was kissing her again. He was an excellent kisser. Perfect pressure. Not too much tongue. And this was the problem. She was thinking about how he kissed her instead of just letting herself enjoy the kiss. She sighed into his mouth and he pulled back again.

'I'm thinking too much,' she said, before she could change

164

her mind. 'I was just wondering what conditioner you use. And now I'm thinking about how you kiss instead of just, you know, kissing you back.'

Nick rolled off her and she grabbed at his arm again. 'No. I'm sorry.'

He reached for her hand and slid his fingers between hers. 'What can I do? Do you want to talk for a bit? Do you want me to be so sexy you can't resist me? Do you want me to lie here and let you have your wicked way?'

Ella rolled onto her side so they were facing each other. 'I like you.'

He grinned. 'I like you too. Is this too much? Do you want me to take you home?'

'No! God, no. I'm having a good time. Unless . . . I mean, unless you want me to go?'

His eyebrows shot up. 'Fuck no. I finally got a girl back here. I need you to at least stay until my roommates see you.'

'Fuck off,' she said, biting her lip to stop herself laughing. 'As if you haven't had loads of girls back here.'

'Oh, that was weak.' He grinned. 'If you want to know my number, you should just ask.'

'God,' Ella said, turning her face into the pillow. 'I don't need to know your number. Unless it's none. Or, like, thousands.'

'It's definitely somewhere between none and thousands,' Nick said. 'And that reminds me. I asked you out. You blanked me. I still don't know your surname. I feel like if we get these things sorted out you'll be able to relax and enjoy my moves.'

Ella rolled her eyes, laughing. She wanted to touch him, wanted to run her finger along his nose. Or press her thumb

165

against his jaw. Or stroke his eyebrows. She reached for his hand instead and he immediately tangled his fingers with hers.

'When did you ask me out?' she said instead.

'I asked for your number. When you bought the book. In the shop. Where I work. And where we first met.'

'I remember,' Ella said, smiling. 'But you didn't ask for my number.'

'I did. Literally as you were paying. I asked for your number. You paid. Bade me a cheery thank-you and fucked off, only narrowly avoiding knocking over a table of *The Norton Shakespeare*, which would have been a nightmare because the pages of those books are tissue-paper thin, and –'

'My PIN number!' Ella said. 'I thought you were asking for my PIN number, you dick.'

'Harsh.'

'How is it harsh? I literally had my card in the machine and you ask for my number? What was I supposed to think?'

Nick bit his bottom lip. 'Now that you put it like that, yes, I can see how the misunderstanding occurred.'

Ella laughed and rolled on top of him, pressing her nose to his. 'At least we got there in the end.'

CHRISTMAS

Chapter 23

Paige woke up late – really late – and the house was quiet. She walked upstairs, expecting someone to be on the terrace or Liane flopped in front of the TV watching one of her Shonda shows, but no. She had the place to herself. She checked her phone and realised it was the twenty-third and everyone had probably gone home. Shit. She'd totally meant to get back from work early enough the night before to say bye to them all.

On the dining table, there was a note written on the back of the electricity bill (Ella had written 'Paid' and the date on the front):

Sorry we didn't see you, Paige! Have a fantastic Christmas!

They'd all signed it. And then underneath, Ella had written

When are you back? Let us know pls.

She hadn't told the girls she wasn't going home. She hadn't told them anything, actually. They'd just assumed she was going home, same as them, and she hadn't corrected them.

Maybe this was for the best. Now she didn't have to lie to them, pretend she was going home too.

She'd been looking forward to having the house to herself, but now it felt too quiet. She curled up on the sofa and watched a Christmas film on the Hallmark channel, then opened up the group chat and typed 'Thanks for the note! I'm back on the seventh, I think. That weekend anyway.'

Lou was the first to reply: 'On train home. Kill me.'

Paige smiled. 'You OK?'

Lou sent back a smile emoji, 'ta for last night' and an aubergine emoji.

Ella appeared with 'something you two want to tell us?' with a shocked face emoji.

Lou: 'I had a boy back, he was a dick. Paige chucked him out. And then found me some spare batteries *aubergine emoji*'

Ella: 'Sorry I asked tbh.'

Lou: 'AND WHERE WERE YOU, YOU DIRTY STOP-OUT'

Ella: *ten heart eyes emojis*

Ella: *aubergine emoji*

Lou: 'OMG. Tell me everything.'

Ella: 'He is so nice.'

Paige: 'Nice?'

Ella: 'Yes. Nice and funny and cute and hot and *heart eyes emojis*'

Lou: 'ARE YOU STILL AT HIS?'

Ella: 'Lol, no. At home already.'

Lou: 'But you're seeing him again yea?'

Ella: 'After Xmas, yeah.'

Ella: 'You ok, Paige?'

Paige: 'Good ta, yeah.'

Ella: *blush emoji* *heart emoji* *Christmas tree emoji*

Lou: 'Where's Issey and Liane?'

Ella: 'No idea.'

Paige: 'I haven't seen them.'

Lou: 'Hmm. Will msg em later. Changing trains now. Love you allllllllllll.'

Paige headed downstairs to check Issey's and Liane's rooms, but both were empty: Liane's pristine and tidy, Issey's like it had been burgled. She closed Liane's open window, turned off Issey's bedside light and went downstairs to make herself a tea.

She was on her own. She was used to being on her own – she'd been home alone a lot when her dad was out at the pub or with his mates, she had no problem with being alone – but the house was really quiet without the other girls.

'What time's Dylan getting here?' Ella asked her mum. They'd made about one hundred mince pies and Ella was desperate for her mum to hang up her apron and crack open the wine.

'I think he said he should be here by six,' Karen said, shaking more flour onto the countertop.

'More, Mum? Really?'

'Just another twelve. You don't have to help.' She opened the fridge and handed Ella a bottle of white wine. 'Take this through to Arthur?'

Ella picked a glass up off the side and carried it and the bottle through to the living room where Arthur was sitting in his chair, in the corner, diagonal to the TV, which was showing *Home Alone* with the sound off.

'Mum sends wine,' Ella said, putting the glass down on the small table between Arthur's chair and her mum's chair.

'Is she still baking?' Arthur asked.

'Yup.'

Ella poured him a glass of wine and held it out to him.

'Thanks, darling.' He took it from her, his hand shaking. 'Are you not having one?'

'I'm going to wait for Dylan, I think. He should be here soon.'

Ella sat on the sofa and looked around the room. Everything was the same. Everything was exactly the same. Apart from Arthur, who was close to half the person he'd been when she'd left for uni. She could barely look at him. She had to force herself. His voice was the same, so if she didn't look at him, she could pretend he was fine. Which is what he and her mum seemed to be doing. The problem with that was that whenever she did look at him, she was shocked all over again.

She pulled out her phone and texted Dylan: 'LMK when you get here. Like before you come in. K?'

She glanced at Arthur. He'd put his wine down and dropped his head back against the chair, his eyes closed. Ella went back to the kitchen and the mince pies.

'We're having dinner together.' Lou's mum was stepping into her boots, holding Lou's shoulder for balance.

'Who?' Lou said.

'Who do you think? Me and you and your dad.'

'Together? The three of us? The three of us – me, you and

172

my actual dad – are having dinner? Together?'

Her mum rolled her eyes. 'Don't be so dramatic.'

She had both boots on now and stalked across the room, her heels tapping on the laminate.

'Mum. Seriously though. Last year, you and Dad practically did a car park handover without looking at each other. What the fuck?'

'Don't say "fuck". And it wasn't that bad.'

'It really was,' Lou said.

When they'd split up it had originally been amicable – they'd just stopped loving each other, they'd told Lou – but then as they'd sorted out the finances and the house and Lou herself, they'd become more and more hostile until they were barely speaking.

Her mum stopped in front of the mirror over the fireplace and ran her fingers through her long hair before spritzing herself with Alien.

'Are you two . . .' Lou started and then shook her head. They couldn't possibly be.

'Hmm?' her mum said.

'Never mind. Is he meeting us there? Where are we going, anyway?'

'Largo.'

'Seriously?' Largo was their first-date restaurant.

Her mum looked shifty. 'Yes. Largo. Are you wearing that?'

Repressing a scream, Lou headed up to her room to get changed.

Issey's dad had given her the one small glass of sherry he

allowed her within about five minutes of her being in the house, so now she and two of her four sisters were huddled together in what their mum called the sunroom – actually their dad's old shed, which their mum had half converted into a garden office, but it still smelled like soil and damp and their dad's cigars. Issey loved it.

'Did you bring this?' Issey asked Aysa, holding up a bottle of cinnamon vodka.

'It's got gold leaf in!' Aysa said. She was trying to roll a cigarette, but she kept dropping it on the floor.

'You can't smoke that in here,' their eldest sister Mel said. 'Mum will come out of the house like a guided missile.'

'I'm not going to smoke it,' Aysa said. 'I'm just practising.'

'Just vape like a normal person,' Mel said, scrolling her phone.

'How do you drink this?' Issey said, swirling the bottle in front of her face, and watching the gold leaf spin and settle and spin again.

'Like . . . shots?' Aysa said. She handed her a plastic cup.

'I only did shots for the first time when we moved into the house,' Issey said. 'How come you've been doing shots?'

Aysa shrugged. 'Everyone does shots.'

'You know Aysa got completely shit-faced in the park and her friends left her and I had to go and pick her up?' Mel said. 'Last summer?'

'No!' Issey gasped.

'And remember where you said you wouldn't tell anyone?' Aysa raised one eyebrow.

'Issey's not "anyone",' she said to Aysa. 'She got sick in my car,' she told Issey.

174

'Bloody hell,' Issey said. 'Didn't it put you off forever?'

'Nah.' Aysa held up the perfectly rolled cigarette. 'Did it!'

'That had better not be a cigarette, Aysa!' their mum called from inside the house.

'Shit,' Aysa said.

Liane lay on the sofa, watching the doctors at Seattle Grace try to save George's life. She'd seen this episode so many times that she didn't need to concentrate at all. Or even properly focus, which was lucky since her eyes kept misting with tears. She was hungover as hell. And her mum wasn't even home.

After she'd kissed Issey she'd apologised, said she was drunk, got up and gone to bed. She'd half expected Issey to come and find her, didn't know what she would have done if she had, but Issey had gone to her own room too. And when Liane had woken up that morning, Issey had already gone.

She didn't even know why she'd kissed her. Just to see what it was like? Because she'd never got a chance to kiss Emily? But she wasn't gay. She liked sex with men. She had the most ticks on the Fuck It List and she was happy with that. She was at uni – that was meant to be a time to experiment and sow oats and just do what felt good, wasn't it?

But none of this felt good. It just hurt.

Paige set up her books, notepads and pens on the dining table. Liane had left her laptop, which Paige hadn't even thought to expect, so it meant she might actually be able to get ahead on her work while the other girls were away. They'd left food too, so she didn't need to do a shop. There wasn't really anything for proper meals, but there was certainly enough ham, cheese, bread and crisps to keep her going.

She put *Lemonade* on loud and sat down to work.

She'd only been writing for about fifteen minutes when her phone buzzed on the table next to her. She glanced over, expecting it to be the group chat again, but it was a call. From her dad. Shit.

She grabbed it, tapped it, said, 'Dad?' But he'd already gone.

'Shit.' She put the phone down and turned back to her screen.

'The subversion of the domestic ideology,' she said out loud. 'Let's do this.'

Her phone buzzed again. This time with a text. Her dad. Again. She picked it up. It said 'Can you come home?'

She closed her eyes briefly and then texted 'No.'

The reply came almost instantly. 'It's Christmas, Paigey.'

As if she didn't know. As if this wasn't the first time he'd contacted her since she'd come back to uni.

And she hated him calling her Paigey. It reminded her of a time when he wasn't always drunk. When her mum was still alive and they both had jobs and sometimes they'd pick her up from school and go to McDonald's and let her eat the chips in the car and then he'd tickle her until she was breathless while her mum said, 'Stop it, Neil! She'll be sick!'

'Princess Paigey', he called her sometimes. Even back then that was more likely to make her sick than the chips were, but he knew she thought it was stupid and said it to tease her. She wasn't a princess. Wasn't even a girly girl. Would rather watch the *Morning Line* racing tips with him than go shopping with her mum.

But then her mum died. And her dad changed. And everything had gone to shit.

'I know it's Christmas,' she typed. 'I'm spending it with my friends.'

She sent the text, shut her phone down, closed Liane's laptop, and went to the pub.

'What's wrong?' Dylan said as soon as he got out of his car. A new car Ella hadn't seen before – a massive black Range Rover that made their mum's Honda look like some kind of toy.

'What the hell is this?' Ella said, gesturing at the car before wrapping her arms around her brother and squeezing him.

'Sponsor thing,' Dylan said, squeezing her back. 'Don't worry about it.'

'Jesus. The life you lead.'

Dylan stepped back and peered at her. 'Is everything OK?'

'Yeah, it's just . . . Arthur is pretty bad. Probably worse than you're expecting.'

Dylan's face fell and he looked about six. 'Yeah?'

'He's lost a lot of weight. And he's exhausted.'

Dylan nodded. 'OK. But Mum said –'

'I think Mum is a little bit in denial.' Ella hooked her arm through her brother's. 'She's made about two hundred mince pies. And she's talking like Julie Andrews.'

'Fuck,' Dylan said.

'Yeah.'

The two of them headed inside the house and straight to the kitchen. Karen was whisking something in a metal bowl, the sound made Ella's teeth itch, but she almost dropped the bowl when she saw Dylan.

'You're here!' she yelled, practically skidding across the kitchen and flinging her arms around him.

Dylan ducked his head onto her shoulder and said, 'Hey, Mum.'

'Can I just say she didn't even stop rolling pastry when I walked in,' Ella said. 'And I think she's forgotten my name. At least Dipsy was pleased to see me.' She bent down and picked up the cat, who butted her head against Ella's jaw.

'Shut up, you,' Karen said, holding Dylan at arm's length and grinning at him.

'See?' Ella said, nuzzling Dipsy.

'I've seen you,' Karen said, swatting at Ella. 'I haven't seen Dylan for months. How long has it been?'

'Months,' Dylan said, and grinned.

'Come and see Arthur,' Karen said, steering Dylan towards the door.

He glanced back at Ella as he left, and he looked so scared she wanted to run ahead of them and stop him seeing Arthur at all. Shit.

'How's it all going?' Lou's mum asked when they were home from the restaurant.

Over dinner her parents had told her that they were 'seeing each other', which sounded ridiculous considering they'd been married. But they both seemed happy so Lou had tried not to take the piss too much.

'Fine, yeah,' Lou said, checking her phone to see if the others

178

had been in the group chat. They hadn't.

'Have you seen Kyle?' her mum asked. She was making them both hot chocolate and Lou knew she really wanted a heart-to-heart, but Lou couldn't face it.

Lou put her phone face-down and looked at her mum. She should tell her. And ask her what to do. More texts had come from Kyle today; she'd read them on the train:

'Saw you at Levels'

'You looked like a slut'

'You left with that dickhead'

'Because you're a slut'

Between each text, he'd sent a photo. Two that he'd sent before and two more of her sleeping. He'd sent so many now, he must have taken photos every time they were together. It made her shudder. And she felt ashamed, even though she knew – she knew! – it wasn't her fault. It was all Kyle. But it was hard to believe that.

'He's kind of been . . . harassing me,' she said.

'How do you mean?' her mum said.

'Sending me loads of texts and stuff.'

'Block him!'

'I have. But he just keeps doing it from different phones and stuff.'

'Lou!'

Her mum looked, as Lou had known she would, outraged and furious.

'I know,' Lou said. 'I was kind of hoping he'd get bored and stop.'

'He's not following you or anything? He hasn't hurt you? I'll come up there and kick the shit out of the little –'

Lou laughed. 'No! He was at a club I was at the other night, but that could've been a coincidence. He's just being a dick.'

'You need to report him. To the university.' She'd shifted right to the edge of the seat.

'I will,' Lou said. 'When I get back.'

'I mean it, Lou. If you don't, I'll ring them.'

'I will,' Lou said again. But she hoped he'd stop before she had to.

'Have you ever kissed a girl?' Issey asked Mel, as they lay on side-by-side mattresses on their parents' bedroom floor.

'All right, Katy Perry!' Mel said, rolling onto her side to look at Issey. 'No. Have you?'

'One of my friends kissed me,' she said, her voice tiny.

'Wow,' Mel said. 'And?'

'Who kissed you?' Aysa asked, dropping over the edge of the bed, her long hair swinging into Issey's face.

'No one you know,' Issey said. She was already regretting bringing it up, but it was all she could think about and not talking about it had made her feel like she was inflating with it. Like the berry girl in *Charlie and the Chocolate Factory*.

'She was drunk,' Issey said. 'I don't think it meant anything.'

'Do you want it to mean something?' their eldest sister, Eve, called from the other side of the bed. Issey had thought she was asleep.

'No,' Issey said. 'I don't know. Maybe.'

'Well, that sounds conclusive,' Eve said.

'Did you talk about it? After?' Mel asked, sitting up slightly to turn her pillow over and then dropping down again.

180

'I didn't see her. When I woke up in the morning she'd already left.'

'You slept with her?' Aysa screeched, which was when Issey realised her mistake.

'No, idiot,' Mel said. 'It's one of her housemates.' She looked at Issey gently. 'Liane, yeah?'

'Yeah,' Issey said.

'You need to talk to her.'

'Talk to her,' Eve said. 'I'm going to sleep.'

'Wow,' Aysa said, clambering back up into bed. 'I never thought you'd be lesbionic.'

'Shut up, Aysa,' the other three all said together.

Chapter 24

Ella had just got into bed when there was a quiet knock on her door and Dylan popped his head round.

'Can I come in?'

'Course you can, dickhead.'

He grinned and pushed the door open properly. He was wearing sweatpants, a blue hoodie that said 'Sorry I was late. I didn't want to come' on the front, and he had his pillow under his arm.

'You staying then?' Ella had already started shuffling over in the double bed she'd begged her mum and Arthur for for about five years before they actually caved and bought it.

'Is that OK?'

'I refer you to my previous answer.'

Dylan flopped down on the bed next to her and Ella marvelled at just how tall he was now. In her head, he was at least a foot shorter. And looked about five years younger. He was a man now, there was no way around that, and it was weird. Although not as weird as him being an internationally famous pop star. That was definitely the absolute weirdest.

'Get your massive feet away from me,' she said, as he pedalled them under the duvet.

He sighed, tipping his head back.

'Didn't want to sleep in the shrine, then?' she said.

Dylan laughed. 'Don't call it that. But yeah. No.'

'I did tell her she should turn it into a gym. Or a craft room.'

'It's weird, right? How she's left it. I mean . . . I'm not dead.'

He shuffled in the bed, so he was on his side, looking at Ella.

'I don't think it's that weird,' she said. 'You left so suddenly. And we were all just waiting for it to end, you know? We thought the arse would fall out of it and you'd come crawling home and you'd be devastated and we'd have to help you get over it. But you just kept getting more and more famous. You wanker.'

Dylan didn't laugh, as Ella had expected. Instead his eyes filled with tears. 'I want to come home.'

'Fuck off,' Ella said. 'You don't.'

'I do. I just . . . I love it. I do. I love the boys and the shows and the fans, but we just never fucking stop. I never get to take a breath, you know? They keep telling us after this show or this album or this promo we'll get a break, a proper break, and then once it's close enough that I start thinking about what I'll do, something comes up and they say "no, sorry, just this one thing". I'm so fucking tired.'

'Fuck,' Ella said. 'I'm sorry. I know it's shit.'

Dylan's eyebrows pulled together. 'It's not. I mean, I feel like a dickhead for complaining about it. Cos, like, this was my dream, right? I wanted this! And so many singers would kill to be in my place. I should appreciate it. I should enjoy it. But I was, like, counting the days 'til I could be home. Who does that?'

183

'That's fair enough, I think,' Ella said. 'I mean, the touring and everything is normal to you now. It's home that's special. I know it's not the same, but I've been looking forward to it too. Even though I was kind of desperate to move out, desperate to get to uni and have some independence. And now I'm there – and I love it – I really look forward to coming home.' Ella wanted to tell him about Nick, but she knew he wasn't really able to have a relationship at the moment either, and she didn't want to rub salt in the wound. It could wait.

Dylan nodded. 'It's not the same for you though. Cos everyone still treats you the same. For me it's like it takes a couple of days for them to realise I'm still Dylan, not, like, Dylan Jewell.'

'Yeah, I know. But – and I know this isn't the same, I'm not saying it's the same – but for me . . . it's kind of nice to be Ella. Not Dylan Jewell's sister, you know? And when I come home, I go back to that again.'

'God,' Dylan said. 'I'm sorry. I do wonder sometimes if it wouldn't have been better if I'd never gone to London. If –'

'Oh, come on!' Ella said, her voice suddenly too loud in the quiet house. 'Don't talk shit. I mean, first of all, it was your dream. You are literally living your dream. Even if it's not quite what you expected it to be, that's an incredible thing. And second of all, you're making shitloads of money. Enough that at some point if you decide you don't want to do it any more, you'll have options. And you can help Mum out. And you paid for Arthur's hospital stuff. It's a good thing.'

'It is, mostly. I know. And I was really happy that I could help out with the doctor like that. But don't you think it's weird?

184

That I'm their kid and I'm the one paying for stuff like that? I mean . . .' He rubbed his hands over his face. 'It's changed us all, the family, so much. And it just feels, I dunno. Weird.'

'I know,' Ella said. 'I'm sorry.'

'You know what I noticed? Arthur doesn't take the piss out of me any more. He used to always go on about my hair or my clothes or the music I was listening to or whatever. But now . . . it's like he's sort of respectful.'

'I did notice all the questions,' Ella said. 'It was like a one-man press conference.'

'Yeah. And then Mum treats me like a VIP. She came into the kitchen when I was emptying the bin and she almost vaulted the breakfast bar to stop me. Like "you shouldn't be doing that!"'

'To be fair, you literally never emptied the bin when you lived here.' Ella grinned.

'Arthur used to do it,' Dylan said. 'I'm thinking he probably doesn't any more.'

'Oh,' Ella said. 'You're right. This is why I hate you. I never would have thought of that. Why do you always have to be so considerate and shit?'

Dylan smiled, but it didn't quite make his eyes. 'He's dying, isn't he?'

Ella gasped, her eyes filling instantly. 'I think so, yeah.'

'Do you think Mum knows or . . .'

'I honestly don't know. I did try to talk to her a bit. Like, it's stage four and, you know, you only have to look at him. But she went all bright-eyed and started talking about booking a holiday to Madeira. I don't know.'

'Fuck,' Dylan said.

Paige planned to run a bath as hot as she could stand and lie in it for as long as possible, reading one of Lou's fashion magazines, and then get into bed and sleep for most of Christmas Day. She'd hated Christmas since her mum had died anyway, but she'd never been able to totally avoid it before. And now her legs were aching and there was something clicking between her shoulder blades. And her key wouldn't turn in the front door.

'For fuck's sake,' she muttered, banging her head gently against the wood. The key was sticky, she knew that. And she knew that if she relaxed, and pulled the key out very slightly, it should turn. She took a breath, she eased the key out, she turned it . . . and it snapped.

'MotherFUCKER,' Paige yelled. She stared at what was left of the key in her hand. She couldn't quite believe what had just happened. Now what? It was late. She was alone. She had nowhere to go and no money and – her chest started to feel tight – no inhaler. Shit.

She sat down on the step and told herself to stay calm. She took a few of the slow, deep, calming breaths she'd learned at yoga once and then stared down at her phone. Who could she call? Her dad would be drunk, she knew from long experience. Plus, what could he do? He wouldn't know how to transfer money or book her a hotel or anything, even if he was capable.

It would have to be Sharda. At least she lived nearby and was relatively flush. Paige had no idea what a locksmith would cost, particularly at this time of night, but whatever it was, she didn't have it. It would probably be better if she stayed the night with Sharda and called the locksmith in the morning. She tapped Sharda's name on her phone, and listened to it ring out. And then it stopped.

'Fuck,' Paige muttered. She had no idea what she was going to do.

Her phone buzzed with a message. Sharda. 'Can't talk. Lola's home.'

Paige's fingers were stiff with cold as she typed her reply, telling Sharda she was locked out, had no money. Asking her if she could come and crash.

'Sorry, no,' Sharda replied. 'I can lend you some cash? PayPal? How much do you need?'

'Fucking HELL,' Paige said, dropping her head back to bang against the door. Her eyes burned with tears. Maybe she should ask Sharda for the train fare, go and spend the night in Lime Street and get the first train home. Yeah, it meant Christmas with her drunk dad, but even that was better than this, wasn't it?

She told Sharda she'd find out and get straight back to her. And then she Googled locksmiths.

By the time Paige got into the house, she was cold and tired and sick from trying not to cry. She climbed into the shower, dropping her clothes on the bathroom floor, and slumped against the wall, sobbing so loudly she almost shocked herself. How had this happened? It was Christmas. She was home alone (she almost – almost – laughed at that), and she had no one.

Leaving her clothes on the floor, she wrapped herself in a towel and sat on the edge of her bed, staring at her phone. She should ring her dad. He was awful, but he was still her dad.

Maybe she should go home. She should talk to him, at the very least. Her chest felt tight at the thought and she rubbed it with the heel of her hand.

She scrolled to her dad's number, but she was already struggling to breathe.

'Fuck.' Her eyes filled with tears and she rubbed at her chest again. She could feel herself wheezing. She reached into her bag for her inhaler, but it wasn't there. It wasn't in the pocket of her coat either. She tried to remember where she'd last had it, but couldn't think.

In her room, she checked her bedside drawer and it wasn't there either. Her breathing was coming faster now, the tears streaming down her face. Trust this to happen when she was home alone. Wasn't that just fucking typical.

And then she remembered using her inhaler the previous night and putting it on her bedside table. It must have fallen off. She got down on the floor and reached under the bed. Her fingers closed around the smooth plastic.

Once she was able to breathe again, she rang her dad – first his mobile and then the home phone. He didn't answer either of them.

JANUARY

Chapter 25

If Paige gave the girls any more free drinks, Jonny was going to start docking her pay. But she was just so happy to have them back. From the moment they'd started messaging to say they were on their way home after Christmas, Paige had felt almost giddy. It was sickening. She'd actually had a moment of wondering if she had a crush on one of them – Liane, maybe? Or Lou? – but she didn't think that was it. It was all of them. And it was a friend-crush. She hadn't experienced anything quite like it for years. It was disconcerting. She'd faffed around the house so much that she'd given up and come into work, even though she wasn't strictly needed – Jonny was there and so was Raimy, the other barmaid – but it was surprisingly busy and Jonny had been pleased to see her. But not nearly as pleased as Paige had been to see the girls.

She'd told them she was at work, and was surprised that they'd just dropped their stuff off and come straight over. Liane first, then Lou, Issey, and finally Ella. Paige was glad she was trapped behind the bar or she'd have been hugging them all. And she'd never really thought of herself as much of a hugger before.

But Christmas had been so . . . She'd expected it to be lonely. And sad. But she hadn't expected it to be quite so soul-destroying. First Sharda making it perfectly clear that Paige was basically a booty call and nothing more. And then her dad – when she finally spoke to him on Christmas Day he'd been drunk and unpleasant. It had all just been utterly grim. She never wanted to experience anything like it ever again.

'My sisters drove me fucking nuts,' Issey said. 'But I made them all watch the Bang! documentary, so that was something.'

'There's a documentary?' Liane asked, one eyebrow arching.

'Yeah, it was a bonus thing with their last album,' Issey said. 'It's only short. But it's hilarious. And cute. Ugh, I love them. Arseholes. We'll have to watch it one night! There's a drinking game that goes with it, I saw it on Tumblr.'

'No fucking drinking games,' Lou said. 'I got so pissed on Boxing Day. I ended up talking about porn with my uncles and my dad's mates from work. I can never look any of them in the eye again, dirty bastards. And then we tried to get a cab and we couldn't, so we started walking, but it was freezing and no cabs came and . . . You know when you have one of those dreams when you're trying to get somewhere and you just can't? It keeps getting further away or your legs aren't moving or whatever? It was like that. I felt like it took years to get home. And I couldn't feel my feet. And when I woke up in the morning I had to make myself sick before I could even get out of bed. Grim.'

'How was your Christmas, Ella?' Liane asked Ella, who had been staring down at her phone all the way through Lou's story.

'Oh, Nick!' Lou said, in an exaggerated high voice. 'I can't wait to see you! I just need to get away from my lovely friends who I haven't seen for aaaaaages and then we can be alone at last!'

'Shut up,' Ella said, putting her phone face-down on the table. 'He was just saying he's not back 'til tomorrow. I'm meeting him for brunch.'

'So that's it for you, then?' Liane said. 'You're ticking "bookseller" off the list and retiring from competition?'

Ella shook her fringe out of her eyes. 'I think . . . yeah. Probably. I hope so, anyway.'

'So much for focussing on your studies,' Lou said. 'What happened to "all work, all the time" and "boys are a distraction"?'

'I know,' Ella said, picking up her Corona. 'I just didn't expect . . .'

'To fall in love?' Lou finished. 'Are you in love with him? Seriously?'

'No!' Ella said, clinging to her beer. 'It's too soon. I just . . . I feel like I could be. Maybe.'

'Fuck me,' Issey said. 'That's amazing. Tell him we're all coming to brunch. We can grill him and ask him about his intentions.'

'That,' Ella said, 'is the absolute last thing I'm going to do.'

'We're going out tonight though, right?' Lou said. 'All of us?' She leaned up over the bar to get Paige's attention.

'If it's free entry, I can come,' Paige said.

'And if it's not, I'll pay you in,' Lou told her. 'You're in, yes?'
'Yes.'

'Excellent,' Lou said. 'Go home. Get changed. Go out.'

'I'm going to puke,' Issey said, standing stock-still in the middle of the Seal Street.

'You're not,' Liane said, holding on to her elbow and swaying slightly. 'You're fine. Come on.'

'I need to lie down,' Issey said.

'Come on!' Paige yelled. 'I want to GO HOME.'

Issey started to bend down towards the road.

'Oh no,' Lou said. 'Iz. You can't sleep here. It's an actual road. You'll get run over! Or sweet-streeped!'

'Sweet-streeped?' Ella said, already laughing almost uncontrollably. 'Have I got my coat?'

'You're wearing it!' Paige yelled. 'COME ON.'

A group of lads piled out of Wetherspoons, yelling and singing and staggering into the road. Issey was still standing at a half crouch and one of the boys hooked his arm around her, underneath her arms, and picked her up.

'Fucking put her down!' Liane said.

'He can carry me home,' Issey said, eyes closed. 'Can you carry me home?'

'Is it far?' he asked. He'd swung his other arm up under her legs now and Issey rested her face against his shoulder.

'Just round the corner,' she murmured.

'Jesus Christ,' Paige said. She'd walked back down to meet the rest of them. 'Why aren't we home yet? I'm dying for a piss.'

'All right, chubs,' one of the other boys said.

Paige rolled her eyes. 'Good one.'

'You shut the fuck up,' Ella told him.

They turned off Bold Street and onto Seal Street.

'You can put her down now,' Lou told the guy carrying Issey.

'Can't he take me up to bed?' Issey mumbled.

'I can, yeah,' the guy said.

'No you can't,' Liane told him. 'Put her down.'

He put her down gently and she immediately curled around Liane.

'Thanks,' Ella told him.

He gave her a thumbs-up and then the three of them joined the queue to get into the club opposite.

'This key had better fucking work,' Lou said, shoving it into the lock. It turned straight away. She bumped the door open with her hip and all five of them tumbled inside the house.

'Are you holding my hair?' Issey asked, turning to try to look at Liane.

'Yes. I think you got a bit of sick in it anyway,' Liane said. 'But I'm holding it now.'

Issey retched and lurched over the toilet bowl again. 'I hate being sick.'

'I don't think anyone likes it,' Liane said. She moved to put her hand on Issey's forehead, but pulled it back at the last second. 'Are you nearly done?'

'I think so,' Issey said. She sat back on her heels, bracing herself against the sink. 'I feel like shit.'

'I'm not surprised.' Liane was far from sober too, but Issey had drunk so much more.

'Sorry.'

'You'd do the same for me.'

'I don't think I would,' Issey said. 'I think I'd leave you to get on with it. Oh fuck. I think there's more.' She lurched over the loo again and Liane held her hair back from her face.

Once she'd finished vomiting, Issey sat down on the tile floor, her back against the side of the bath.

'Did you have a good night though?' Liane asked, shuffling along the floor to sit next to her. Issey's bare arm was cold against hers. Liane thought about moving it away, but she was determined they were going to carry on as they'd been before. Neither of them had mentioned the kiss. Liane was trying hard to never think about the kiss.

'Come on, get up,' Liane said. 'You're freezing.'

'Can I sleep with you?' Issey asked, dropping her forehead down on Liane's shoulder. 'I'm really cold.'

Liane stared at the wall. She didn't want to look at Issey. 'I think you're better off in your own room. You might vom.'

Issey nodded. 'Yeah. OK.'

Chapter 26

Ella saw Nick through the window of the cafe. He was looking down at his phone and his glasses had slid down his nose. As she watched, he pushed them up, and something unfurled in Ella's chest. She liked him. She really liked him.

As she pushed open the door, he looked up and his face transformed into an enormous smile. She grinned back and bumped into a table in her eagerness to get to him. She apologised to the two women sitting there, squeezed through the gap, and then she was standing right in front of Nick.

'Hey,' he said, looking up at her.

'Hi.' She thought about kissing him, but instead she curled her hand around his cheek, fingers brushing over his jaw, thumb pressing into his dimple. He smiled wider.

'You missed me,' he said. 'I can tell.'

'I didn't,' she said, sitting down opposite him, even though she wished she could sit next to him and press into his side, maybe hook one leg over his thigh. 'I was much too busy.'

'Oh, me too,' he said, passing her the menu. 'It was wall-to-wall parties. But in the occasional quiet moments in between, I think I missed you a bit. Just a bit.'

Ella grinned. They'd texted a lot in the few days they'd been away. They'd texted and called and whatsapped and facetimed. But she'd missed him anyway. More than she'd expected.

While the waitress was taking their order – a bacon butty for Nick and smashed avocado on soda bread for Ella – Nick inched his hand across the table until his little finger was curled around Ella's. When the waitress had gone, Ella turned Nick's hand over and rubbed his palm with her thumb.

They were still smiling dopily at each other – Nick's ankles linked around Ella's under the table – when their food arrived.

'Why did you let me get so drunk last night?' Issey asked Liane as they crossed Bold Street towards the coffee shop.

Issey had drunk a pint of water and close to a pint of tea, and taken two paracetamol, but her head was still banging, so when Liane suggested popping over the road to Bean, she was all for it.

'I'm not your mum,' Liane said. 'And you don't take any notice of me.'

'It was a good night though, wasn't it?' Issey said. 'Until the puking.'

'It was,' Liane said.

She pushed open the door and Issey followed her in. It was much warmer inside, the windows were all steamed up and the scent of coffee beans almost overwhelming.

'Oh my god,' Issey said. 'I knew I needed a coffee, but I didn't know just how much I needed a coffee until right now. No one's ever needed a coffee as much as me.'

'Sit down,' Liane said, laughing as she pointed to a table

near the back of the shop. 'I'll get you a coffee. Jesus.'

Issey sat down and fiddled with the sugar sachets as she rolled her shoulders back and stretched her neck, listening to it crackle. She needed a new pillow. Liane's pillows were better. She definitely slept better in Liane's bed. But obviously Liane hadn't wanted that last night. She'd said it was in case Issey was sick – which was a legitimate concern – but Issey knew it was probably also because they hadn't talked about the kiss.

But maybe they were going to talk about it now. If Liane didn't mention it, Issey could. She could say it didn't have to mean anything. They could just forget about it and never speak of it again. But maybe Liane didn't really want that? Issey really had no idea.

'He's bringing them over,' Liane said, sitting down opposite Issey. 'Don't look. But the guy . . . the barista? The black guy?'

Issey turned to look.

'I said don't look!'

Issey rolled her eyes. 'Obviously I was going to look. He's cute. Do you know him?'

'He comes into the shop sometimes. He's lovely. I'm going to ask him out.'

The sugar sachet Issey had been fiddling with ripped in half and sugar tumbled over the table.

'Shit,' Issey said, gathering it into a pile with the side of her hand.

'Hey,' Alfie said, appearing at the side of the table and putting a tray down between Issey and Liane. 'Don't worry about that. I'll get a cloth.'

He put Issey and Liane's coffees down in front of them, along with a glass of water each, and picked up the tray.

'I'll just be a sec,' he said.

'What do you think?' Liane whispered to Issey, leaning forward over the table, one of her curls dangling dangerously close to her coffee.

'He's cute,' Issey said. 'He's got dimples.'

'Right?' Liane said. 'And a gorgeous smi—'

She cut herself off because Alfie was back. He wiped the table, picked up the empty wrapper, gestured at the coffees and said, 'Enjoy!'

'So?' Liane said, once he'd left for the second time.

Issey thought that one of them should mention the kiss. Issey thought that was maybe, possibly – and aside from her hangover – why they'd come to the coffee shop in the first place. Issey thought they were probably never going to talk about it now. They'd go back to being friends and Liane would start going out with Alfie and it would just be this thing that had happened that neither of them ever acknowledged. Issey thought she should probably just accept that and stop being such a needy dick about it.

'I think you should go for it,' she said.

Lou found that she was constantly looking for Kyle now. She was always aware that he could be somewhere nearby, watching her. She hadn't even seen him or heard from him since Christmas, so she tried to tell herself she was just being paranoid, but just knowing that he was here in Liverpool was enough.

Most of the Austen lecture had passed her by because she thought Kyle was sitting down near the front – a skinny guy with black leather jacket and cropped hair. Literally the only bit of the lecture she'd paid attention to was when the tutor had read 'Why do I not see my little Fanny' and brought the house down. It was only when the lecture was over and everyone started filing out that Lou realised it hadn't been Kyle at all. It was a mature student, with a close-cropped beard and glasses, not remotely like Kyle. She'd had to grab someone from her seminar group and beg to borrow their notes.

She sat in the cafe now, looking out of the window at the drizzle, a limp cheese sandwich and weak tea on the tray in front of her. She knew she should talk to someone about it. Knew she shouldn't carry on like this. She'd promised her mum she'd report it. But. She hadn't heard from him. So maybe he'd accepted it and just . . . stopped. It was possible. He could've met someone else. Or just got bored. She hoped it was the latter. She didn't wish him on anyone else.

The boy was in the library again – the one who'd helped Issey pick up the books after she'd knocked them all off the shelf last term. He was sitting at one of the computer desks, his elbow on the desk, chin on his hand, staring at the screen. There was no way Issey was going to get his attention unless she actually walked right up to him, and she wasn't planning on doing that.

Instead, she walked over to one of the bigger tables and spread her books and notebook out in front of her, along with her water bottle and phone, remembering (for once) to put it on silent.

She was halfway through noting down her highlights from the Social Psychology lecture when a shadow fell over her books. She counted to three before looking up. It was him.

'Hey,' Mickael said.

'Hi,' Issey said, smiling. He was cute. Actually cuter than she'd remembered. Since she'd last seen him, his face had become a bit vague and unformed in her mind. She'd remembered his jacket, his hands when he'd passed her the books she'd knocked down, even the way his hair fell over his face, but she hadn't been able to picture his actual face. It was nice.

'We go for drink?' he said, one eyebrow raising hopefully.

Issey wasn't sure about that. What would they talk about? How would they talk? But she didn't know what else they could suggest – the cinema would be a plan, but that seemed like something you'd suggest in advance. Instead they walked to the nearest bar. There was an outside terrace, but it was packed with smokers, so they pushed their way inside. Inside was less busy, but much noisier. The music was loud and the ceilings were high so the sound of glasses and talk was amplified.

'Beer!' Issey yelled into Mickael's ear and watched him walk up to the bar.

Issey got her phone out while she was waiting. Nothing from Liane. Which was what she expected – they'd hardly messaged at all since The Kiss – but she was still disappointed. And confused. The kiss had been amazing. And if Liane wanted more, Issey thought she would definitely be up for more. But if Liane didn't want more . . . if Liane wanted Alfie . . . then she wanted her friend back.

But if they weren't going to talk about it, maybe that wasn't going to happen. She couldn't think about that, though. Not now.

Mickael came back with their beers and leaned up on the pillar next to her, clinking the necks of the bottles together. Issey drank too much too quickly, some of the liquid spilling down her chin. Mickael reached out and brushed her chin and bottom lip with his thumb, the rest of his hand curled around her cheek.

'Ohh,' Issey breathed.

Mickael was still looking at her mouth, his hand still on her face. Issey tipped her face up and his mouth was on hers, his tongue pushing straight in. Issey slipped one hand into his hair, partly to push him back a little since she couldn't pull away because her head was pressed against the pillar. Mickael sucked on her bottom lip and she turned her body to press up against him.

Mickael curled one arm around her neck and tipped his head back to drain his beer. Issey pressed her mouth to the side of his neck. He smelled really good. She curled her hand in the front of his T-shirt..

'We go, yes?' Mickael said.

Issey nodded. She felt almost dizzy. Mickael kept his arm around her as he guided her through the bar and out onto the street. They made it as far as the next building before Mickael pressed her up against the doorway, his hips pushing into hers, one hand sliding up under her top, thumb brushing over her nipple.

'God,' Issey gasped. 'My place, yeah?'

Mickael looked at her quizzically and Issey thought about getting her phone out, bringing up Google Translate, trying to explain, but instead she just grabbed his hand and tugged him towards the traffic lights. He came easily.

Liane was on her third coffee when she finally approached Alfie. And she'd lost count of how many times she'd been into Bean and failed to approach him. It was a good job she had a loyalty card. He'd served her the first two times, but apart from 'Hey, how are you?' and 'Good, thanks' they hadn't exactly chatted. Now her hands were shaking and her mouth was dry (despite the coffees) and she was standing at the counter staring at him in his apron. With his dimples. And that smile.

'Same again?' he said.

He was looking straight at her. She knew he was one of those people who always gave you their full focus. She liked that. Although it also made her feel too much. Like she had nowhere to hide. But she didn't want to hide, did she? That was the point.

'No,' Liane said. And then cleared her throat and tried again. 'No. Thanks. I was just wondering . . .'

An alarm sounded – short beeps – and Alfie frowned and said, 'Just one sec,' before turning and doing something with a piece of machinery behind him.

'Sorry about that,' he said, turning back. His hands were on the counter in front of him, fingers spread. He had really nice hands. Liane needed to not be looking at his hands.

'That's OK,' she said. 'I was just wondering if, um . . .'

'We don't have any vacancies, I'm afraid,' Alfie said. 'But if you've got a CV –'

'No, no, it's not about a job.'

'Oh!' Alfie said. 'Yeah, sorry. You work in Tesco, right?'

'I do, yeah.' Liane was slightly disappointed that he only just seemed to have realised where he knew her from, but still. At least he knew her. 'I sold you the Phish Food.'

Alfie frowned, as if he wasn't sure what she was referring to, and then his face broke into a smile. 'Course, yeah. So how can I help?'

She took a deep breath and balled her hands into fists. 'It's not that. I was wondering if you'd like to go for a drink with me sometime?'

His eyes went wide. 'Oh. Right. Thanks. That's . . . I . . .'

There was a customer behind Liane now. She wished they'd go away.

'I actually have a girlfriend,' Alfie said.

'Right,' Liane said. 'Of course you have. Sorry. It was just . . . my friend Paige works in the White Rose? You know, on the corner?' She was babbling. She couldn't seem to stop. 'So I just thought . . . But, yeah, OK. Never mind.'

Alfie smiled. Kindly. He was so nice. Liane wanted to die.

'Did you want another latte?' he said. He lowered his voice, dipping his head. 'On the house?'

Great. A pity latte.

'No. Thanks,' Liane said. 'I think I've had enough caffeine for one day. I'm just going to . . . bye.'

She managed to make it out of the coffee shop before she started to cry.

Issey had folded her tenner into a fan and when the other girls joined her in the lounge, they found her lying back on the sofa, flapping her face with it.

'The guy didn't speak English?' Lou asked, snatching the tenner from between her fingers and crossing the room to find the pot with the Fuck It List money in.

'Yup,' Issey said.

'How was it?' Ella asked, lifting Issey's legs so she could sit down. Issey held them in the air for a few seconds then dropped them down on Ella's lap.

'It was good. We didn't need words. We spoke the language of lurve.'

'Christ,' Lou said, flopping down on the other sofa. 'You're as bad as Ella.'

'How is Nick?' Issey asked Ella.

'Lovely,' Ella said, the human version of the heart-eyes emoji. They all laughed.

'Are you going to see him again?' Lou asked Issey.

'Nah,' Issey said. 'No point. We can't talk to each other so what would we do?'

'The thing you already did?' Lou suggested. 'You don't need to donate a tenner every time.'

'It wasn't that good,' Issey said. 'Not good enough to postpone the rest of the list. But, you know, if we're ever both at a loose end . . .'

'You'll have another go on his loose end?' Lou said, reaching for the remote.

'Tight end,' Issey said. 'Very tight end.'

206

'What's happening?' Liane said, walking in and straight across the room to close the balcony door, to keep out the cold air.

'Issey pulled,' Lou said.

'Yeah?' Liane stayed over by the door, her hands in her pockets.

'Someone who doesn't speak English,' Ella said. 'So she's ticked that one off.'

'And paid up,' Lou said.

'Great,' Liane said tonelessly.

Issey's stomach felt twitchy. She wanted to curl over herself. She really wished Liane hadn't walked in right then.

'How about you, Li?' Lou asked Liane. 'Any prospects?'

Issey looked at Liane, who looked as uncomfortable as she felt.

'There's this guy John in my Victorians class. He's a mature student. Kind of hot.'

'You've already ticked off someone twice your age, haven't you?' Ella said.

'Yeah,' Liane said, her eyes flicking to Issey and then back to Ella. 'But he invited us over at the weekend. A few of us. He's got a flat in Albert Dock. I think he used to work in IT or something. Seems like he's got a bit of money.'

'So you're going to go?' Lou said.

'Yeah.'

'Not just you, though?' Ella asked.

'No,' Liane said. She'd taken one of her hands out of her pockets and was chewing at the skin around the nail. 'A few of us. Like, I dunno, six of us, maybe? Violet and Matt from my seminar group, I think.' She glanced at Issey, but Issey was staring down at her phone.

'Good,' Lou said. 'Like, I don't want you to go round to some random bloke's house and get murdered.'

Liane rolled her eyes. 'I won't get murdered.'

'Probably,' Ella added.

'Ring me,' Issey said, before she could stop herself. 'So I know that you haven't been . . . you know.'

Liane nodded. 'I will. But I'm sure it'll be fine.'

'If you do get murdered,' Lou said, 'can I have your room?'

Chapter 27

'Am I first?' Liane said, as she followed John into the flat. She actually felt slightly apprehensive. Bloody Issey and her murder jokes.

'No, no,' John said. 'Matt's in the loo.'

Matt was in their seminar group too, but Liane hadn't really spoken to him. He seemed nice though. Quiet.

The flat was much smaller than Liane had expected. And plainer. White walls, boring beige carpet and curtains, no pictures or plants or homely touches. The view over the dock from the end of the room was the only interesting thing. John looked the same as he did at uni – slightly scruffy in well-worn jeans and a baggy black jumper, hair all over the place. The only difference was that he'd shaved and he wasn't wearing shoes. He was hot at uni and possibly even hotter at home. Not as hot as Alfie, but Alfie wasn't interested, and maybe John was.

Matt came out of the bathroom, Violet arrived, and John brought them all drinks, before disappearing into the kitchen again. Liane, Matt and Violet wandered over to the balcony, looking out across the dock to the Liver Building.

'Has he invited any other mature students, do you know?' Violet asked. One of her plastic extensions was hanging partly over her face. Liane wanted to put it back in its rightful place.

'Dunno,' Matt said. 'Why? You worrying he actually wants to harvest our youthful organs or something?'

Violet laughed and Liane noticed she had a tongue stud. 'No. I mean . . . probably not, no. But it's a bit weird, isn't it?'

'My friend was worrying I was coming here to get murdered,' Liane said. 'Actually, I should probably text her. She's a bit melodramatic, she'll be calling the police if she doesn't hear from me.'

Liane tapped out a text, feeling slightly guilty for taking the piss out of Issey behind her back. But honestly.

'My mum made me promise I wouldn't go anywhere on my own,' Violet said. 'Before I came to uni, I mean. Like, literally anywhere. How would that even work?'

They sat out on the balcony for a while, looking down at the dock and talking about university, but when Liz, another mature student, arrived they moved back inside.

Liane thought she should probably go home. It was all a bit weird. She didn't really know these people, didn't think they had much in common, but then Violet started telling a story about her first year and John kept bringing out more beers and she just slumped back against the sofa and relaxed.

'Do you think this whole thing was just because he fancies Liz?' Violet whispered to Liane. They were out on the balcony so Violet could smoke, the door mostly closed.

Liane peered inside before reaching out for Violet's cigarette. She handed it over without questioning it.

'They are sitting very close together,' Liane said. 'But why wouldn't he just ask her out on her own?'

'Maybe he was nervous,' Violet said. 'He was married before and I don't think it ended very well.'

Liane nodded. 'This is still a bit weird, though. I mean, if she likes him too what are they going to do, ask us all to leave so they can get it on?' She blew out some smoke.

Violet laughed. 'We just need to make sure we all leave until it's just them.' She took her phone out and squinted at the screen. 'It's already eleven, actually. I need to go soon.'

'Shit,' Liane said. 'I need to make sure I ring my friend.'

'So she knows you're not murdered,' Violet said, nodding. 'I mean, they do call me Violent.'

Liane laughed. 'I don't think it was you she was worried about.'

'Well, that's sexist.' Violet took the cigarette back from Liane and took a long drag. 'Women can be murderers too.'

Liane let out a bark of laughter and raised one fist. 'Girl power.'

Violet laughed so much she started coughing. Liane thumped her on the back.

'It's true though,' Violet said once she'd recovered. 'That whole virgin/whore thing boils my piss.'

Liz and John both got up and left the room.

'Are they going to shag?' Matt asked, too loudly.

Liane and Violet both laughed and shushed him.

'I think so,' Violet said. 'But maybe not now. That would be rude.'

Liane started to laugh, imagining the three of them sitting there on the sofa while John and Liz shagged in the next room.

Liz came back and sat down on the edge of the other sofa. She looked nervous, fiddling with her bracelet and biting her lip. Liane realised she'd seen her doing that at university too.

'You OK?' she asked her.

Liz nodded. 'Just . . . I don't really do this. Drinking. Or smoking. Or . . . dating.'

Violet snorted, and Liane shoved her with her elbow.

John came back with a small rectangular Tupperware box of weed and started rolling.

Liane needed to ring Issey before she started smoking. She'd never remember once she was high.

John rolled two spliffs and lit them, handing one to Matt and offering the other to Liz.

'You first,' she said.

'Do you want to go first?' Violet asked Matt.

'I don't know what to do,' Matt said.

'Just, like . . . like a cigarette,' Violet said.

'I've never smoked a cigarette either,' Matt said.

'Fucking hell, Matt,' Liane took the spliff from between his fingers. 'Who even are you? Were you just hatched or something?'

'I've got really strict parents,' he said.

Liane lit the spliff and leaned closer to him, holding it up just in front of her own lips. 'So you put it in your mouth, yeah. And then you breathe in. Gently. Or you'll choke yourself. Do that.'

She put the spliff between Matt's lips, holding his face still with her other hand. His eyes went wide.

'Breathe in,' she said.

He sucked in a breath, choked, and yanked the spliff out of his mouth as he coughed.

'That always happens,' Violet said, as Liane took the spliff from his hand.

'Fuck,' Matt gasped.

'What if I did it for you?' Liane suggested.

'Fucking hell,' she heard Violet say.

'What? It's easier, particularly your first time. That's how I –'

'No,' Violet said, nudging her. 'Not that.'

Liane turned to look at Violet, but she didn't even need to because as soon as she looked away from Matt, she spotted what Violet was referring to: John and Liz grappling with each other on the opposite sofa.

'That was fast,' Matt said.

'Nicely done with the weed, John,' Violet said.

John didn't respond, just pressed even closer to Liz, who was already slipping down the sofa onto her back.

'Are you going to do the thing?' Matt said.

'Eager,' Liane said, taking a drag herself.

'I just . . . I might not get another opportunity. So I want to make sure that I, you know, have a go.'

'Right,' Liane said. 'Hold still, OK. Open your mouth a little.'

She held his jaw with her hand again, using her thumb to drop his mouth open. She inhaled and then pressed her lips up to Matt's – not properly touching, but only a hair's breadth away. And then she breathed out. She watched Matt's eyes widen and then the lids drop. He tipped his head back against the sofa cushions.

'That was better,' he said.

213

'Well, you're not coughing up a lung,' Liane said.

She took another drag. She could already feel it flowing through her blood. Her limbs felt heavy. And, as usual, she was starting to feel horny.

'Do me,' Violet said.

Liane tried to hand the spliff back to her, but Violet ran one hand down her arm.

'No, do me. The same.'

'Oh shit,' Liane said. 'OK.'

Violet was sitting up straight, her legs crossed underneath her, hands resting on a cushion in her lap.

'You ready?' Liane said.

Violet nodded, staring at her mouth.

Liane clambered up onto her own knees on the sofa and braced herself with one hand behind Violet on the wall. She breathed in, leaned in, breathed out into Violet's mouth. She could smell beer on her breath, along with faint traces of her perfume – a Thierry Mugler one she wasn't sure she liked.

'More,' Violet said.

'Fuck,' she heard Matt murmur.

Liane did it again. She was about to move back to Matt when she felt Violet's fingers in her hair, tugging her closer. She closed her eyes and let herself be pulled the short distance to Violet's lips. They were soft and Liane felt a throb of arousal. She half wanted to swing one leg over and straddle Violet's lap, but instead she opened her mouth and slipped her tongue along the underside of Violet's bottom lip. Violet moaned into her mouth and Liane heard Matt say 'Oh shit.'

She laughed against Violet's lips and opened her eyes long enough to see Violet grinning back at her. She closed them again and saw Issey. Shit.

'Can I . . .' Matt said and Liane felt him take the spliff from between her fingers. Which was probably for the best – she could quite easily have dropped it and set the sofa on fire.

She kissed Violet again, moving her free hand up to stroke her face, her thumb slipping over her bottom lip.

'You're a good kisser,' Violet mumbled.

'Could you . . .' Matt said. 'Could I . . . I feel like a bit of a spare prick right now.'

Liane leaned back. 'Shit, yeah. Sorry. Are they still . . . ?'

She sat back down on the sofa and looked across at Liz and John. Liz was on her back now, John half on top of her, his hand pushed up under her top.

There was a knock at the door.

'Shit,' Liane said. 'Are we being loud?'

There was music on, but only quietly, as they'd turned it down a while ago.

'Ignore it,' John said, his face buried in Liz's neck.

There was another knock. This one harder and louder.

'Should I get it?' Violet said.

Liane glanced over at John and Liz again.

'I can't really . . . I've got a bit of a . . .' John said, half turning on the sofa and gesturing at his crotch. Liane could see Liz's hand was inside the front of his trousers.

'That escalated quickly,' Violet said and Liane laughed.

'I'll go,' Liane said, shuffling to the edge of the sofa and using Matt's knee to push herself up.

She wobbled for a second, but took a breath and then a step. On the way to the door, she thought about how weird it was that she was somehow in this situation with these people she barely knew but saw almost every day. As she got to the door, she realised she still had the spliff in her hand and that it could, theoretically, be the police at the door.

'Hang on,' she said, knocking on the door from the inside. And then detoured to the kitchen and dropped the spliff down the sink.

Whoever was out there hammered on the door again – it sounded like both hands this time – and Liane said, 'Hang ON!' again as she headed back from the kitchen and turned the lock, opening the door to find Issey.

'Are you OK?' Issey said immediately.

'M'fine,' Liane said. She couldn't quite work out what the other girl was doing there. They weren't in their house, were they? No. They were in Albert Dock. It wasn't that far from Bold Street, but it was far enough. And it was the middle of the night. 'Are you?'

'You were supposed to ring me!' Issey said.

'Ohhhh,' Liane said, resting her head – which suddenly felt quite heavy – against the door jamb. 'I forgot. Sorry.'

'Have you taken something?' Issey said.

'Can you come in?' Liane heard John say, presumably still from the sofa. 'The neighbours –'

'Come in,' Liane said, reaching for Issey's elbow and pulling her inside, before closing the door quietly behind her.

'I was really fucking worried,' Issey said, her mouth close to Liane's ear. It reminded her of Violet. Of kissing Violet.

Which reminded her of kissing Issey. She couldn't think about kissing Issey.

She looked over at the sofa where Matt and Violet were kissing each other. John and Liz were still lying down on the other sofa, but her hand was out of his pants, at least. Both of her hands were now on his arse.

'What the fuck?' Issey said.

'It's OK,' Liane told her. 'They're all good.'

'But . . .' Issey said. She was standing in the middle of the room, next to the coffee table, turning slowly in a circle. 'What have you –'

'We had a few drinks,' Liane said. 'And then we smoked some weed. Oh fuck, I dropped it down the sink.'

'Can we go?' Issey asked Liane. 'This is fucking weird.'

'It's not,' Liane said. 'It's fine. But yeah. I'll find my coat.'

'On my bed,' John said. 'Past the kitchen.'

'What even was that?' Issey said once they were outside.

It had obviously rained at some point during the evening, because the cobbles were wet and slippy. Liane hooked her arm through Issey's to make sure she could stay upright. She probably shouldn't. But she didn't want to fall. And she was meant to be acting normal. She wasn't sure she was doing a great job of it, but still.

'It was fine,' Liane said. 'And I can tick two more off the list. I mean . . . I didn't fuck either of them, but –'

'I don't care about the list!' Issey said, stopping and pulling her arm away from Liane's. 'I was so fucking scared. I phoned you and phoned you and you didn't answer and I knew it would probably be fine, but then I kept thinking . . . what if it wasn't? What if I decided it was fine and went to bed and then in the morning found out you were dead? So I had to come down. And you made me feel like –'

'I'm sorry,' Liane said, trying to wriggle her arms around Issey's waist under her stupid pouffy coat. 'John got the weed out and it all went a bit hazy and . . . but it was fun. I had fun.'

Issey shook her head. 'Well . . . I mean, I'm glad you did. But still. That was fucked up. I came all the way down here.'

'It's not that far,' Liane said. 'And you didn't have to.'

'That's not the point!' Issey almost shouted. 'Fuck!'

'I know,' Liane said, squeezing Issey's waist and rubbing her face into Issey's neck. 'I'm being a dick. I'm still drunk. And stoned. I'm sorry. Forgive me?'

She tipped her head back and looked up at Issey. 'You look pretty,' she added hopefully.

'Oh my god,' Issey said. 'You're the fucking worst.'

Usually Liane would say 'but you love me' or kiss Issey on the cheek or nose. Or she'd snuggle up against her and make her laugh. But she couldn't do any of that now, could she? Cos she'd fucked it all up.

FEBRUARY

Chapter 28

Lou was running late. She'd slept through her alarm, couldn't find anything to wear, had forgotten she'd loaned her straighteners to Ella and had turned her room upside down looking for them. She had a seminar first thing and she couldn't miss it. She was struggling with the essay – Colonialism in Victorian English Literature – and really wanted to talk to her tutor about it before she got back to it, and it was due at the end of the week.

She made herself a coffee in a takeaway cup and left, slamming the door behind her. She turned on to Bold Street and had to step into the road to avoid a street sweeper on the pavement. It was only when she stepped back up again that she saw Kyle. He was leaning against the plate glass window of the new cafe on the corner.

'Hey,' he said.

'I'm late,' Lou said and carried on walking, biting at her lip. Her stomach had clenched at the sight of him, but she couldn't stop; she wasn't going to engage with him. It had been so long since she'd last seen him that she'd really started to believe he'd given up coming after her. She should have known better.

And then he grabbed her arm.

'What the fuck?' she said, yanking it out of his grasp and spilling some of her coffee. She yelped, licking the back of her hand.

'I want to talk to you,' Kyle said.

'Not now,' Lou said. 'I'm late. I'm sorry. I've got to go.'

'I'll walk with you,' Kyle said.

Lou shook her head, but carried on heading up towards the main road. She couldn't believe she'd apologised to him, what the fuck. And what was he even doing there, waiting for her? Tears pricked her eyes and she glanced down at the back of her hand, which had turned pink. That was why she was almost crying. Not Kyle. She'd burned her hand.

At the lights, she sipped tentatively at her coffee, the steam prickling her top lip.

'What are you doing for Valentine's Day?' Kyle said.

Lou stopped and stared at him. 'Are you joking? I told you. I'm not interested. And I really don't think it's OK for you to turn up here . . .'

The lights changed and Lou crossed, Kyle keeping pace with her.

'There's a party,' Kyle said. 'For Valentine's. And I thought you might –'

She stopped on the other side and turned to him. 'Look. Please. I can't . . . I just need to get to uni. And I've hurt my hand and I've had a shit morning and I can't –'

Kyle reached out and ran his fingers over the back of Lou's hand and she yanked it away. Again.

'OK. Then meet me for lunch,' Kyle said.

222

Lou wanted to say no. She almost said no. But she knew he wouldn't accept it, knew he wouldn't let her go if she said no. So she said yes.

Issey woke up to find Liane pressed up against her back, one arm curled around her waist, hand dangling over her belly. One of Liane's legs was between Issey's, their ankle bones knocking together.

'Fuck,' Issey murmured. She was already turned on. She'd woken up turned on. What if Liane's hand moved just a bit lower . . .

She shuffled forward, away from Liane, swinging her legs out of bed and letting Liane's arm fall down onto the mattress. She grabbed her dressing gown and tiptoed out of the room and down to the kitchen.

Paige was sitting at the dining table, fully dressed, eating an enormous bowl of cereal.

'Big night?' she said, pausing with the spoon just in front of her mouth.

'Sort of. Not really. Weird night.'

'Get a tea,' Paige said. 'You'll feel better.'

Issey put a teabag in a mug and flicked the kettle on. She walked around the other side of the table and leaned back against the units.

'Can I ask you something?'

Paige looked up and nodded, pointing at her mouth to show it was full of cereal.

'I . . . You said you were bi, right? When we first moved in here?'

Paige swallowed and wiped her mouth with the back of her hand. 'Did I? I think I'm pan.'

'Oh, OK,' Issey said. Her bare feet were freezing on the tiled floor. She stepped one on top of the other. 'I don't think I know what that is exactly.'

'Well, some people think bi suggests binary gender – so, male or female, right?'

Issey nodded. The kettle started to boil and she walked around the breakfast bar to get to it. Paige shifted in her seat so she was half turned towards Issey.

'But if you believe gender is a spectrum, then bi doesn't really work because there's not just two. I mean, it works for some people, that's how they identify and that's fine. But it didn't feel right to me. And pan does. So.'

Issey poured hot water into the mug and then turned around again.

'How did you know?'

'What?' Paige said, reaching back and picking her phone up off the table. 'Sorry, I've got to go in a bit . . .'

'Oh, sorry.' Issey crossed the room to get milk from the fridge.

'No, it's OK,' Paige said. 'I've got, like, a minute. How did I know I was queer, do you mean?'

Issey frowned. 'I think so. Yeah.'

Paige shook her head. 'I think I sort of always knew. I had crushes on boys at school and on girls too. And there was never a time that I really thought about one more than the other. I mean, specific people, yeah? But it was always just there. Both.'

'Right,' Issey said. 'I remember you mentioned a girl you were seeing when we first moved in?'

'Yeah,' Paige said. 'That's not really a thing any more.'

'Oh, right,' Issey said. 'I'm sorry. I never . . . I didn't ever really think about girls.'

'But you are now?' Paige asked.

Issey nodded, biting her lip. 'I mean, I always had crushes on boys. You've seen my room – I've got Bang! and 1D and Justin Bieber posters on my wall.'

'You've got Beyoncé too,' Paige said.

Issey smiled. 'Everyone loves Beyoncé. But I don't think I fancy her.' She frowned. 'Do I?'

'I don't know,' Paige said. 'But I know I do.'

'I think . . . you know when people ask who you'd fancy if you were gay? I mean, when you're not gay?'

Paige nodded.

'I'd probably say Beyoncé. But I don't, like, get turned on when I look at her.'

'But there is someone, right? Which is why you're asking me.'

'Yeah,' Issey said. 'And I don't know . . . I think about her. Like that. I do get turned on when I think about her. I think about touching her and kissing her and stuff.'

'And stuff,' Paige repeated and waggled her eyebrows.

Issey smiled.

'Sorry,' Paige said. 'You just look terrified.'

'I kind of am,' Issey said. 'It's just . . . it freaks me out. And I think – is it just cos we're spending so much time together? Or because she's my friend? I remember reading a thing in *Glamour* or somewhere about how it's natural to fantasise about other women, it doesn't mean you're gay. But I . . . I don't know.'

'Can you talk to her about it?' Paige asked gently.

Issey shook her head. 'Fuck. No. No. I don't think so.'

'If she's your friend, she'd understand, right? Unless she's homophobic.' She glanced at her phone. 'Oh, shit. I'm sorry. I've got to go!' She stood up, dropping her phone in her pocket, and pulled Issey into a quick hug. 'Don't worry about it so much, OK? And you can talk to me any time. Will you be all right?'

Issey nodded. She felt small next to Paige. Small and young and stupid.

'She's not homophobic,' Issey said.

'Good,' Paige said. 'Talk later, yeah? Come to the Rose?'

Issey nodded. 'OK. Yeah.'

Paige grabbed her bag and coat and ran out of the room. Issey heard the front door slam and picked up her tea, blowing across the surface of the liquid.

Her phone buzzed in the pocket of her dressing gown and she pulled it out. It was a text from Liane. The text had three coffee cups and the face with the medical mask.

'I feel like shit,' Liane said when Issey took her up a cup of tea and a plate of toast. 'Actual shit. Shit in human form. Like the poo emoji. But not smiling.'

'You'll feel better when you've had some tea,' Issey said, putting Liane's mug on the bedside table and perching on the end of the bed with her own.

'Do you need to go?' Liane said. She didn't look like her eyes were actually open, but they must have been open enough to see Issey.

'No?'

'Good. I know we haven't hung out much lately.'

'No,' Issey said. She wanted Liane to say why. To either say she didn't regret the kiss or she did. Just something. Instead of pretending it hadn't happened.

'We could go and get breakfast, maybe? I've got some vouchers for McDs.'

'OK,' Issey said. 'I need a shower first though.'

'OK,' Liane said. Issey was almost out of the door when she said, 'Iz? I feel bad about last night. I need to know you forgive me for my wangery.'

Issey stopped and leaned against the doorjamb. 'You were a dick.'

'The biggest dick,' Liane said. 'And not in a good way. I'm sorry. Does it help to know I feel like actual shit?'

'Little bit,' Issey admitted. 'But I feel a bit shit too. For turning up like that. It was really nothing to do with me –'

'No,' Liane said. 'I mean, yeah, it was nothing to do with you.' She smiled. 'But you were worried. And I said I'd phone. And I didn't phone.'

'So we're good?'

'We're good.'

Chapter 29

Lou stood in the doorway of the canteen and watched Kyle. He was sitting by the window and staring down at his phone. Every now and then he pushed one hand back through his hair. Lou could just about see the tattoo of a crown on his wrist. She'd loved that tattoo when they'd first started seeing each other, she remembered kissing it, in bed at Kyle's place. Before it all went to shit.

She didn't bother getting anything to eat – she had a KitKat, a packet of Quavers and a bottle of water in her bag. She crossed the room before she could change her mind, and sat down opposite Kyle.

He looked up and his face split into a smile and . . . he had a good smile. And a good face. Lou could remember what it was like to like him, to wait for him to look at her and smile at her. She remembered what it was like to want him to want her. But she didn't want that any more. Not now she knew what a shit he could be.

'Kyle,' Lou said. She was gripping the edge of the table with both hands. 'If you don't stop . . . bothering me . . . if you don't stop texting me and waiting for me . . .' She took a breath.

'I'll have to report you.'

She looked up from her hands and into his eyes. He was staring straight back at her, his expression blank.

'You don't mean that,' he said.

'I do,' Lou said. 'I do mean it. Please.'

She pushed her chair back. Stood up. And left.

'I can't talk now, Dad, I'm at work,' Paige said.

She turned her back to the bar and held her phone between her ear and shoulder as she sliced a lemon, dropping the slices into a jar of iced water.

'I really need to talk to you,' he said.

Usually, telling him she was at work was enough; he'd say 'Oh, sorry' or 'I'll call back' or even just grunt, but then he'd hang up and she could get on with whatever she'd been doing before. But not this time, apparently.

'What's up?' she said now, keeping her voice intentionally casual.

'I'm going to sell the house,' he said. He sounded sober. Could he possibly be sober? Maybe he was just less drunk than usual and that sounded sober to her now.

'I've found a little flat,' he said. 'You know the new development? Down by the park?'

'Yeah,' she said, even though she didn't.

'It's only small, but it'll do for me. But half the house is yours. And I hope there'll be some money for you too. So I need you to come and sign some documents. As soon as you can. Maybe at the weekend?'

Paige's brain had stopped functioning properly at 'sell the

house'. Last time they'd talked about this, her dad had cried and then got so drunk he'd been sick all over himself on the sofa and Paige had left in the middle of the night and slept on a bench in the bus station. He couldn't really be planning to sell it, could he? Not just planning either, but actually taken concrete action? She wasn't going to get her hopes up, let herself think that this might actually solve her problems, that her dad would give her some money from the sale, come through for her when he never had before.

'I'll have to call you back,' Paige said. And hung up.

Ella sat at the dining table in the lounge with the flat's bills spread out in front of her and her bank account open on her laptop. Something wasn't adding up, and she wasn't sure what. She grabbed a notebook and pen and listed the outgoings and the incoming monthly payments and then she spotted it: Paige hadn't paid her portion of the bills.

Her phone buzzed on the table and she grinned as she opened a selfie from Nick. He was at work, pouting, a full trolley of books next to him.

'Come and help?' he texted.

'Can't,' she replied. 'Busy with grown-up household stuff.'

Ella scrolled back through a couple of months' bank statements, wondering how long this would take and if maybe she could actually chuck it in and go and meet Nick after work, and found Paige hadn't paid last month either. Annoyance flickered through her. It was bad enough that she had to be responsible for all this shit, without the others fucking up. She took a breath. She was sure Paige hadn't done it on purpose.

Maybe she'd had a problem with her bank. It would have been better if she'd told her, but perhaps she hadn't noticed either.

Once she'd cross-checked all the other payments and confirmed everything else was sorted, she closed her laptop and texted Nick: 'What if I came to meet you when you get off?' She regretted the phrase as soon as she'd sent it, but laughed when Nick replied with a string of aubergine and tongue emojis. She grabbed her coat off the back of her chair. She could talk to Paige tomorrow.

Shit. Shit. Shit.

During her break, sitting in Jonny's office while Jonny covered the bar, Paige stared at her bank account on her phone. There was a crack running across the middle of the screen, but it couldn't hide the fact that she not only had no money, but that she hadn't paid the house bills for the past two months. How could she not have noticed? She'd thought one day that there was a little more in the bank than she'd expected, but she'd done a couple of extra hours at the pub and so she'd just assumed it was that. She should've been keeping a closer eye on it, she knew, but it had always been her instinct to stick her head in the sand when things started to go to shit. It was either that or run away.

Maybe she should call her dad back like she'd said she would. Ask him exactly what he was planning to do about the house, and if there really was going to be any money for her. But she wouldn't be able to trust the answer anyway. No matter what he said, she wouldn't believe she was getting anything from him until she actually had it in her hand.

What were her other options? Could she run away? Not yet, no – she didn't have enough cash to get her to Birkenhead, let alone anywhere she might want to go – but when she got paid. Or when her next loan payment came through. She could just pack up and go. Start again, somewhere else. The thought of it made her feel sick. But so did knowing that Ella knew she couldn't pay her bills.

Chapter 30

Lou knocked on Ella's door and pushed it open.

'Hey,' Ella said from the bed. She was leaning back against the headboard, her laptop on a pillow on her lap. 'You OK?'

'Not really,' Lou said, crawling into bed next to her, even though there wasn't room. 'Can I show you something?'

'Course.' Ella pushed her laptop away and turned towards her friend.

Lou took a deep breath and unlocked her phone. 'Do you remember Kyle?'

Ella nodded.

'I bumped into him a few weeks ago. He was being a dick. You know I told him last year that I didn't want to see him any more? Turns out he didn't believe me.'

'Lou,' Ella said, gently.

Lou looked up at the ceiling. 'And then one day he was waiting for me outside the library – remember the day I came to meet you in the bookshop?'

Ella nodded. The day she'd thought Nick would ask Lou out.

'And I told him again. That I wasn't interested. That we were, you know, never ever getting back together.' She laughed humourlessly. 'So that night he sent me this.' Lou turned the phone and Ella only had enough time to register that it was a photo of her best friend, naked, before Lou took the phone away again.

'Lou,' Ella breathed. 'Fuck.'

'I know. He's got more. He's sent a couple more. But he says he's got loads. He took them while I was asleep. And once when I was . . .' She let out a huge breath. 'Blowing him.'

'Oh my god,' Ella said. 'Why didn't you tell me before? How long – that was ages ago, that day at the bookshop. Is that the day he sent the first one?'

Lou nodded.

'You've been on your own with it all this time?'

It was that that made Lou's eyes burn with tears, and she nuzzled her head into Ella's shoulder.

'Fucking hell, Lou. You should've – why didn't you tell me?'

'I knew you'd say I had to report it.' Lou's voice was strained, her throat tight. 'I didn't want to . . .'

'Didn't want to report it?'

'Didn't want to be that girl. You know.'

'Fuck,' Ella said again. 'What do you think he's going to do?'

Lou shook her head. 'I don't know. Probably nothing. I just fucking hate the idea that he's got them at all, you know?'

Ella nodded, her cheek brushing against her friend's hair. 'What a piece of shit.'

Lou huffed out a laugh, draping her arm over Ella's middle and snuggling even closer.

'I can really pick them, you know?'

'No,' Ella said. 'Fuck that. This is not on you. Him being a shithead is nothing to do with you.'

'That's OK for you to say. You with your perfect boyfriend.'
She tipped her head back and smiled so Ella knew she was
joking.

'He's not perfect,' Ella said. But her cheeks had flushed
pink and her eyes were sparkling because, well, Nick wasn't
perfect. But he was pretty fucking awesome.

'I never should've shagged him,' Lou said. 'I knew he was
a dick.'

'But not this much of a dick.'

'No,' Lou said. 'And, I mean, everyone's got nudes, yeah?
It's not like . . . even if he showed people, they'd just be like
"yeah, nudes, whatever". It's not that big a deal.'

'Exactly,' Ella said.

'I mean, I know you haven't –'

'I have,' Ella said.

'You have not.'

'Not *nudes*,' Ella said. 'But I sent Nick a tit pic once. Just
because . . . I don't know. Cos it was so not me. So I thought
I should try it.'

Lou laughed. 'And?'

'He opened it at work. He spilled his coffee into the till.
Short-circuited it. There was a whole big thing. I won't be
doing that again.'

Lou fiddled with the edge of the duvet cover.

'I just don't know what to do about it, you know?'

'We can go and see your student advisor,' Ella said. 'They'll
know what to do.'

'Is it confidential?'

'I don't know. I think so,' Ella said. 'I'm sure you can tell her you don't want it to go any further. But you have to do something. You can't leave it like this.'

'He hadn't been as bad lately,' Lou said.

'Lou,' Ella said gently.

'I know,' Lou said. 'I just . . . I thought he'd stop. I thought he'd get bored.'

'He's enjoying it,' Ella said. 'It's like a power thing, I would think.'

Lou nodded.

'And you know if he stopped doing it to you, he could still be doing it to someone else.'

'I know,' Lou said again. 'I've been thinking about that. He needs to learn that it's not fucking OK.'

'I'll come with you,' Ella said.

'Yeah?'

'Course.'

'We could go now,' Lou said. 'I've got a seminar last thing. We could go before that? Or after, if she's not there.'

'No problem.'

'You're not doing anything?'

Ella had been planning on doing some revision and ringing her brother, but both of those things could wait.

'Nope,' she said. 'I'm all yours.'

MARCH

Chapter 31

Paige was running late. She'd spent the afternoon in the library working on yet another essay, but she'd lost track of time and now the only way she was going to make it to her pub shift was . . . well, she wasn't going to make it. But if she hurried, at least she'd only be a few minutes late.

'Paige!' a voice called as she stepped out onto the quad.

Paige stopped. It had sounded like her dad, but there was no way it could be her dad. He didn't know where she was, she knew he didn't.

'Paigey.'

He was there. Right in front of her. He was there and he looked so much better than the last time she'd seen him. He was clean-shaven and he'd had his hair cut and even his skin looked better – not as dry, not as florid.

'Dad,' Paige said. She was embarrassed to find that her throat felt tight. 'What are you doing here?'

'You didn't want to come to me,' he said. And then he shook his head. 'I don't blame you. Honestly. But I've got these forms and I need you to sign them.'

'How did you know where to find me?' Paige said. She still

couldn't quite believe he was there, was half wondering if she hadn't fallen asleep in the warmth of the library and was dreaming right now.

'The library? I guessed. I've been in that cafe over there.' He pointed to the canteen.

'No,' Paige said. 'The university.'

Her dad looked confused. 'I always knew you were coming to Liverpool. Did you think I didn't?'

Paige blinked back tears. 'No. I knew you knew,' she lied.

'So, can you sign this stuff now? Have you got somewhere you need to be?'

'No,' Paige said. 'I'm free.'

All the way home from her day's lectures at uni, Ella had been wondering whether she should call a house meeting. Yes, Lou would totally take the piss out of her control-freakiness and bullet journal, but it had been a while since they'd all hung out and things seemed to be falling apart a little.

As much as she claimed to be OK, and as helpful as her student advisor had been, escalating it to the Dean of the School and referring Lou for counselling, Ella knew Lou well enough to know that it was stressing her out. Ella still hadn't spoken to Paige about the missed payments, she'd just made the money up herself, but she knew she had to do that soon, before another month became due. And there was something funny going on with Issey and Liane; a weird tension that hadn't been there before.

Maybe she should've bought pizza and made everyone sit down together.

Ella had just put her key in the front door and was muttering, 'Turn, you stupid sticky bastard!' – the new lock was as temperamental as the old one had been – when someone touched her arm and said, 'Els.'

'Christ!' she said, yanking her arm away and then turning to see her brother tucked up in a coat with a fur hood, a beanie pulled low on his face.

'You scared the shit out of me!' she said, punching him on the arm.

'Ow,' he said. 'Fuck. Sorry. But I've been waiting for fucking ages and I'm freezing.'

'What are you doing here? Where've you been waiting?'

Dylan pointed slightly further up the road. 'Doorway. Three people tried to buy drugs off me.'

'Jesus, Dylan!' Ella said, finally managing to get the key to turn in the lock. She stopped before opening the door and peered at him. 'Are you all right?'

He nodded. 'Better now you're home. Freezing. Hungry. Tired.'

'Shit. OK. I don't know who's in, so stay quiet.' She opened the door and headed straight up the stairs, Dylan close behind her.

'Hey, Els?' Issey called from the kitchen.

'Hiiiii!' Ella called back, opening her bedroom door and pushing Dylan inside. 'Nick's with me. We'll be in my room.'

'Oh, don't worry,' Issey called out, faux-sweetly. 'We won't disturb you . . .'

'We'll let you have your pri-va-cyyyyy,' Liane added.

'Use protection!' Issey yelled.

241

'Fuck off!' Ella shouted down the stairs and then shut the door, turning the key in the lock.

'So that was horrifying,' Dylan said. He was standing at the foot of her bed, his coat half off.

'Serves you right for sneaking up on me,' Ella said. She kicked her shoes off and dropped her coat over the chair in the corner of the room, gesturing for her brother to do the same.

Dylan pulled off his beanie, his curly hair following it for a moment before falling back down, slightly enlivened by static.

'It's so good to see you,' Ella said, pulling him into a hug.

He rested his forehead on her shoulder and squeezed her back. His face was freezing against her neck and she could feel how cold his hands were even through her jumper.

'You too,' he murmured. 'I miss you so much.'

'Fuck,' Ella said, pushing him away and then down onto the bed. 'What's wrong?'

Dylan shook his head, the tears Ella had been able to hear in his voice welling in his eyes. 'I'm tired and I'm homesick and I'm worried about Arthur and Mum and I'm just . . . sick of it.'

'Have you –' Ella crawled up the bed to sit back against the pillows. 'Has something happened with one of the other boys?' She knew that Dylan didn't always get on well with Calum. And he and Noah had an intense friendship that sometimes crossed over into passive aggression.

'No. The boys are fine.' Dylan sat down at the foot of the bed, turning to look at Ella. 'I mean, we've all been getting on each other's tits, you know, but nothing bad. I'm just so sick of not having any freedom. I asked if I could come and see you. They said no. The other night I sneaked out of the hotel and walked around in the dark. And I couldn't remember the last time I'd gone anywhere on my own.'

'It was at home. Christmas,' Ella said.

'Oh, yeah,' Dylan said, frowning. 'It seemed like longer. But even so, that's months. I haven't done anything on my own for months.'

'You used to hate being on your own,' Ella said. When they were growing up, that had been the best way to get Dylan to do something for her – to threaten to leave him on his own. It used to make him cry and then actually beg her to do the thing he'd just been refusing to do. Ella would have liked to say she had been kind and gentle with him and not taken advantage of it, but that would have been a lie.

Dylan flopped down next to her. 'It's too much pressure, you know.'

'It's the touring, I think,' Ella said. 'You'll be fine when you stop touring.'

'I don't think we're ever going to stop touring though, that's part of the problem. They're already booking the next one. It's like I told you at Christmas, there's always one more thing.'

'That's ridiculous,' Ella said, turning slightly so she could look at him. She could see now how run-down he looked. His skin up close was pale and greasy and slightly unreal-looking. She reached up and tugged on one of his curls, letting it straighten and then coil up again.

'I'm just so tired,' he said again. 'We do press in the day and then the show at night and we still have to record. The other night I slept for like forty-five minutes. That was it. None of it feels real cos I'm spaced out with tiredness.'

And weed, Ella thought, but didn't say.

'I know what you're thinking,' he said. 'But it helps me relax. That's the other thing – it's really hard to sleep after being a performing monkey all day.'

'Performing monkey,' Ella said, smiling. 'That sounds like Noah.'

Dylan laughed. 'Yeah.'

'How is he?'

'Furious. All the time. Hates management. Hates the record company. I'm worried about him actually. He's smoking too much. And going out too much. I thought about bringing him with me. But I knew we'd be too conspicuous together.'

'You're pretty conspicuous on your own, dickhead.' She kicked at his ankle. 'I can't believe you were hanging around waiting for me for so long.'

Dylan shrugged. 'People don't recognise me so much when they're not expecting to see me.'

'Your life is weird,' Ella said, dipping her head to rest it on his shoulder.

Dylan rubbed his face. 'I miss all of you. Everything. Just being at home, you know? I keep thinking about one day when I came back from school and you were already there and I think you and Mum were making something? Corned beef hash, maybe? And you had the radio on and you were singing along and the windows were steamed up and it was just nice. I think about it all the time.'

'I remember that day,' Ella said. 'It *was* corned beef hash. Cos we fucked up the tin and Mum stabbed it with a knife. And you stood on Dipsy's tail.'

'I think that was a different day.'

'Maybe,' Ella said. 'Ugh. Now I'm homesick too. When can you get back?'

Dylan shrugged, jolting Ella. 'No idea. They'll probably have me on house arrest after this.'

Ella lurched up to look at him. 'They don't know that you're here?'

Dylan bit his lip. Ella knew that look. 'Fucking hell, Dyl!'

'There's no way they would've said yes. So I just left.'

'Where were you?'

'Manchester,' Dylan said. 'At the BBC. I got the driver to drop me here. He didn't even question it.'

'You got him to drop you where? At the house?'

'No, I'm not an idiot. At the top of the road.'

'And you didn't tell anyone you were going? They'll be worried. Fuck, it's probably on the news –'

'I told Noah. It'll be fine.'

Ella shook her head. 'Knowing Noah, he'll have told them you were kidnapped just to fuck with them.'

Dylan snorted. 'Actually, you might be right. Shit. I should've told Calum.'

'How is Calum?' Ella asked, her face warming. She'd had a huge crush on Calum when Dylan first joined the band. He was just so ridiculously handsome.

'How's Nick?'

245

'Fuck off.'

Dylan laughed. 'I mean it, though. Tell me about him. Clearly you've brought him here and had him in your room with the door locked.' He fake-shuddered.

'He's lovely,' Ella said. 'Honestly, Dyl, he's so fucking lovely. I can't even tell you. He's just . . . I keep thinking it's a trick. Cos it's too easy. He's just nice to me. And he likes me.'

'And you like him?'

'I really like him, yeah.'

'That sounds good. That doesn't sound like a trick.'

'I know,' Ella said. 'That's what I keep trying to tell myself.' She ran a hand through her hair and said, 'He asked me if I was related to you.'

Dylan frowned. 'Yeah? What did you tell him?'

'I said no. I said people always ask me that. Which they do. But I said no. I didn't want it to become a thing. It was early on. We were only just together. And I wanted him to know me, Ella. Not Dylan Jewell's sister. But now . . . when do I tell him? And how do I explain why I lied? And also, it just feels shitty because I want to say "Hell yeah, I'm his sister!" cos I'm so fucking proud of you, you know?' She punched his knee. 'But . . . part of university for me is to, like, find out who I am. Or get to be Ella. Just Ella. Not Anne's daughter or Arthur's step-daughter or Dylan's sister or Jake's cousin. Just Ella.'

'And then I had to go and get famous and fuck it all up.'

'You haven't fucked anything up, dickhead. It's just . . . it's made it a tiny bit harder.'

Dylan grinned, his dimples showing, and Ella knew what he was going to say before he said it. And he knew she knew. But he said it anyway.

'That's what she said.'

Chapter 32

'*Scandal, Grey's* or *Murder?*' Liane asked Issey.

Issey was sitting at the dining table, her laptop open in front of her and a pile of books on her left.

'Hmm?' she said, glancing up and then back at her screen.

'When you've finished that,' Liane said, gesturing at Issey's laptop. 'Do you want to watch *Scandal, Grey's* or *How to Get Away with Murder?*'

'Or maybe something not Shonda?' Issey said.

'I mean, I can see how you might think that would be an option, but nah,' Liane said.

Issey grinned. '*Grey's?* An old one, though. One of the horrifying season finales.'

'Plane crash? Shooter?'

Issey frowned at her screen. 'Plane crash, maybe? I feel like a good cry.'

'Plane crash it is,' Liane said.

'Haven't you got any work to do?' Issey asked her after she'd typed six words into her own document.

Liane was lying on the sofa, but she propped her head up on the arm. 'We've got this seminar project, but I can't get hold of the girl who's meant to be doing the reading list, so I'm stuck until she calls me back.'

Issey typed another few words and then Liane said, 'I mean . . . I could probably start my statistics essay, but . . .' She rolled on her back.

'What?' Issey said.

'I can't be bothered,' Liane said passionately.

Issey grinned. 'I know that feeling.'

'Can we go out instead?' Liane said, rolling back onto her belly. 'Do you have to finish that now? What if you just, you know, didn't. And instead we go and get pissed.'

'I really need to finish this,' Issey said. 'I'm sorry. We can have a bottle of wine with the plane crash though. If you like?'

Liane groaned. 'I guess. I just wanted to get out of here. I feel like I'm going stir-crazy.'

'You've only been home a couple of hours!' Issey said.

'Feels like years.'

Issey laughed. 'OK. Just shut up for a bit, yeah, and I'll finish this and it'll be plane crash and wine time.'

'Fine,' Liane said.

Issey tried to work on her essay, but once she started thinking about being on the sofa with Liane, drinking wine and crying over *Grey's*, she couldn't concentrate. She felt like she was just getting more and more confused. She thought maybe she wanted Liane to kiss her again. No. She definitely wanted Liane to kiss her again. But clearly Liane didn't want that. But she still wanted to be friends. Best friends. And Issey wanted that too. She just wasn't sure how that could possibly work.

She closed her laptop.

'I'm never going to get this done tonight.'

'Yay!' Liane said, waving both arms in the air. 'Plane crash!'

At work in the pub, Paige's mobile hadn't stopped ringing all night. Well, she'd stopped it ringing, but it was still buzzing on the shelf behind her. She'd ended up putting it face-down since every time she saw the notifications on the screen it made her stomach lurch. Her dad kept telling her the house sale was going through, everything was in order. He'd sounded good every time she'd spoken to him, but she was still waiting for the time he didn't.

'Boyfriend?' Jonny asked, eventually. 'Just tell him to do one. Easier.'

'Not a fucking boyfriend,' Paige said and then glanced round to make sure none of the customers were listening.

'Girlfriend?'

Paige shook her head. 'My dad.'

Jonny sucked a breath through his teeth, dragging a cloth across the top of the bar. 'Family are the worst.'

Paige laughed. 'No shit, Sherlock.'

'Anything I can help with?'

A customer came to the counter before Paige could answer and she served them, thinking about how maybe she should have asked someone – probably not Jonny, but someone – for help in the past. How her tendency to try to deal with everything on her own had never really worked for her. How, even though her dad seemed to be doing OK, she couldn't let herself trust that he really was.

The customer went to sit in what Paige now thought of as the girls' snug – even though they hadn't actually been in the pub for a few weeks; they were all too busy. Paige turned back to her boss.

'There's nothing you can do, no. But thanks for asking.'

'No problem.'

'But I do need money, so if you could throw some extra shifts my way?'

'You're already doing as many as I've got,' he said, shrugging. 'And I'm already worried about how you're fitting your uni work in.'

Paige smiled. 'You're not my dad.'

'Shut it, you,' Jonny said. And then went back to his office.

Paige wasn't really fitting her uni work in. She was squeezing it in last thing at night and between shifts. And she was skipping lectures and getting notes from a couple of different people on her course, but she could tell it was starting to piss them off. But there was no way around it.

She just had to keep going until she didn't have to any more.

'Oh shit, who's that?' Issey said from the sofa, where she and Liane were gripped by McDreamy, his arm trapped in the detached plane door while Cristina searched for her shoe.

Someone was ringing the bell.

'I'm not getting it,' Liane said. She was lying on the other sofa, her feet up on the arm.

Issey laughed, swinging her legs down. 'Maybe you should,' she said, as she headed out of the room. 'Stop them coming back again.'

She could hear Ella and Nick's laughter as she passed Ella's room. Maybe she'd knock on the way back up. She hadn't talked to Nick much and she thought he should come and meet her and Liane, tell them his intentions towards Ella. She grinned to herself at the thought. Ella would kill her.

Issey opened the door.

'Hey,' Nick said.

Issey grinned, stepping out of the way to let Nick in. She could smell the cold air on his big black coat.

'I didn't hear you leave,' Issey said, as she turned back towards the stairs.

'No,' Nick said. 'I just got here.'

'I was just thinking you should come up and have a chat with me and Liane,' she said over her shoulder. 'She's got a face mask on so she looks like shit, but –'

Before they'd even got to the landing, Issey could hear a male voice coming from Ella's room. She stopped on the landing and Nick stopped just behind her.

'Fuck off, Els!' the male voice said. Ella giggled. And then the boy did too.

Issey turned to Nick, holding her hands up. 'I'm sorry. I thought – She said it was –'

'Fuck,' Nick said, his cheeks flushing pink, eyes wide. He turned and headed back down the stairs, Issey following.

'I brought her a coffee,' he said once they were back at the door. He held out a cardboard cup from Bean. 'She brought me one at work the other day and she said she was studying, so . . .' He ran his other hand back through his hair, which had already been sticking up at mad angles and was now an absolute disaster. Issey wanted to smooth it back down. She took the coffee instead.

'Nick, I'm sure –'

'No, it's OK.' He shook his head and tried to pull open the door. 'We never said – I just assumed – Shit, I can't open –'

'You need to turn the lock at the same time,' Issey said. She handed him the coffee and opened the door.

'Can you give her that?' Nick said, giving her the coffee back again. 'I'm gonna go. Thanks.'

He pulled the door closed behind him.

'Shit,' Issey said to the closed door.

Chapter 33

'Shit. Fuck. Shit.'

'Who was it?' Liane said.

'Nick.' Issey turned the coffee in her hands. The cup was still hot and the coffee smelled really good.

'I thought he was in Ella's room already.'

'So did I. But it's someone else.'

'Seriously?' Liane sat up, folding her arms on the back of the sofa. 'Go, Ella!'

'No. Fuck. He was really upset. Shit. What do I do? He brought her a coffee. He's so nice.'

'Maybe she's just not that into him,' Liane said, shrugging.

'I need to go and tell her, yeah? That he was here? I need to give her the coffee.'

'She might be busy,' Liane said.

'I don't know. They were laughing. They didn't sound like they were –'

'Some people laugh during sex, Iz.'

'I'm going to go and knock. If they're busy she can just tell me to go away.'

'Rather you than me,' Liane said, lying back down and

un-pausing *Scandal*.

'Shit shit shit,' Issey muttered under her breath on the way back down the stairs to Ella's room. She could hear the guy's voice and Ella laughing. At least it wasn't sex noises.

She sipped the coffee without thinking and then muttered 'Shit' again.

Then she knocked on Ella's door before she could change her mind.

'Hang on,' Ella called.

'It's me,' Issey said. 'Issey. Sorry to interrupt. But . . . I need to tell you something.'

'Do you need to tell me right now?' Ella said from the other side of the door. The boy had gone quiet.

'Yeah. Sorry. And I've got something for you. I just . . . I know this is weird. It's weird for me too. I'm sorry. But if you could just open the door –'

Ella opened the door, but only about a foot. 'Hey,' she said.

Issey couldn't help looking down to see what she was wearing. She was fully dressed.

'I . . . sorry,' Issey said. 'Um . . .'

Ella raised her eyebrows. 'What's up?'

'Nick came round,' Issey whispered, unable to resist a glance past Ella into the room. Not that she could see anything. 'He brought you a coffee. This coffee.' She passed it to Ella.

'Shit,' Ella said. 'Um. You didn't tell him, did you? That I had someone here?'

'I . . . yeah. I mean, I didn't tell him. But I thought he'd popped out and was coming back. So he came up with me.

And then we heard that you were with someone. And he left.'

'No,' Ella said, stepping back into the room. 'No, no, no. Shit.'

'What?' the boy's voice said. 'What's wrong?'

'Nick came round,' Ella said. 'Fucking SHIT. I need to go and . . . Where's my phone?'

'Ella?' Issey said from the door, which was still only partly open.

'Oh, fuck it,' Ella said. She yanked the door open. 'Issey, Dylan. Dylan, Issey. Where's my fucking phone?'

Issey stared at the boy sitting on the chair in the corner of Ella's room. Dylan. Dylan Jewell was sitting on a chair in the corner of Ella's room.

'Jesus McFuck,' Issey said.

'I know,' Ella said. 'He's my brother. I'm sorry I didn't tell you. But I knew you'd freak out. You're freaking out, right?'

'Yeah,' Issey breathed.

'Nice to meet you,' Dylan said, standing up and holding his hand out to Issey.

She looked at his hand and then at his face and then she turned and ran up the stairs to the third floor.

'Dylan Jewell,' she said, in the doorway of the lounge. 'Dylan Jewell from Bang!'

'What?' Liane said, sitting up. 'Has he died?'

'He's in Ella's room.'

'Fuck off!' Liane jumped up and half ran across the room, before following Issey back down the stairs.

'Holy shit,' Liane said, standing in the doorway.

'Hi,' Dylan said, smiling.

'I'm wearing a fucking face mask,' Liane said. 'Fuck my life.'

256

'He's my brother,' Ella said. 'I know I said he wasn't, but I lied. He is. Now can we all stop freaking the fuck out so I can find my fucking phone?'

'Els,' Dylan said. 'Calm down. Do you know his number?'

'Of course I don't know his fucking number! Who knows anyone's number? Where's my bag? Shit!'

She turned to Issey and Liane who were still standing in the doorway, mostly staring at Dylan. 'Can you go and look for my bag?'

'I don't think you even had a bag,' Dylan said. 'When you got home, I mean. I remember thinking that. I think.'

'Why would you remember that?' Ella said, lifting up her duvet and looking underneath it.

'Cos as I walked up I was thinking that you might think I was about to rob you. And I noticed that you didn't have anything for me to steal. No bag.'

'Fuck.' Ella sat down on the end of her bed. 'I don't remember when I last had it.'

'Where were you before you came home?' Dylan asked.

'I stopped at Lou's salon on the way back. Fuck. I left it there. Give me your phone.' She held her hand out to her brother.

Dylan pulled a rose gold iPhone out of his pocket and handed it to her.

'Wait,' he said, reaching for it. 'I need to put the PIN in.'

'I know your fucking PIN, dickhead,' she said, already tapping away on his phone. 'You've had the same one since you were, like, twelve.'

Dylan smiled and looked over at Issey and Liane.

'So you're Ella's housemates?'

'Two of them,' Liane said. 'There's also Paige and Lou.'

'But they're not here right now,' Issey added.

'Can you two go away for a bit?' Ella said. 'Sorry, but the two of you standing there staring at my brother is really distracting.'

'Yeah,' Liane said. 'Sorry.'

'Good luck with Nick,' Issey said. 'Sorry I let him in.'

The two of them stepped away from the door and Ella stood up and closed it, still looking down at Dylan's phone.

'No one's answering at the salon,' Ella said. 'Shit shit bollocks.'

They heard a door slam, followed by an extended scream, and then laughter.

'Did she really think we wouldn't be able to hear that?' Dylan said, mouth twisting with amusement.

'She's got a poster of you on her wall,' Ella said. 'Ugh, I don't know what to do.'

'You really like him,' Dylan said.

'I really do. I hate that he thinks I'm here with someone else. I hate that he's hurt right now.'

'Just go and see him,' Dylan said. 'Seriously. I'll be fine.'

'If I'm really quick. And I get food on the way back?' She was already pulling on her boots. 'I don't know where the fuck Lou is, she's usually back by now. She'd better have my bag, shit.'

Dylan handed Ella her coat. 'I'll be fine. Promise. Take as long as you need.'

'And you won't leave before I get back?'

Dylan hugged her, resting his chin on her head and grinding

258

it into her skull in the same annoying way he had done since he grew taller than her. 'Nope. I won't leave until you get back.'

'OK,' Ella said, taking a deep breath. 'OK.'

Chapter 34

Ella sat on Nick's front step. Lou had already left the salon and Ella didn't want to go home in case he was on his way back from wherever he'd gone after he'd left her place. But she really couldn't just sit on his step all evening. She reached behind herself and knocked on the door again – in case one of his housemates had been on the loo or in the shower or otherwise ignoring the door, but . . . nothing.

'Shit,' she muttered. She looked straight down the road ahead, as headlights shone off the shop windows and cars turned into the car park opposite the Premier Inn.

She tried to think where he might go if he left her house and he was upset. He'd turn up Seal Street onto the main road, and then would he have gone to the pub? Paige's pub, maybe? It was worth a try. Ella stood up, leaning back against the door for a second, and looked both ways. She was sure he'd be home any minute. She could almost see him, walking towards her in his long black coat, his ridiculous hair standing straight up in the wind. It made her heart hurt. She wanted to slide her hands inside his coat, under his shirt, across his warm skin. She wanted to press her face against his chest, the V of dark hairs brushing her cheek. She wanted to kiss his neck and smell behind his ear. She wanted to curl up with him in his bed until they were breathing in sync. She wanted to fall asleep with him and wake up with him and eat breakfast with him and lick melted butter off his fingers and his lips.

She pushed open the door of Paige's pub and walked round to the far end of the bar before returning to the front door and checking the snug. Which was empty. She should take Nick there. He'd love the snug. If he ever spoke to her again.

She walked back to Nick's house and knocked again, before heading home.

'No luck?' Dylan asked when she got back. He was still in her bedroom, but he had her laptop propped up on a pillow on his lap.

'Nope. No sign of him. You'd better not be watching porn.'

'Oh my god!' Dylan said, turning the laptop round to show her. 'Netflix.'

'*Gilmore Girls*,' Ella said, sitting next to him. 'Typical. Why are you still hiding in here?'

'Remember when we used to watch it with Mum?' Dylan said. 'And I'm not hiding.'

Ella tapped the space bar to start the show playing again. 'Yeah. She so wanted me to be Rory.'

'Remember when you used to write Jess fanfic?'

'Shut up,' Ella said. 'Or I'll show you some of the Bang! fanfic Issey told me I should read.'

'No,' Dylan said.

'Yep. She's a big fan.'

'Of me and –'

'Of you and everyone. You're a bit of a fanfic slut.'

'I can't believe I'm getting so much imaginary action. That doesn't seem fair.'

'You should read it. Might be the next best thing to actual doing it.'

'Yeah. No. You haven't –'

'Oh my god! God, no. Of course not. Ew.'

They watched a few minutes of Lorelei and Luke bantering in the diner and then Ella said, 'How come you're still in here?'

'I did go out. Talked to Paige a bit? She's nice.'

'She is. She's great.'

'It just felt weird being in the house without you.'

'Scared of Issey?'

'Little bit.'

Ella laughed. 'She's lovely, really. She'll be fine once she's calmed down.'

'I don't know if I'm staying that long.'

Ella rested her head on his shoulder. 'I kind of don't want you to go.'

'I can stay 'til tomorrow, I think.'

'Yeah? We could get a takeaway and watch a film.'

'Is that the Real College Experience?'

'Well, there's the Fuck It List, but if you're not up for that . . .'

'What the fuck is the Fuck It List?'

Dylan paused *Gilmore Girls* while Ella told him.

'Someone with a tattoo,' Dylan said, tapping the page with his finger.

'Who?' Ella asked.

'Remember that German girl in Majorca?'

'She had a tattoo?'

'Butterfly. On her ankle. Don't think I've ever slept with a waiter/waitress . . .'

'I used to work in a diner,' Liane said. 'Just saying.'

Issey elbowed her and Dylan grinned at them both. They were sitting on the other sofa and so far hadn't done much other than stare at him. Issey's cheeks were still flushed, her eyes wide. Plus she'd put on make-up and changed into tight jeans and a loose, low-cut top.

'Someone off a reality show,' Dylan read and his cheeks flushed.

'Ooh!' Issey leaned forward. 'Who?'

Dylan glanced sideways at Ella. 'I can't really say. Sorry. But they were in a band as well, so I can tick that one off too.'

'Was it Perrie Edwards?' Issey said.

Dylan nibbled his bottom lip, looking at Ella again.

'No point looking at me, mate. I don't know who you've shagged.' She grinned.

'I really can't say,' Dylan said. 'I'm in enough trouble as it is.'

'When you're already in trouble,' Paige said, 'you might as well get into more, that's what I always say.'

Dylan laughed. 'You sound like Noah. You know, from the band? Yeah. No. I think it's more, sort of, baby steps for me.'

'Goody two-shoes,' Paige said. 'Like your sister.'

'Well brought up!' Ella argued. 'Standards! Morals!'

'You know it says "friend's brother or sister"?' Dylan said. 'What if it was your sister's friend?'

'Who?' Ella shrieked.

'Standards! Morals!' Paige mocked, laughing.

'Jessica Wilkins gave me a hand job at your eighteenth,' Dylan said.

'Holy shit,' Ella said, punching him on the thigh. 'I knew you weren't charging her fucking phone.'

'I mean, I did charge her phone too,' Dylan said.

'Ugh,' Ella said. 'At my own party. Dirty little bastards.'

'Someone who doesn't speak English,' Dylan said. 'There was a fan in Amsterdam.'

'Just one?' Paige asked. 'Come on.'

'No, really!' Dylan said, sitting up straighter. 'I don't like . . . It's not the kind of thing . . .'

'You don't sleep with fans?' Issey asked.

Dylan dipped his head and rubbed the back of his neck. 'I mean . . . I have. But usually I'm drunk or . . . something. And I don't really remember.'

'Morals,' Ella said, sarcastically. 'Standards.'

'But I said a while ago I wasn't going to do that any more. It's too risky. And it's just kind of . . . sad. The other guys in the band . . .' He shook his head. 'I mean, we're young. And there are opportunities. But it's not for me.'

'Any more,' Paige said.

Dylan glanced at her and smiled. 'Yeah. No. Not any more.'

'I always kind of thought you'd be having orgies,' Issey said.

'You've mixed up fanfic and reality again there, Iz,' Ella said, rolling her eyes.

'Definitely no orgies,' Dylan said.

'Unless they just don't invite you,' Paige suggested.

'Fuck,' Dylan said, his eyebrows pulling together in a frown. 'Maybe they don't invite me to the orgies. Shit.'

Chapter 35

'Where've you been?' Ella yelled, as she ran down the stairs.

'I've got your bag,' Lou called out, turning straight into the kitchen.

'I know!' Ella said. She followed Lou into the kitchen. 'I really need my phone.'

Lou had put Ella's bag down on the breakfast island and Ella immediately started rooting through it for her phone. 'Where've you been?'

'I went for a drink after work. What's up with you?'

Ella pulled her phone out, half hoping for a message from Nick, but at the same time scared of what it would say. There was nothing.

'Fuck,' she muttered.

Lou was drinking milk straight from the bottle.

'We need to talk about that,' Ella said, pointing. 'But I need to tell you some other stuff first.'

'What?' Lou wiped her mouth with the back of her hand.

'OK,' Ella said, taking a breath. 'OK. So.'

'Is it something bad?' Lou asked, frowning.

'Not . . . bad. But. Basically I didn't tell you something. And now I need to tell you. And you're probably going to be pissed off that I didn't tell you. But I had a good reason and –'

'Just tell me!' Lou said. 'You're stressing me out.'

'OK. OK.' Ella fiddled with her phone, then put it face-down on the table. 'OK.'

'Ella!'

'Sorry. OK. So Dylan Jewell is my brother.' She wrinkled her nose. She really hadn't wanted to just blurt it out.

Lou burst out laughing. 'Fuck off.'

'No. I'm serious. He's my brother. I know I should've told you. I wanted to. Loads of times. But I just . . . I didn't want to be Dylan Jewell's sister here. I wanted people to get to know me. So I'm sorry that I lied, but –'

'Why are you telling me now?' Lou said. She still looked incredulous.

'Oh, right. Yeah. Because he's upstairs.'

'Fuck off,' Lou said again. 'Seriously?'

'Yeah. He's kind of going through some stuff and he wanted to get away. I didn't know he was coming.'

'Is he staying?' Lou said, heading for the door.

'Just tonight.'

'I'm still expecting this to be a joke, OK?' Lou said, as she walked up the stairs. 'I want you to know that even though I'm going up to have a look, I don't actually believe you. I haven't fallen for it. OK?'

'Noted,' Ella said, smiling.

'Holy shit,' Lou said, stopping in the doorway to the lounge.

Dylan turned round on the sofa and smiled at her. 'Hi. I'm Dylan. You must be Lou.'

'Holy shit,' Lou said again. She crossed the room and held out her hand. Dylan shook it.

'Good to meet you,' he said. 'Ella talks about you a lot.'

'I need a cig,' Lou said. 'Do you smoke?'

Dylan shook his head. 'No. Not really. Sometimes. I –'

'Want one?' Lou said, holding the pack of Marlboro Lights out to him.

He looked over at Ella.

'Fucksake, Dyl, you're a grown man. If you want a fag, have a fag.'

Dylan stood up and followed Lou out onto the terrace, the door squeaking obnoxiously as she slid it open.

'I'm totally telling Mum though,' Ella said, under her breath.

Paige grinned at her. 'He's nice. Your brother.'

'No,' Ella said.

'What?'

'He's my brother. He's in a band. He's got a tattoo. He was on a reality show.'

'Holy shit,' Issey whispered, eyes wide. 'He's the holy grail.'

'Absolutely not,' Ella said. 'Out of bounds.'

'Hey, Els,' Dylan called from the terrace. 'Remember when you were going out with Oliver Hall and I said I was going to tell him to keep his hands to himself and you said it wasn't up to me to . . .' He did air quotes. '"Police your sexuality"?'

'Not the same,' Ella said.

'Exactly the same,' Dylan said.

'It does seem fairly similar,' Paige said.

'Shut up, all of you.' Ella stood up. 'I need to go and phone Nick.' She turned and looked at Dylan. 'Will you be OK?'

'God,' Dylan said, cigarette still in his mouth. 'I'm fine.'

'Don't worry, Ella,' Liane said. 'We'll look after your brother.'

'Your hot, tattooed, brother-in-a-band,' Paige added.

'I hate all of you,' Ella said.

Nick's phone went straight to voicemail. Ella hung up. And then pressed redial. She should just leave a message telling him it was her brother and – She hung up again. There was too much to say to leave a message. He probably wouldn't believe Dylan was her brother anyway. Or that the boy in her room had been her brother. She wouldn't believe it if the situation was reversed. If Nick had phoned and said 'Hey, guess what, my brother's the singer in one of the most famous bands on the planet', she'd think it was a wind-up. She definitely needed to actually talk to him. She opened her texts. The last one from Nick said: 'Bored. Miss you. Wish you were here. You could help with the shelf-stacking. Not a euphemism. (Or is it?)' She read it in his voice. His voice was so clear in her head. He always sounded like he was smiling. It was one of the things she liked the most about him. God, she hated picturing him unhappy, it just seemed wrong.

She tried ringing again. And then went back to texts. But she had no idea what to say. 'It's not what you think' was ridiculous. Clichéd. Like something from *EastEnders*. 'We need to talk' sounded too ominous. Same for 'I need to see you'. But she wanted to know if his phone was on. If it was off, she might as well give up for now and go and see him in the morning. Although she hated the idea of him being upset overnight. Fuck.

She typed 'Nick' and sent it before she could change her mind.

Underneath it said 'Delivered' but it didn't change to 'Read'.

Muttering 'shit shit shit' to herself, she went back upstairs to the lounge.

Chapter 36

'Are you going to be OK?' Ella said the following morning. 'Going back?'

They'd stayed up talking for half the night, but finally they'd slept and then Dylan's alarm had woken them and Ella had made breakfast. Her other housemates were either sleeping in, letting them have some time alone, or already at uni. And Dylan was going back to face the music.

Dylan rubbed the back of his neck. He'd been doing that since he was a little kid. It made Ella feel ridiculously fond of him.

'Yeah. It's fine. I mean, I can't complain about it really, can I?'

'You can,' Ella said. 'You can complain to me. I mean, I might tell you to get over yourself, but you can still do it. You should ring me more.'

'Could we, like, Skype, maybe? I know I don't have that much time, but it's better if I can see people's faces. Talking on the phone's a bit lonely, I think.'

'Course we can.' She poured him another cup of coffee. 'Mum's finally got WhatsApp and she wants me to set up a family group chat, so I'll do that.'

'Oh my god,' Dylan said, grinning as Ella slid the coffee over to him. 'That's going to be ridiculous.'

'Right? Which is why I haven't done it already. But, you know, it might help you to feel more connected. To us. I don't want you to feel . . . I want you to know that we're always there. No matter what.'

'I do know that,' Dylan said.

By the time she got to Nick's shop, she was shaking with nerves. She'd texted him again in the morning – going with 'I promise it's not what you think' when she just couldn't stand it any more – but again, she couldn't tell if the text had even been read. She'd thought about going and sitting on his step first thing because he must have come home and he'd have to leave the house to go to uni or eventually work, but she thought she was dipping deep into stalker territory there, so she'd made herself go to uni – to her lectures, a tutorial, lunch – as usual. Lou had met her for lunch and reassured her that it would be fine once she'd explained to Nick, but to Ella it felt like every minute that passed without getting to speak to him was taking him further and further away. It had been so long now she was scared she wouldn't be able to get him back.

She saw him as soon as she opened the door. He was standing behind the circular information desk, the first place she'd ever seen him. He was wearing black-rimmed glasses she hadn't seen him wear before and his hair was swoopy and out of control. Her hand itched to smooth it down. Her stomach flipped as she walked through the shop, never taking her eyes off him in case he darted away. He was leaning on the counter, writing something down, and then he ripped some paper, poked it into a book and crouched down under the counter. Ella had a mad vision of him crawling away before she got there, but he straightened back up just as she reached the desk.

'Hey,' she said.

He startled a bit and his cheeks flushed pink as he turned to look at her. 'Oh! Hi.' He pushed one hand back through his hair.

'Nick, I –'

'I can't talk. Sorry.' His eyes darted around the shop. 'Not here. I –'

'When are you on break?'

'I'm not . . . I've only just got here, so I won't get a break til, like, six? I'm on 'til closing tonight. Nine.'

'OK. So if I come back at six?'

'Yeah,' Nick said, his eyes settling back on her for a second. He was chewing his lip. Ella wanted to reach out and smooth her thumb over it. 'I'll only have, like, ten minutes.'

'That's OK. I –'

'Sorry,' Nick said. 'I have to go and get something from the –' He stepped out from behind the desk, but walked around the back so he was as far from Ella as he could get, the enormous circular desk between them. 'Stockroom. I – See you at six, yeah?' He looked over at the stairs, where Leila, one of his colleagues, was coming down the stairs. 'Lei – can you cover for me? I need to go to the stockroom.'

Leila looked confused, then saw Ella and looked thunderous. 'No problem.'

'See you at six,' Ella said.

'Ella's going to kill you,' Lou said, staring at her phone.

'Seriously?' Issey asked from the other sofa. 'Why, though?'

'She has spent almost two years lying to people who asked her if he was her brother. And now you've outed her on Instagram.'

Issey picked her phone up off the coffee table and stared at it. As if it would tell her she'd been right to post a photo of Dylan. Instead she saw that her notifications were blowing up – on Instagram and on Twitter (she'd totally forgotten that her Insta posted directly to Twitter).

'Maybe she won't care if she's all loved up with Nick,' Liane said. She was sitting next to Lou, one foot on the coffee table, painting her toenails.

'Have you met Ella?' Lou said. 'Issey is totally dead.'

'It's just . . .' Issey held her phone out to Lou. 'You can barely even see him!'

The photo was of Ella and Lou with Dylan almost, but not quite, out of shot. His hair was partly covering his face, but his dimple was showing. And the neck of his T-shirt was gaping, showing the musical notes tattoo on his left collarbone. The tattoo was pretty identifiable, Issey had to admit.

'That's not the point!' Lou said. 'Anyway, you tagged him! And Ella, and now the photo has had – how many likes?'

'Not loads,' Issey said, putting her phone down again.

'Hundreds?' Lou asked. 'Thousands?'

'Like, seven hundred and something,' Issey said.

'You should prob delete it,' Liane told her.

'Not much point,' Lou said. 'There'll be screenshots and everything now.'

Issey flopped back on the sofa. 'I'll apologise.'

'Good luck,' Lou said.

Ella spent the next ninety minutes in the library. She wasn't entirely concentrating, but she hoped she'd actually managed to make some notes that might be useful for her next essay. She'd checked the time on her phone pretty much every five minutes – even though she'd set an alarm – and she'd jumped every time she got a notification, even when they were tweets or Facebook posts. There was nothing from Nick. At quarter to six, she packed her books away, put on her coat and headed back to the bookshop. It was already dark, but the quad was lit with fairy lights strung between the trees and street lamps and the cafe was still open, flooding the area with a warm golden light. It was probably Ella's favourite place in the whole university, she thought as she headed towards Nick's shop.

He was already outside, wearing his big black coat, his hands pushed into the pockets. He still had his glasses on.

'Hey,' Ella said, stopping directly in front of him. Her hands reached out instinctively and she pulled them back against herself and crossed her arms. 'Do you want to go somewhere?'

'I haven't really got time,' Nick said. 'I've literally got, like, ten minutes.'

'Do you want to go and sit down? I –'

'You can just tell me,' Nick said. 'You don't need to give it a big build-up or sit me down or get me a drink or anything. I'm not going to freak out or make a scene. Just, you know, say it. And I can get back to work and you can get back to –' He shook his head.

'Nick,' Ella said. She wanted to touch him so badly. 'It was my brother. In my room. I know you probably won't believe that. I wouldn't believe it. But it's true. It was my brother.'

Nick looked at her, his eyebrows furrowed. God, he had great eyebrows. 'You told Liane – or Issey? You told her it was me.'

'I did. Because I didn't want them to know who it was. Who my brother is.' Ella looked around, in case anyone was standing nearby who might overhear. 'You asked me if I was related to Dylan Jewell. And I said no. Well, I lied. He's my brother. And I didn't want the girls to know, which is why I said it was you.'

Nick was tugging on his bottom lip with his forefinger and thumb. 'Seriously?'

'Yeah. I know I should've told you. But I didn't know . . . I hardly knew you then. Even though I liked you, obviously. And it was just . . . it was one of the things that was really important to me, about coming here. That people didn't know. That they got to know me as me.'

'I thought you'd come to break up with me,' Nick said.

'No,' Ella said. 'I've been . . . God, I've been so fucking miserable thinking that you thought – I would never do that. To you. I came to your house last night. I sat on your step. I couldn't stand it. Thinking that you thought that. Thinking that you'd be upset and hurt. Because of me. I was going to go and sit there again this morning, but I thought it was stalkery and – Oh! Fuck. Also, I'd left my phone at Lou's. That's why I couldn't ring straight away. She didn't get back for hours and by then . . . It was late. And I texted. But I didn't want to tell you all this over text. I just wanted to talk to you and –'

Nick reached out and wrapped his hand around her wrist.

'You sat on my step? Last night?'

Ella nodded. 'For about an hour. And then I went to look for you in the pub. But you weren't there.'

'I went to my friend Charlie's flat. Up by the cathedral.'

'Right,' Ella said. 'OK.' She was distracted by the feeling of his fingers on her wrist, his thumb rubbing over the skin. She wondered if he could feel her pulse racing.

'He's really your brother?' Nick said.

'He really is,' Ella said.

'Is he still at your place?'

'No. He had to go back to the band. He sort of . . . ran away. For a bit.'

Nick tugged on her wrist and she took a step closer.

'Do you . . .' Ella started. 'What are you . . .'

'I'm sorry,' Nick said. 'I freaked out. I started thinking that we hadn't said we were, like, exclusive. And I know it's uni and you've got that Fuck It List and everything. And I felt like an idiot. Like I hadn't realised it was a casual thing.'

'It's not,' Ella said. 'I don't . . . It's not a casual thing for me.'

'No?' Nick said.

Ella took another step until she was right in front of him. Another half step and she could press up against him. She wanted to.

'No. It never was. I was fucking gone for you from the first time I saw you.'

Nick laughed then and Ella almost shivered with how good it felt to hear it.

'I'm completely in love with you,' Nick said.

'Holy shit,' Ella said. She ducked her head, pressing the top of it against his chest, before straightening up and closing the gap between them. She slid her hands inside his coat, under his top, across his skin, pressing her fingers against his ribs. She tipped her head back. 'Me too. I'm completely in love with you too.'

'Yeah?' Nick said, his eyes twinkling behind his glasses.

'I like the glasses,' Ella said.

And then she kissed him.

Chapter 37

When Paige got back from work she'd sneaked straight into her room, rather than go to the living room and hang out with the others. Another utilities payment was due and Paige still hadn't paid last month's. She'd managed to get the first lot to Ella, but that was all. And Ella was being sweet and understanding in her totally Ella way, but Paige felt like shit. And she didn't know how she was going to be able to catch up.

She'd actually accepted a couple of paid promotions on her Instagram, which she said she'd never do. Particularly since one was fucking tummy tea or something, which made it look like she was trying to lose weight. The whole point of her Instagram was that she was happy with how she looked, but she couldn't turn it down – they had offered double what anyone else was offering. It still wasn't enough, though. It had paid for food and a book she needed that the library didn't have and she couldn't find used since everyone else had their shit together and had bought it already.

Ella had loaned Paige her laptop so she could do her essay. The essay she'd had to get an extension for, her tutor telling her it was the last time. Her eyes had actually welled with tears when he'd said that and she'd been mortified. He'd been kind and suggested she see a counsellor, the usual shit. But that wasn't happening. She just needed to organise her time better. Work a bit more, if she could. Sleep a bit less. Then it would all be fine.

After about ten minutes, she stopped and googled the university's hardship fund. She'd have to remember to clear the history, this was Ella's laptop after all. There was a form, she had to collect it from Student Services. She could do that. She could do that tomorrow. Her chest felt instantly looser. And then she saw that the deadline for applications was the end of March, presumably since they thought as the term was ending the students wouldn't need additional funds. Tears stung her eyes again. She had to pay Ella before the end of term. She just had no idea how she was going to do it.

She stretched her arms over her head, hearing the tiny bones in her neck crackling. She was so tired.

'I hated thinking you were hurt,' Ella said. She tracked one finger over Nick's shoulder and down his arm.

He shivered. 'I was all right. I got hammered.'

Ella laughed. 'So I was picturing you crying yourself to sleep and you were –'

'Playing *Guitar Hero*, yeah.'

Ella kissed his collarbone. 'Did you win?'

'Nah. Couldn't really see the screen through my tears.'

'Shut up.' She leaned up and kissed his mouth.

'I hated it,' Nick said, against her lips. 'Hated thinking you were with someone else. Hated thinking I wouldn't get to be with you again. Do this.' He ran his hands down her sides until she giggled.

'I know,' she said. 'Me too. I'm sorry.'

'Let's never speak of it again!' he said dramatically, rolling over so he was on top of her. He kissed down the side of her neck. 'Can you stay?'

'I probably shouldn't,' Ella said. 'I've got an essay –'

'I can help,' Nick said, sliding down the bed until his head was resting on her shoulder. 'I'm good at essays.'

'You're an English student.'

'That's what I'm saying!'

'It's a microbiology essay.'

'God, I love having a genius girlfriend. I could help with spelling? Grammar? Paragraph indents?'

Ella laughed, brushing her hand through his hair just because she could. 'I think I've got that covered. But thanks.'

'Talk it through with me then. Order your thoughts. But I'm warning you, it's definitely going to get me hot.'

'Noted,' Ella said.

Paige was in the kitchen pinching one of Issey's Jaffa Cakes – Issey never noticed – when Liane came down.

'Is there vodka?' she said, yanking open the freezer, barely even glancing at Paige. 'I need vodka. Want one?'

'I've got coffee,' Paige said. 'Got an essay to finish.'

'God,' Liane said. 'I don't know how you do it.'

Paige laughed. 'Me neither, to be honest.'

Liane poured herself a generous measure of vodka, topped it up with orange juice, and turned to look at Paige.

'Do you ever feel like you're losing your mind?' she said. 'Like you literally can't trust your own thoughts?'

Paige smiled wryly. 'All the time.'

'God. I don't know what I'm doing,' Liane said. She swigged the vodka. 'I kissed Issey.'

'Yeah?' Paige said, sipping her coffee. 'Cool.'

Liane laughed. She didn't know what she'd been expecting Paige to say, but 'cool' wasn't it.

'But then we haven't talked about it or anything,' Liane admitted. 'I've just kind of been pretending it never happened.'

'Why?'

'Because . . .' Liane frowned. 'Because I don't want anything to change. She's my best friend and I love her. And I don't want to lose her.'

'What makes you think you'd lose her, though? Did she kiss you back?'

'She . . . yeah.' Liane hadn't let herself think much about the kiss. It was too stressful. Too much. But Issey had definitely kissed her back.

'It was a good kiss?'

Liane nodded. It had definitely been a good kiss. She drank some more vodka.

'So maybe it wouldn't ruin everything? Maybe it would be amazing. The two of you together.'

'Issey's not gay, though,' Liane said. She sounded stupid even to herself.

Paige rolled her eyes. 'She might be bi. She might be pan. She might just be gay for you.'

Liane shook her head. 'That's not a thing.'

'Why not? You kissed her. You liked it. She liked it. What's the problem?'

'I always wondered . . .' Liane's voice cracked. 'Like . . . in the back of my mind. Not even in the back of my mind, actually. I would think of it and then –'

'Not let yourself think of it,' Paige finished. 'Yeah, I've been there.'

'And I like boys. Men. I like dick.'

'Me too,' Paige said and then grinned. 'Sometimes. In its place.'

Liane laughed, covering her face with both hands. 'God, this is awful. I don't know what I'm doing.'

'You've never been with a girl before?'

Liane shook her head. 'No. I've had crushes, I think. Not that I ever thought of them as crushes. My friend Zack – he died – I thought I was in love with him. But I don't know. I used to think about him and his girlfriend a lot. A lot. And now I wonder . . . And then I met this guy, Alfie. And I asked him out but he had a girlfriend and now I wonder if I even liked him or if I was just trying to distract myself. From Issey. Like, I told myself I liked Zack, but maybe it was actually his girlfriend. And then I told myself I liked Alfie, but –'

'Maybe you did,' Paige said. 'Maybe you liked them both. Alfie and Zack. Maybe you actually liked Zack's girlfriend. That's OK. It's all OK. You don't have to beat yourself up about it.'

Liane shook her head. 'I know. I mean, I sort of know. But also maybe I just miss the feeling of being with someone properly, you know? The list is great – it's been fun – and hook-ups are

283

fine and everything, but that feeling of anticipation, you know? Butterflies and thinking about someone all the time and . . .'

Issey. She had that with Issey.

'God,' she said, dropping her head down onto the table. 'I am an idiot.'

Paige rested her hand on the back of Liane's neck. 'You're not an idiot. You're just in love with your best friend.'

Nick was snoring lightly next to her, but Ella couldn't sleep. She texted with Dylan for a bit, but he was exhausted – the band had been in crisis meetings with their management and record company since he'd got back – so she had to let him go. She checked her bank account and noted that Paige still hadn't transferred the money in. She needed to talk to her again, she knew, but it was so awkward. This was why she hadn't wanted to be responsible for the bills in the first place. Particularly since she could tell that Paige was struggling, but every time she'd tried to say something, Paige apologised and said she was sorting it and would be able to pay soon.

She scrolled through Tumblr for a while and then went to Instagram. It was so irritating now it wasn't in chronological order. She was constantly wondering why someone was at Starbucks in the middle of the night before realising the photo had been taken hours or sometimes days earlier.

She almost scrolled right past Issey's photo – her eyes were already starting to lose focus and she thought she could probably fall asleep – but then she stopped and stared.

'What the fuck?' she muttered.

'Hmm?' Nick said in his sleep, shifting slightly towards Ella.

Ella stared at the photo Issey had posted. It was of Ella and Dylan with Lou in the background. Lou was standing behind the sofa, leaning on it with both arms, her head hanging down, hair almost touching the cushions. Dylan was right on the edge of the photo, in profile, his fringe curling down over his eyes. He was grinning, the dimple popping in his cheek. Ella was grinning back at him, and she could actually see for once why people sometimes said they looked alike. People who knew they were siblings. So, people at home in Lancashire, not at university.

It was a really good photo. Issey had put a filter on it that made Ella's skin look smoother, her hair warmer. It was the kind of photo she'd have had as the lockscreen on her phone if she wasn't at university. But she was. And now Issey had permanently linked her with Dylan. She was going to kill her.

Chapter 38

'I am going to kill you,' Ella said, pushing Issey's bedroom door open.

She'd woken up with Nick and had breakfast with Nick and walked as far as she could with Nick until he had to go up the hill to work and Ella had to go down the hill to home. They'd stood on the corner kissing until Nick had realised he had five minutes to do a fifteen-minute journey and had run off, his black coat flying behind him.

Issey was leaning back against her headboard, her laptop on her knees. Her curtains were still closed, but the window was obviously open – Ella could feel the breeze and the fabric was fluttering.

'Seriously, Iz! What the fuck?'

Issey rubbed one hand over her face.

'Are you crying?' Ella said, frowning.

'No,' Issey said, rubbing her face again. 'Just tired. Couldn't sleep last night.'

'Guilty conscience?' Ella knocked the end of Issey's bed with her knees.

'I'm really sorry, El,' Issey said. 'I didn't think.'

Ella shook her head. 'I don't believe you. I love you, you know I do. But this is classic Issey. Act first and think later. I just . . . I've spent almost two years hiding this and you just casually fuck it all up.'

'Is it that big a deal though?' Issey said, leaning forward on the bed. 'I mean . . . why does it matter if people know?'

'That's not up to you though, is it? I mean, that's not your decision to make. And you know that. So it wasn't OK for you to, like, out me.'

'Oh, come on!' Issey said, dropping back against the pillows again and throwing her hands up. 'Don't be so dramatic. It's nothing like being outed. I mean –' Her voice cracked.

'I don't mean outed like that,' Ella said. 'Of course it's not like being outed like that. But you knew I didn't want people to know. And you told them anyway.'

Issey had both hands over her face and she rubbed them back through her hair. 'Yeah,' she breathed. 'Yeah. You're right. I'm sorry. I just . . . I got overexcited. I didn't think about how it would affect you. You know I'm a big fan. And I've posted stuff about him on there before. So I just, like, couldn't resist. I'm sorry.'

'Thank you,' Ella said. 'Are you OK?'

Issey shook her head. 'Not really. There's some stuff I need to sort out, deal with, I dunno. Doesn't matter now. Do you forgive me?'

Ella blew out a breath. 'You're not the only one who's got shit going on, you know? I've got house stuff to deal with, I have to pay all the bills, the kitchen's always a shit tip, Dylan turned up and then Nick. There's just . . . The world doesn't revolve around you.'

'I know,' Issey said.

'And what's going on with you and Li? You're both being weird.'

'Yeah. I don't know. It's all got a bit fucked up and I don't know –'

Ella's phone rang.

'Sorry,' she said. 'It's my mum. I'd better get it.'

'Course,' Issey said.

'Hey,' Ella said into her phone. 'How's things?'

Issey tapped open her Instagram and stared at the photo of Dylan. She should delete it. But Ella hadn't asked her to, so . . .

'Oh,' Ella said, next to her. 'Oh no.'

'What's happened?' Issey said.

Ella's shoulders were shaking. 'Oh no,' she said again. 'Mum.'

Issey draped herself over Ella's back and squeezed her with both arms.

'You don't need to come,' Ella told Lou, who was trying to make her sit down and drink the tea she'd made her. 'I'll be fine. It's only, like, just over an hour on the train.'

'Do you actively not want me to come?' Lou asked, taking Ella's favourite hoodie out of the drawer and dropping it next to the weekend bag Ella was stuffing with anything she could get her hands on. 'Or are you worried about inconveniencing me or whatever?'

'We've got exams. And you've got work. And uni. And counselling. When are you seeing the Dean?'

'Never fucking mind that,' Lou said. 'It doesn't matter now. Do you want me to come?'

Ella shook her head and then pushed her hair back with one shaking hand. 'I don't want to go home on my own. But I know I'll be fine when I get there. I mean, I think I will. God.' She sat down heavily on the bed. 'You should've heard her. My mum. She could hardly speak.'

'I'll come,' Lou said, sitting down next to her and curling an arm around Ella's shoulders. 'I'll come, don't worry.'

Ella snuffled against Lou's shoulder. 'You know what my first thought was? Once I realised what she was telling me? It was "I need to get away". Who the fuck does that? Like, I should've wanted to go straight to her. To . . .' Ella swallowed. She hadn't been able to say Arthur's name yet. She'd tried to tell Issey, but had only managed 'my step—' before she'd been crying too much to speak.

'You're too hard on yourself,' Lou said. 'I think it's completely understandable to want to run away. This shit is hard! You think I didn't want to run away from the Kyle situation? I thought about a new identity and everything. And what you're going through is so much worse. I can't even imagine.'

Ella sniffed. 'I bet Dylan didn't want to run away.'

'Well, Dylan is an actual angel,' Lou said, kissing the top of Ella's head. 'Also, he already ran away once. And he ran towards you.'

'Yeah,' Ella said. 'I love him.'

'We all love him,' Lou said.

Ella laughed, snottily. 'God. He's going to be heartbroken.'

Lou squeezed her friend. 'And you'll take care of each other. And you'll both take care of your mum. And I can hide out in

289

your room or make tea or endless toast or get you all hammered, dye your hair, whatever you want.'

'I don't think you should dye anyone's hair.'

'OK,' Lou said, kissing her again. 'Will you be OK if I go and pack a bag?'

Ella nodded. 'Maybe . . . can you ask Issey or Liane to come in?'

They both went in and sat either side of Ella while she cried and tried to think what she needed to take with her.

'I can't find my laptop,' she said.

'I think Paige might have it,' Liane said. 'I can go and ask –'

'No,' Ella said. 'It's OK. Is she at work?'

'She's always at work,' Issey said.

'I know.' Ella stood up and started zipping the various pockets on her weekend bag. 'I was going to talk to her about it. I'm worried about her.'

She stopped zipping and let her head hang down, a tear dropping off the end of her nose.

'Oh, El,' Liane said, sliding her arms around Ella's waist. Issey cuddled her from the other side.

'All packed!' Lou said, walking in. She dropped her bag and draped herself over the other three girls.

'Let us know when the funeral is,' Liane said, kissing Ella's temple.

'You don't have to come,' Ella said.

'Of course we're coming,' Issey said into Ella's hair.

Chapter 39

'I'm glad it's raining,' Ella said.

The five of them were standing outside the church, underneath a shelter. Water ran off the corners and splashed onto the ground at their feet. Ella's legs were already soaked to the knee, from walking from the car to the church in the first place.

'It would've been weird if it had been sunny,' she continued. 'This way it feels like the sky's crying too. Fuck.' She clamped a hand over her mouth, glancing back over her shoulder at the church. 'Sorry. That was such a ridiculous thing to say.'

'It's OK,' Lou said. 'We're going to get struck down now anyway. Who says "fuck" in a church?'

Ella snorted. 'God. I think I'm hysterical.'

Her mum and Dylan were inside saying bye and thank you to everyone, but Ella had had to escape. She kept wanting to laugh. It was awful.

'Have you got cigs?' she asked Lou.

'Wow, we're really rebelling today, aren't we? What's next? Want me to find a young vicar for you to ravish?'

'I can ravish Nick later,' Ella said, her shoulders instantly relaxing at the thought of him.

'He texted me,' Lou said. 'I'd show you but I don't want to drown my phone. He said to look after you. He's gutted not to be here.'

'I know,' Ella said. 'But he's going to be here later. And you're all here now.'

Issey leaned against her and Ella looked past her at Liane and Paige.

'I've thanked you for coming, right?'

'About a hundred times,' Paige said, half smiling.

'Sorry. It does make it easier, having you here.'

'Of course we'd be here,' Liane said. 'Where else would we be?'

Ella laughed and it turned into a sob.

'I keep remembering things to tell him. Like about today. That it was raining. That Alan from the pub came but Phil from golf didn't. And every single time I have to remember that I won't be able to. When's it going to stop happening?'

'It'll happen for a while, I think,' Lou said.

'Have you got cigs?' Ella asked again.

'Seriously?'

'Unless you've got, like, a hip flask.'

'I have not got a hip flask,' Lou said, taking out a pack of Marlboro and a lighter. 'Want to go somewhere else?'

'Nah. I'm an adult. Allegedly. And if my mum comes out I'll say you made me do it.'

'Can you believe how long we were in there for?' Dylan said, coming outside and standing directly in front of Ella.

His cheeks were flushed, eyes bright. He reached out and took the cigarette out of Ella's hand and put it between his lips.

'I started to think they were going round the back and coming through again!' he said around the cig.

'Like a clown car,' Paige said.

Dylan barked out a laugh. 'Exactly that, yeah.'

'Are you OK?' Ella asked him.

'Fuck no,' he said, and then glanced over at the door of the church just as Ella had. 'I feel awful. But, you know, we get to go and get drunk now.'

'How's Mum?' Ella asked. She felt terrible for abandoning her, but she was so sad that Ella felt overwhelmed with it. She had to keep running away from her.

'That woman,' Dylan said, pointing over his shoulder with his thumb. 'Big hat?'

The girls nodded.

'She said, "So you're the popstar" and then when I said yes, she said, "It doesn't mean anything, you know? And I hope you're investing wisely."'

'What?' Ella said. She had an irrational urge to go and push the woman into a puddle. Even though she looked about ninety.

'Who is she?' Lou asked.

'Dunno,' Dylan shrugged. 'Probably didn't even know him. Grief tourist or something.'

'I don't think that's a thing,' Ella said.

'Maybe she just fancies a free buffet? Anyway. Keep away from her. She's mean.'

Dylan took another drag of the cigarette and held it out to

293

Ella. She shook her head. Dylan dropped it to the ground and stubbed it out with his shoe.

'Where's Mum now?' Ella asked him.

'Talking to the vicar.'

'Is he hot?' Issey said.

Ella snorted. Dylan looked horrified. 'God, no.' He looked from Lou to Paige, via Ella, Issey and Liane and then said, 'Wait. Is there a vicar on your list?'

'Oh my god, Dyl, no!' Ella said, closing her eyes.

'There should be,' Lou said, bumping her with her shoulder.

'Mum's coming out,' Dylan said, flicking the cigarette butt away with the toe of his shoe.

Lou squeezed Ella quickly and then held back as Ella walked ahead to join her mum and brother in the car back to their house.

'She'll be OK,' Dylan told Ella, his mouth right up against her ear.

They'd been home for a couple of hours and pretty much everyone was well on the way to being hammered.

For the first half hour their mum had fussed around everyone, fiddling with the buffet, topping up drinks, but now she was in the garden with her friend Cheryl, and Ella could hear them screeching with laughter.

Ella nodded. Her mum had good friends. She didn't need to worry as much as she did. She finished her wine. She'd told herself it was the last one she was going to have, but when Dylan held out the bottle, she let him fill her up again.

'Hey,' she heard from behind her and she was already crying as she turned.

Nick wrapped his arms around her and Ella felt Dylan take the wine glass out of her hand.

'Can we go upstairs?' Ella said against Nick's neck. 'To my room.'

'Course, babe,' he said.

She half pushed him out of the room and stopped in the hallway to kiss him.

'I'm so glad you're here.'

He stroked her hair away from her face. 'I'm sorry I'm so late. I wish I could've –'

Ella shook her head. 'It doesn't matter. The girls were here. You're here now. Come on.'

He followed her upstairs to her room and she sat down on the edge of her bed.

'Are you all right?' he said, shaking his coat off and hanging it over the back of her office chair.

'No,' she said. 'But I will be. Come and lie down.'

She swung her legs up on the bed and shuffled up until her head was on the pillow. Nick lay next to her, his hand on her waist.

'I'm so glad you're here,' she said again.

Nick kissed her. 'Me too.'

Ella shuffled closer until her whole body was pressed up along Nick's side. And then she fell asleep.

Chapter 40

'I think we all need a night out,' Lou said.

Apart from Paige, who was working at the dining table, they were all lying across both of the sofas. *Scandal* on the TV. A family bag of Kettle Chips on the coffee table. Lou had heard from the university that Kyle had been asked to leave with immediate effect, and his behaviour reported to the police. She hadn't been contacted by the police yet, but it was only a matter of time.

'Same,' Ella said. 'No money though.'

'You know what we should do?' Issey said. 'Use the Fuck It List money. I mean, there must be, like . . .' She screwed her face up as she worked it out in her head. 'Eighty quid? At least.'

'If everyone's been putting in,' Liane said. 'Has everyone been putting in?'

'I'll go and get it,' Lou said, jumping up from the sofa.

'Wait,' Paige said, pushing her chair back from the table. 'I'll get it. I need a break from –'

Lou was already at the door. 'You're OK. I'm going to grab a drink too.'

When Lou came back up, she had a bottle of Corona in one hand, the Illy coffee can in the other.

Paige had moved to sit on the sofa next to Liane. Lou put the can on the coffee table and reached out to unscrew it.

'Dying to know how much there is,' she said, grinning at the other girls. 'Maybe we could get dinner as well?'

'There's not going to be enough for dinner,' Ella said. 'Unless you've all been getting way more than me.'

'Not more,' Issey said. 'Just with more people.'

'Wait,' Paige said, leaning forward and grabbing Lou's wrist. 'Wait. Don't open it.'

'You think we should wait 'til the end of term?' Ella asked.

Paige shook her head. 'It's empty. I borrowed the money.' She closed her eyes for a second and when she opened them, looked around at the other girls. 'I mean, I took the money. I was going to pay it back. I promise you. I'm behind on the bills. I've missed payments on my cards. My laptop's knackered. I'm working all the shifts I possibly can.' She shook her head. 'I'm so sorry. It sounds total shit to say I never thought you'd find out, but that's how I justified it to myself.'

'Why didn't you tell us how bad it was?' Ella said.

Paige pushed her glasses up on her head and rubbed one eye with the heel of her hand. 'My dad's selling our house and he's said I'll get some money from that, so I thought even if I didn't manage to pay it back sooner, I could pay it back then. I thought I still had some time. And I didn't want to be the one who couldn't pull her weight, you know? You've all got your shit together. And I'm eating twelve-p cup-a-noodles and fucking everything up.'

'We absolutely have not got our shit together,' Lou said.

297

'Jesus. I've been stalked. I'm waiting for the police to call me for a statement. And even mostly perfect Ella's been hiding her famous fucking brother like something from, I don't know, *Hollyoaks*.'

'I asked out the guy in Bean and he said no. So now I can't go there any more,' Liane said. 'And it turns out that's the least of my problems.'

She glanced at Issey before she could stop herself but, to Liane's relief, Issey was looking at Paige and didn't see.

'I went on a date with a sixteen-year-old, Paige!' Issey said. 'I should be locked up.'

It was only when Paige laughed wetly that they realised she was crying. She rubbed her face again. 'I'm so happy I met you all. I'm sorry I'm such a fucking mess.'

Lou was the first to put an arm around her, but the other three quickly followed, all piled on top of one another on the sofa, arms and legs tangling and feet bashing against the coffee table.

'We're meant to be a mess,' Lou said, when they eventually detangled themselves. 'It's what uni's for.'

Chapter 41

'Come and dance with me!' Liane yelled, trying to make herself heard over the sound of DJ Khaled's 'All I Do Is Win'.

The club had free entry and they'd all agreed they could manage it if they stuck to the cheapest drinks, paced themselves, and split own-brand shopping for the next couple of weeks.

Lou shook her head. She was grinding against some boy who was wearing glasses Liane hoped were ironic: huge and rimless, possibly also tinted. Hideous.

Liane looked around the club for Ella, but she hadn't seen her since not long after they'd arrived. She was probably off in a booth somewhere kissing Nick. Paige was standing at the bar, talking to a tiny woman in an even tinier dress.

'I'm going to go and find her,' Liane said – pointlessly, since no one was listening.

She pushed her way off the dance floor, apologising as she bumped into a boy just as he held a beer up to his mouth.

'Bitch,' he spat out, wiping his chin with the back of his hand.

Liane paused for a second, one foot on the step, the other still on the dance floor. She wanted to yell at him, tell him it was an accident, ask him why he was so aggressive, but she also suddenly felt like she was about to cry, and there was no way she was going to be the girl crying in the club. She kept walking.

She found Ella and Nick exactly where she'd thought they'd be. In a booth, Ella sitting sideways on, her legs hanging over Nick's, his hand on her thigh under her sequinned skirt.

'Come and dance!' Liane said. 'I love this song. And we should all be together. Don't you think?'

'OK,' Nick said, his mouth against Liane's ear. 'I just need the loo. Meet you down there.'

He kissed Ella on the mouth, before heading off to the loos. Liane watched him weave through the dancers. She saw him say something to Lou, who laughed and pressed a kiss to his cheek. He glanced back at Ella, looking partly bashful and partly something else. Liane felt rather than heard Ella laugh and she turned to look at her. Ella was looking at Nick with such happiness and love that Liane felt her eyes well with tears. God, what was wrong with her? Was she due on? That must be it. She felt Ella squeeze her hand – she hadn't realised Ella was even holding her hand – but she squeezed back and then tugged on her arm.

'Let's go and dance.'

On the way past the bar, they grabbed Paige, who left the tiny woman behind. When Nick came back from the loo, he'd found Issey.

By the time they all made it to the dance floor, DJ Khaled was over, but they carried on dancing anyway. Liane loved it. The music was loud, the lights were flashing, she was with her friends who she loved. Nick and Ella were trying to dance and kiss at the same time while Lou yelled at them to get a room.

Paige turned out to be an incredible dancer. Issey was filming them all on her phone. She turned to Liane, her eyes bright, shouting, 'I love this!'

Liane felt like the music had stopped. Like the room had gone dark. Like she was the only person there. Just her. And Issey.

She grabbed Issey's arm. 'Can we go somewhere?'

'Now?' Issey yelled back.

Liane nodded.

And then they were moving through the club. They weren't touching any more, but Liane could feel Issey right next to her. She didn't even look back. Their friends would be fine. They were all going to be fine.

At the door, Liane put her key in the lock, but of course it wouldn't turn. She kicked the base, muttering 'fuck fuck fuck' to herself as she twisted the key.

'Don't,' Issey said from behind her. 'You'll break it. Let me do it.'

Liane moved to one side, leaning back against the wall. The bricks felt rough through her thin dress. Her hands were shaking.

Issey pushed the door open and Liane followed her inside.

'What's wrong?' Issey asked, as Liane pushed the door closed.

'I kissed you,' Liane said.

Issey's eyes went wide.

'And then I just fucking bottled it,' Liane said. 'And there's a few reasons and I want to tell you about them, but really I just . . . I want you to know that I don't regret it. And I'm sorry if you do, but –'

'I don't,' Issey said. 'I never did.'

'I thought . . .' Liane said. 'I mean . . . I was so drunk. And I wasn't thinking. And then you didn't say anything about it. And I told myself I shouldn't have done it. And it was better just to forget it.'

'Do you still think that?' Issey said.

Liane stared at her. She took a breath. 'No. I'm glad I did it.'

'I've missed you so much,' Issey said. 'I mean . . . you're my best friend. And it felt like you were trying to keep away from me –'

'I was,' Liane said. 'A bit. Cos I was scared I was going to kiss you again.'

They stared at each other across the hall.

'Kiss me again,' Issey said.

Issey didn't even see Liane move, but suddenly Liane's mouth was on hers. She kissed her softly at first, but then Issey heard or felt herself gasp and Liane pressed up against her and her mouth became more insistent. Issey didn't know what to do with the rest of her body. She wanted to touch, but she wasn't sure if she was allowed. And anyway, her arms felt dead. Fucking cheap vodka.

'This OK?' Liane whispered.

'God,' Issey said before she could stop herself. 'Yeah.'

Liane kissed her again, and Issey felt her tongue sliding against her lips. She opened her mouth and Liane's tongue slipped against her own. Issey gasped again and pressed her hands flat against the wall. If she didn't, she knew she'd grab Liane's hips, maybe hook her legs up around her waist.

'Can we go upstairs?' Issey said against Liane's mouth.

'God,' Liane said. 'Yeah.'

They practically ran up the stairs. Issey wanted to laugh. Laugh and shout, 'Oh my god! Liane kissed me! Again! Finally!'

'Here?' Liane said, as they reached Issey's door.

'Yeah.'

Liane pushed the door open and Issey followed her in, only having a moment to notice that her bed and floor were covered in clothes and magazines and textbooks, before Liane was kissing her again.

Issey let her own tongue stroke against Liane's, ran it along her bottom lip, gently sucked her top lip for just a second before letting Liane take control again. Liane tasted like beer and smoke and lipstick. Issey had thought – when she'd let herself think about kissing Liane – that tasting lipstick, the feel of it sliding against her own lips, might be weird. But it wasn't. It was soft and sweet and she wished she hadn't wiped her own lipstick off earlier in the evening so she could have imagined the colours swirling together on their mouths.

Issey had no idea how long they kissed for. It sort of seemed like forever, but it also felt like only seconds later that Liane was pulling back and saying, 'Wow.'

'Yeah,' Issey said, her voice cracking.

'Good?'

'Yeah.'

Liane leaned in and kissed her once more. Just quickly, the kind of peck she would have given Issey in the past. When they were friends. Just friends. And now they were more than friends. There was no question of that.

Issey thought about asking if they could kiss more. If they

could maybe do more than kiss. But she couldn't make the words come out. Instead she took the couple of steps across the room to her bed and shoved everything onto the floor.

'You're such a slob,' Liane said, laughing.

Issey lay down on the bed and looked up at Liane.

'You look beautiful,' she said, her voice small.

'God, Iz,' Liane said. She was still standing at the foot of the bed, looking down at her. For a second, Issey worried Liane didn't want this after all. That she was going to turn and leave. But instead she lay down next to Issey.

Issey's fingers twisted in the bedding. She felt flat, like a rock was holding her down. But she also felt lighter than she had maybe ever. Like she could float up off the bed. Before she realised she was doing it, her hand was stroking down Liane's side, curling into her hip.

'I thought it might be weird,' Liane said, her voice low. 'After everything. But it wasn't.'

'No,' Issey whispered. She brushed her fingers over the fabric of Liane's dress, wondered what Liane would do if she pushed her dress up, slid her hands up over her skin, rolled on top of her and kissed her collarbones, braced her legs either side of one of Liane's and rolled her hips.

'I can stay in here, yeah?' Liane said.

'Course,' Issey said.

Chapter 42

'Oh god, I feel like shit,' Lou said.

She was sitting on the terrace, her head resting on her arms, eyes closed, hoodie pulled up and covering most of her face.

'I'm not too bad,' Ella said from the other side of the table. 'I think I might still be pissed.'

'Are you seeing Nick today?' Lou asked, resting her chin on her arms long enough to squint at Ella before flopping back down again.

'Nah. Thought I'd hang out with you guys.'

'Is he busy?'

Ella snorted. 'No! Well, I mean, he's working. But I totally could've gone to hang out with him at the shop.'

'Where are Liane and Issey?' Lou said after a while.

Ella looked up from her phone. Nick wasn't meant to have his phone on the shop floor, but he did anyway. 'In Liane's room, I think.'

Lou looked over at the patio door, a small frown on her face, and then said, 'Do you think they're doin' it?'

'No!' Ella said. 'Really?'

'I was just thinking . . . When I went to Liane's room last night, they were both flushed and giggly and Issey had sex hair.'

'Wow,' Ella said. 'But you know they're close. They might've just been messing.'

'Nah. I think they're lesbian loverssssss.'

'Wow,' Ella said. 'So they can tick that off the list then.'

Lou laughed. 'Did you forget the point of the Fuck It List was not to worry about relationships so we could focus on work? We've all failed miserably.'

'I haven't,' Ella said. 'I'm working and I've got a relationship.'

'Yeah, all right, you smug cow,' Lou said. 'We're not counting you.'

Ella grinned. 'I don't even care.'

By the time Paige joined them, Ella was reading on her phone and Lou was asleep with her head on the table.

'I've just been talking to my dad,' Paige said, both hands wrapped around a mug of tea. 'He sounded much better. The house sale is going through and he's exchanged on the flat. I should get a cheque sometime soon, but he doesn't know exactly when.'

'That's good,' Ella said. 'And how are you doing?'

'I'm feeling better too,' Paige said. 'Thank you. Again.'

Ella shook her head. 'It's fine. As long as you're OK. And you promise to tell us if you need us in future.'

'We're all nosy cows,' Lou said, her voice muffled by her sleeve. 'We'll all be in your business all the time now.'

'I thought you were asleep!' Ella said, kicking Lou lightly under the table.

'I am.'

'Oh, here's the lovebirds,' Ella said, spotting Liane and Issey through the patio door. They were both in sweats, Issey's hair all over the place, Liane's held back with a scarf.

'You told them?' Issey said, shoving Liane.

'I didn't, dickhead,' Liane said, stepping out onto the terrace. 'But I think you just did.'

'Shit,' Issey said.

'Seriously?' Ella said, looking at Issey and then Liane.

Lou sat up, her eyes bleary. 'I just said that, but I was joking. Mostly. Are you really?'

'Yes,' Liane said. 'But it's very new. So don't, you know, shit all over it.'

'I would never,' Lou grinned. 'God. I'm so happy for you!'

Issey dropped her forehead down on Liane's shoulder, hiding her smile against her arm.

'Oh god,' Paige said. 'PDA.' But she was grinning at them too.

'So we need to work out who won,' Lou said, standing up suddenly and then grabbing the table. 'Shit. Head rush.' She sat back down again.

'Won?' Ella said.

'The Fuck It List. Obviously. Keep up.'

'I'll get it,' Paige said.

When she came back, she'd brought a bottle of cheap Prosecco with her. Someone had won it in the quiz at the pub and then left it behind, so Jonny said she could have it.

'I am not drinking that,' Lou said. 'My poor fucking head.'

'Hair of the dog,' Paige said. 'And anyway, we have to toast the List.'

'She's right,' Liane said, pulling one of the wrought iron chairs up to the table.

'So how are we going to do this?' Ella asked. 'I'm kind of hoping everyone remembers what they did and who they did it with?'

'Mine's easy,' Lou said. 'Nothing. With no one. But at least I focussed on my studies. Oh shit, no. I didn't do that either. Ah well, always next year.'

'You'll be fine,' Ella said, reaching across the table to squeeze her arm. 'You had enough to deal with.'

'Just Nick for you, right?' Lou said. 'Trust you to immediately meet a total sweetheart and fall in love. So not in the spirit of the Fuck It List.'

Ella grinned. 'I'm not even sorry.'

'Two for me,' Paige said. 'A girl. Which, by the way, was a pretty easy so-called challenge. And someone who once went to jail. Guy from the pub.'

'So it's down to you two,' Lou said, pointing at Liane and Issey. Ironic.

Liane looked at Issey. 'I don't really want to say . . .'

Issey smiled at her. 'Me neither.'

'If you don't say, you can't play,' Lou said. 'Honestly, am I the only one taking this fucking thing seriously?'

'Can we split it?' Issey suggested.

'There's nothing to split,' Paige said. 'Not until I pay back the money.'

'So we just toast it then,' Ella said.

Paige stood up and twisted the cage off, then held the cork with the hem of her hoodie and twisted it off. Air hissed out and Issey gave a weak cheer.

'Oh, shit,' Liane said. 'We didn't get glasses.'

'Doesn't matter,' Lou said.

'I can go and get some,' Ella said, starting to stand.

'We can totally drink out of the bottle, Ella,' Lou said. 'Sit down.'

Ella rolled her eyes. But she sat back down.

'To . . .' Paige said. 'What are we toasting to?'

'To mostly totally failing the Fuck It List,' Lou said. She took the bottle from Paige and swigged some. 'Jesus Christ.'

'To surviving this fucking year,' Paige said, and drank, wincing. It was not good Prosecco.

'To Issey and Liane,' Ella said. 'Who not only won the list, but found each other.'

'Oh god,' Liane said, but she was grinning.

'And to Ella and Nick,' Issey said. 'For being so disgustingly cute.'

'To all of us then?' Lou said.

'To all of us,' Ella, Paige, Liane and Issey agreed.

And then they finished the bottle.

Acknowledgements

As always, hugest thanks go to my agent, Hannah Sheppard, and everyone at Hot Key, particularly Georgia Murray, Jenny Jacoby and Tina Mories. Thanks to Anneka Sandher for the fabulous cover. (Special thanks to Naomi Colthurst, even though she wouldn't let me call it *The Fuck It List*.)

To Jenni Nock, Katey Lovell, Alicia Brooks and Lucy Powrie, who read a super-early version of this book and bowled me over with their enthusiasm.

To Vicki Hall for being my biggest fan (but not in a scary way).

To Jenni, Georgie, Lindsay, Alicia, Kevin, Rachael, Alice and Hayley for being the best of pocket friends (best of women) (and one man). Thanks to Froukje Muller for Dipsy.

The idea for this book came out of a Twitter chat with Sara Bernard, L.D. Lapinski and Louise O'Neill. Thanks for letting me run with it.

Thank you as always to the readers, the bloggers and the booksellers, without whom I wouldn't get to do this. Which would make me sad. Because it's fun.

And thank you to David, Harry and Joe for putting up with me abandoning literally everything else in favour of deadlines.

Keris Stainton

Keris Stainton was born in Winnipeg, Manitoba, which, by all accounts, is very cold. And also hot. But when she was four months old, her parents moved back to the UK, and now she lives in Lancashire with a fellow northerner, their two ridiculously gorgeous sons and a pug. OK, they haven't got a pug, but Keris hopes if she writes it here it will come true. If you write it, pugs will come.

Keris has been writing stories for as long as she can remember, but she didn't write a novel until 2004 when she took part in National Novel Writing Month. She hasn't quite finished that one yet, but she has finished a few others, including *One Italian Summer*, *Counting Stars*, *Jessie Hearts NYC*, *Della Says OMG!* and *Emma Hearts LA*. Find out more about Keris at www.keris-stainton.com or follow her on Twitter: @Keris

Thank you for choosing a Hot Key book.

If you want to know more about our authors
and what we publish, you can find us online.

You can start at our website

www.hotkeybooks.com

And you can also find us on:

We hope to see you soon!

Want to read
NEW BOOKS
before anyone else?

Like getting
FREE BOOKS?

Enjoy sharing your
OPINIONS?

Discover

READERS FIRST

Read. Love. Share.

Get your first free book just by signing up at
readersfirst.co.uk